Phoenix Rising
FIREBASE
FREEDOM

PHOENIX RISING
FIREBASE
FREEDOM

WILLIAM W. JOHNSTONE
with J. A. Johnstone

PINNACLE BOOKS
Kensington Publishing Corp.
www.kensingtonbooks.com

PINNACLE BOOKS are published by

Kensington Publishing Corp.
119 West 40th Street
New York, NY 10018

PUBLISHER'S NOTE
Following the death of William W. Johnstone, the Johnstone family is working with a carefully selected writer to organize and complete Mr. Johnstone's outlines and many unfinished manuscripts to create additional novels in all of his series like The Last Gunfighter, Mountain Man, and Eagles, among others. This novel was inspired by Mr. Johnstone's superb storytelling.

All Kensington titles, imprints, and distributed lines are available at special quantity discounts for bulk purchases for sales promotions, premiums, fund-raising, educational, or institutional use.
Special book excerpts or customized printings can also be created to fit specific needs. For details, write or phone the office of the Kensington special sales manager: Kensington Publishing Corp., 119 West 40th Street, New York, NY 10018, attn: Special Sales Department; phone 1-800-221-2647.

This book is a work of fiction. Names, characters, businesses, organizations, places, events, and incidents either are the product of the author's imagination or are used fictitiously. Any resemblance to actual persons, living or dead, events, or locales is entirely coincidental.

PINNACLE BOOKS and the Pinnacle logo are Reg. U.S. Pat. & TM Off.

ISBN-13: 978-0-7860-3059-0
ISBN-10: 0-7860-3059-3

First printing: December 2012

10 9 8 7 6 5 4 3 2 1

Printed in the United States of America

PROLOGUE

Washington Mall, Washington, D.C.

There were at least 10,000 people gathered on the mall, all of them looking toward the 555-foot-tall obelisk that had stood there since its completion in 1884. The area immediately around the Washington Monument was roped off so that nobody could get any closer to the monument than 17th Street.

Loudspeakers had been erected so the people assembled could hear the words of Imam Mohammad Akbar Rahimi. Rahimi stepped up to the microphone to speak to the crowd.

"All praise be to Allah, the merciful. Whomsoever Allah guides there is none to misguide, and whomsoever Allah misguides there is none to guide. Today, this symbol of heresy that has long been worshiped by the people of this country, will no longer lead our people into the sin of apostasy. This we do in praise of Allah."

Looking back toward the Washington Monument, Rahimi pushed a button on the electronic device he was holding. There was a loud, rumbling explosion, and the obelisk came crashing down, lifting in its place a towering column of smoke and dust.

The World War II Memorial, the monument to the Korean War, and the Vietnam Memorial Wall had already been taken down. So, too, had the Lincoln Memorial. Gone also were the Roosevelt Memorial, the Jefferson Memorial, the Einstein Memorial, and the Holocaust Museum.

In New York Harbor, Liberty Island was now bare, the Statue of Liberty being the first of the heretical symbols to have been destroyed. The Gateway Arch in St. Louis had been taken down, and, on Mount Rushmore, the stone-carved faces of all the presidents had been obliterated.

All the artifacts in the Smithsonian Institute were destroyed, and the books, newspapers, photographs, sound recordings, videos, and movies of the Library of Congress were removed from the building and burned. Soon, the only record of what had once been the United States, the greatest nation in history, became nothing but a memory kept alive in the minds and the hearts of those who still held the country dear.

CHAPTER ONE

When Mehdi Ohmshidi was elected President of the United States, he campaigned on the promise of "fundamentally transforming America," and that is exactly what he did, carrying out that promise in a way that few could imagine. The result was devastating; a complete breakdown of America's infrastructure to include a total rupture of the power grid; dissolution of the military and law enforcement; the destruction of all commerce to include distribution of food, clothing, and services; as well as the cessation of all newspaper, radio, television, telephone, and Internet access. Paper money lost its value, and hundreds of billions of dollars lay undisturbed in worthless trash piles. Taking advantage of the collapse, Islamic terrorists detonated three nuclear bombs, and the United States ceased to exist.

All across the nation millions of Americans

died, and their unburied, decaying, and putrefied bodies not only created a horrific landscape, but spread diseases that took the lives of millions more. One third of the remaining population became homeless, while nearly as many turned to crime as their only chance for survival. Within one presidential term, what had been the most powerful nation in the twenty-first-century world, was thrust back into the eighteenth century.

Here and there across the country, groups of Americans had formed enclaves of mutual assistance, and one such team was headed by army veteran Jake Lantz. Jake Lantz, a major when the army collapsed, was thirty-two years old. A helicopter pilot and flight instructor in the Army Aviation School at Fort Rucker, Alabama, he was at the peak of physical condition, having scored a perfect 300 on his last PT test, maxing out on the three required events: push-ups, sit-ups, and the two-mile run. A not-too-prominent scar on his right cheek, the result of a wound he received in Afghanistan, ran like a bolt of lightning from just below his eye to the corner of his mouth. He had blue eyes and he wore his light brown hair closely cropped in the way of a soldier.

Raised in the Amish community, Jake had no reason to doubt that he would be a farmer, as his father, grandfather, and great-grandfather had been. Like all Amish boys, he had learned the skills necessary to live in a world that shunned modern conveniences. He was a good carpenter, he knew farming, he understood nature, and he knew what wild plants could be eaten and what plants would have medicinal value.

But even as a child he used to watch airplanes pass overhead and wonder about them. One day an army helicopter landed in a field nearby. The occupants got out, opened the engine cowl and made a few adjustments, then closed the cowl, got back in, and took off. Jake knew on that day that he wanted to fly a helicopter. He also knew that such an ambition was not for an Amish boy.

When he was eighteen years old, Jake, like all eighteen-year-old Amish, went through *rumspringa,* a period of time in which they were exposed to the modern world. Once this coming-of-age experience was over, the Amish youth would face a stark dilemma: commit to the Amish church—or choose to leave, which meant severing all ties with their community and family forever. Jake made the gut-wrenching decision to sever those ties.

Because of that, he was excommunicated from the church, and being excommunicated meant being shunned by everyone, including his own family. When he went back home, in uniform, after graduating from Officer Candidate School, his mother and father turned their back and refused to speak to him. His sister shunned him also, but he saw tears streaming down her face and he knew it was not something she wanted to do.

After OCS, Jake went to college on the Serviceman's Opportunity College program, getting his BA degree from the College of William and Mary in two and a half years. After that, Jake attended flight school, fulfilling his ambition to be a pilot. His love for flying was not diminished, even though he had three combat tours; one to Iraq and two in Afghanistan. There he flew the Apache armed helicopter and was awarded the Distinguished Flying Cross as well as the Air Medal with "V" device for heroic action against the enemy. He also received a purple heart when a shoulder-launched missile burst in front of the helicopter, killing his gunner/co-pilot, and opening up gaping wounds in Jake's face, side, and leg. He managed to return to his base, but had lost so much blood that when he landed, he passed out in the cockpit, not regaining consciousness until he was in the hospital. That was where he met the nurse, Karin Dawes, who was then a first lieutenant.

Jake had never married, partly because before he met Karin, he had never met anyone he wanted to marry. He had been giving a lot of thought to asking Karin to marry him, but with the nation in turmoil, he wasn't sure it was the right thing to do.

* * *

If you had asked any of Captain Karin Dawes's childhood friends about her, they would all say that the last thing they ever expected was for her to wind up in the army. Would they think of her as a nurse? Perhaps. All agreed that she was someone who tended to look out for others, but nobody expected her to become an army nurse. And certainly no one ever thought of her being in a combat zone, though not because anyone questioned her courage or her physical stamina, because she had always been very athletic.

Karin was a distance runner and a cheerleader, both in high school and at the University of Kentucky. She continued to run after graduating from college, and the last year before the collapse of America, she came in first place among all women in both the Atlanta and the Chicago marathons.

While in college, Karin fell in love and planned to be married upon graduation. But only three days before the wedding, Tony Mason, her fiancé, was killed in a car wreck. Karin was so distraught that she joined the army. She was sent to Afghanistan immediately after her training, and there she encountered a captain with severe wounds to his face, side, and leg. The wound in the captain's leg got infected and there was a strong possibility that it would have to be amputated. Karin made a special effort to tend to the wound, keeping him dosed with antibiotics, keeping it clean and aspirated, and treating it with antiseptic—sometimes spending the night in the room with the patient in order to attend to it—and the captain's leg was saved. His doctor told the wounded officer, Captain Jake Lantz, that Karin had saved his leg.

It was not entirely by coincidence that when both returned to the States, they wound up at Fort Rucker, Alabama: both had applied for the station. Karin thought she would never feel about another man as she had felt about Tony, but Jake Lantz had changed her mind. She would marry him in a minute if he would ask her, and if he didn't ask her, she might just ask him.

Seeing the coming collapse, Jake assembled a team of survivors, starting with Karin Dawes.

Marcus Warner was a helicopter mechanic who worked on the flight line. In all the time Jake had been in the army, he had never run across a better helicopter mechanic. He was also one of the most resourceful men Jake had ever met, and he knew that he wanted him to be a part of his team.

Sergeant first class Willie Stark was thirty years old. An avionics specialist, Stark could practically build a radio from scratch. He knew all the inner workings and hidden mechanisms of any radio, and he could read and send messages in Morse code. Stark, who others referred to as an "electronics geek," was also a wizard with computers.

Sergeant Deon Pratt was a powerfully built black man who had been an instructor in SERE, the Survival, Evasion, Resistance, and Escape course at Fort Rucker. The consummate warrior, Deon was skilled in hand-to-hand combat. He was also an expert in firearms and explosives. Deon had won a Silver Star in Afghanistan for killing fifteen enemy fighters and rescuing, under fire, his captain and first sergeant who had been wounded and trapped beneath a collapsed building. Jake had thought long and hard about including a combat expert, but he realized that if there was a complete breakdown of civilization, Sergeant Pratt would be a good man to have on his side.

Sergeant Julie Norton had been Karin's recommendation. She worked in the hospital with Karin, primarily as a clerk, but the beautiful twenty-two-year-old black woman was an organizing genius, an efficiency expert who had taken the post hospital from a barely functioning mess to one of the best organized hospitals in the army.

These were the members of the group that reconstructed a Vietnam-era Huey UH-1D helicopter, which had been on display in the Army Aviation Museum, and used it to leave Fort Rucker and begin a new life.

* * *

It was not just happenstance that the group Jake assembled wound up at Fort Morgan. Fort Morgan is an old fort, built long before the civil war, at Mobile Point, a little spit of land that separates Mobile Bay from the Gulf of Mexico. During the Civil War Admiral Farragut's famous line, "Damn the torpedoes, full speed ahead," was delivered while he was under the guns of the fort, and facing the torpedoes that blocked the entrance into Mobile Bay.

When Jake and his team showed up at the fort, there was nothing there but old casements and stone walls. Jake had chosen Fort Morgan for a number of reasons, number one being the most obvious. It was a fort, and Jake knew that as conditions deteriorated even further in the country, it would spawn armed bands of hooligans, preying on anyone they thought might have something they could use. As Jake and his group were going to be well off, relatively speaking, he knew they would be a prime target for such groups. He knew, also, that the fort would provide them with protection against such groups.

Inside the fort was a rather large area of arable land, probably the only place down on the beach that had real soil, rather than sand. Immediately after arrival, Jake and the team planted the seeds they had brought with them. There was also plenty of fish, and there was a considerable amount of game, from rabbits to possum to alligators.

Once the group reached Fort Morgan, they encountered three families who were living in beach houses, next to the fort. One was Bob Varney, a retired army warrant officer and former helicopter pilot, who had done three tours in Vietnam. Bob was also a novelist, who, until the collapse of the nation and currency, had been doing quite well. Now, however, money was useless, and Bob welcomed the invitation from Jake to join his team. James Laney and Jerry Cornett were the other two families Jake and his team encountered. Laney was a jack of all trades who could fix anything, and Jerry Cornett was a consummate sportsman who, very early, proved his worth in providing the little survival group with fish and wild game.

Although the national electric grid was down, James and Willie Stark managed to bring electricity to the survival group by adapting solar panels that they had stripped from some of the abandoned houses. One evening after they had been there for several weeks, they were shocked to pick up a television broadcast. And it wasn't just any broadcast, it was the broadcast of George Gregoire, a man who, in what they were now calling the "before time," had been the leading spokesman for conservative America, before the collapse of the Republic.

"Hey, you guys!" Stark called. "Jake, Deon, Marcus! Come look! We have television!"

The others hurried to the TV set to watch the broadcast.

Hello, America.

This is a simulcast over shortwave radio, and satellite. That's right, I'm back on TV, though the size of my audience is probably less than a cable access show on the joys of scrapbooking. Nevertheless, I am extremely proud of our little group of technicians who have managed to put our show up on the satellite so that those with electricity, a TV, and satellite access can see us.

First, I will bring you up to date on the latest news we have been able to gather.

It appears that the so-called Islamic Republic of Enlightenment holds only Washington, D.C. and Detroit. The fact that they hold our capital city has given them a great deal of cachet in the rest of the world, but we, here in America, know that they are unable to expand beyond that. Already there have been isolated and uncoordinated raids against the Enlightened ones, none of which, at this point, have been much more than a nuisance. In the meantime the Enlightened atrocities against our people, especially the women and children, continue.

Ohmshidi is alive and well, somewhere, we know not where. From time to time he will make a shortwave radio broadcast to rally his base.

Really? Rally his base?

Tell me, friends, does he even have a base any longer? I think not. I think that once we reestablish control, put decent Americans back to work and reconstitute our government, we will then have time to find Ohmshidi and bring him to justice for all the crimes he has committed.

That means we have much to do, America, and since last I spoke to you much has been done. I have been contacted on 5110-LSB by several groups of brave Americans who have banded together to fight this evil that has come into our midst. I will not disclose at this time how many groups I have been in contact with, where they are, or what their strength is. I will only say that for the first time since Ohmshidi was elected president, I am feeling optimistic.

It is my sincere belief that there are many, many more groups that have not yet made contact with me, so I feel that, even though Americans made the colossal mistake of sending an arrogant, incompetent fool to the White House, those same Americans are now prepared to rectify that mistake.

During those days when we existed as a democratic republic we often heard one party or another—whichever party was out of office— adopt the political slogan, Take Back America.

Well, my friends, this is no longer empty political rhetoric. This is a real and vital battle cry. And I urge you, with all that is in my being,

*to hold yourselves in readiness until we can
coalesce as a mighty revolutionary army to
do that very thing.*

*Now you may well ask, From whom are we
to take back our country? Is it from Ohmshidi
and his State Protective Service? Is it from
the Muslim extremists who have captured
Washington and who, even now, are persecuting
Americans under the guise of their religious
indoctrination? Or is it from the roving bands of
brigands and thugs, people from among us, who
prey upon the weak and helpless, Americans by
birth, but not by any moral code that we all hold
dear?*

*The answer, my friends, is that we must be
prepared to do battle with all of them. I urge
those of you who are watching this program,
and those of you who are within range of
this broadcast, to establish contact with the
Brotherhood of Loyalists, and join forces in
this new revolution.*

Contact was made, and an alliance formed. It
was good to know they weren't entirely alone.

CHAPTER TWO

After detonation of the nuclear bombs and the complete dissolution of the United States, a tremendous power vacuum was created. That vacuum was filled by a fundamentalist Islamic sect that called themselves the *Moqaddas Sirata*, or the Holy Path.

Initially those Americans who had survived the total collapse of the nation under Mehdi Ohmshidi welcomed the *Moqaddas Sirata* because they began to restore order across the country, punishing thieves and murderers. They also brought in fuel and food, and reestablished electricity, water, telephone service, and the Internet. They even put radio and television broadcasts back on the air. Schools were reopened, newspapers were printed. The American Islamic Republic of Enlightenment applied for membership in the United Nations, and though they were denied full membership, they were admitted on a nonvoting observer status. They were accorded membership in the OIC, the Organization of Islamic Cooperation.

Muslimabad, formerly Washington, D.C.

The governments of Iran, Iraq, Libya, Syria, Afghanistan, Lebanon, and Saudi Arabia received a message from Caliph Rafeek Syed demanding that they recognize the Greater Islamic Caliphate of Allah, with him as the Grand Caliph. Every government contacted acquiesced to the demand. What had been the United States, and was, for a while, the New World Collective, was renamed the American Islamic Republic of Enlightenment, and Mohammad Akbar Rahimi was made Minister of Culture for *Moqaddas Sirata* in the new country.

Rahimi was an American, and had been born in Omaha, Nebraska, as Warren Church, the son of a school teacher and a union official. Before the collapse of the United States, Church had been a professor of Ethics and Diversity at Colorado State University. He first broke onto the national scene with his claim of being full-blooded Sioux Indian, using that to his advantage to secure a professorship. That claim was subsequently proven to be bogus, and his next appearance on the national stage was with the publication of an article entitled: *Chickens Come*

Home to Roost: The Oppressed Push Back. It was about the September 11, 2001, attacks, in which he wrote:

> The attacks were entirely justified
> by America's treatment of the Islamic
> nations. The absolute center of the US
> financial hegemony was located at the
> World Trade Center, and those who
> made their living working in the trade
> towers, mostly Jews, were little more
> than vampires, sucking the blood of
> the rest of the world. The 9/11 attacks
> by the martyrs were not only justified,
> but were the righteous acts of courage,
> and all nineteen martyrs are now in
> glory in paradise.

Rahimi was sitting in his office, the Oval Office, in what used to be called the White House, but was now called the Palace of Peace. He looked up when his secretary stepped into the room.

"Imam, President Mehdi Ohmshidi has been found, and brought here as you directed," his secretary said.

"He is president, only if I permit him to be president," Rahimi said.

"But of course, Imam."

"Allow him to enter."

It was a very nervous and frightened Mehdi Ohmshidi, the last freely elected president of the United States, who was brought into the Oval Office, at the bidding of Rahimi. Halfway between the door and the famous Resolute Desk, behind which Rahimi was sitting, Ohmshidi dropped down to his knees. He then bowed so low that his forehead touched the carpet. He extended his arms out before him, his hands palm down.

"Oh, merciful one, I have come as you requested," Ohmshidi said.

"It wasn't a request, Ohmshidi, it was an order."

"Yes, as you have ordered," Ohmshidi said, his words muffled by the carpet, against which his forehead was still pressed.

"You may rise."

Ohmshidi stood.

"Do you wonder why I have sent for you?" Rahimi asked.

"I do wonder, oh merciful one, and beg that if you have found fault with me, that you will show me mercy."

"You are the last connection between what this country is now, and what it once was."

"Yes," Ohmshidi said.

"There are those who will say that America ceased to exist because of your incompetent leadership."

"Imam, it was the detonation of the nuclear

bombs that destroyed this country," Ohmshidi defended. "I was bringing it into the way of the Holy Path."

"Yes. Be that as it may, this once powerful country was brought to its knees by you."

Ohmshidi bowed his head, not knowing what to say.

"And for that, I say Allah be praised!" Rahimi said.

Hearing the change in the tone of Rahimi's voice, Ohmshidi looked toward him.

"You are not displeased?"

"Why should I be displeased, Ohmshidi? For many years, we of the United States occupied the lands of Islam in the holiest of places, plundering its riches, dictating to its rulers, humiliating its people, terrorizing its neighbors, and building military bases in Muslim lands from which to launch attacks against the neighboring Muslim peoples.

"Those crimes and sins committed by misguided Americans were a clear declaration of war on God, his messenger, and Muslims. But, by your presidency, you brought death to millions of the infidel Americans, you depleted the nation of its power to wage war on Muslims, and today the once mighty nation lies prostrate before us."

"Yes, yes, that is so!" Ohmshidi said, getting into the spirit of things, now that he realized that he wasn't going to be punished. "And, Imam,

I did this thing to bring my people into the Holy Path."

"If you are prepared to subject yourself to the *Moqaddas Sirata,* I am prepared to allow you to resume your position as president of the American Islamic Republic of Enlightenment."

"Imam, it would be with gladness of heart that I serve *Moqaddas Sirata* in such a fashion."

"We have announced to the public that money will soon be printed and distributed. As it is now, all commerce is being done by barter. But soon, there will be money, and by controlling the money, we will control the people." Rahimi said.

"Yes, Imam, that is true."

"We will print bills in denominations of one, five, ten, twenty, fifty, and one hundred dollars."

"Imam, if I may make a suggestion?" Ohmshidi offered.

"You may."

"Let us not call the currency dollars. It was dollars when the United States was a pariah to the world, and America derived their power from the dollar."

Rahimi nodded. "Yes, that is true," he said. "Have you a suggestion?"

"I do have a suggestion. I would call the currency Moqaddas."

Having made the proposal, Ohmshidi studied Rahimi's face, ready to withdraw at the slightest suggestion of disapproval. To his surprised satisfaction, Rahimi smiled approvingly.

"Yes," he said. "Calling the currency holy is an excellent idea. And, I will instruct the engravers to put your picture on every bill."

"I am humbled, Imam, and I thank you."

"Now, as to police authority. The military and the police are no more."

"If you would allow it, Imam, I will reactivate the State Protective Service. They will act as a super police force, in control of all local and state police. They will also act as our military."

"I will allow this, Ohmshidi, only if every member of the SPS is sworn to the sacred duty of serving Allah through *Moqaddas Sirata.*"

"They will be so sworn, Imam," Ohmshidi said. "I will send them out to enforce the Holy Path, and to wreak destruction upon the Christian and Jew enemies of Islam."

Rahimi held up his finger. "Not just the Christians and Jews," he said. "We must punish anyone who does not follow the Holy Path, and that includes other Muslims who do not see the way."

"Yes, Imam, this we will do."

"How quickly can the SPS be reactivated?"

"By executive order, I will absorb all the police as an arm of the SPS, and since many cities have already reestablished their police force, that gives us an instant presence. I think that, within a month, we will have a core group of SPS, enough to act in conjunction with the police. After that it will just be a matter of extending the SPS so that we also have a military. And there will be no difficulty in recruiting new members, for the SPS will be the most elite organization in the country."

"Who will you get to run such an organization?"

"Reed Franken was the head of the SPS in the before time. I know where he is, and I believe he will be able to reactivate and greatly expand the SPS."

"Very well. Do so," Rahimi ordered. Rahimi stood up, then took in the Resolute Desk with a wave of his hand. "Come, sit behind your desk."

"My desk, Imam? This is to be my desk?" Ohmshidi asked, gratified by the offer.

"Yes. If you are to be the President of the American Islamic Republic of Enlightenment, and you shall be as long as you please me, then you should occupy this office and this desk."

"I thank you, Imam. From the bottom of my heart, I thank you."

As soon as Rahimi left, Ohmshidi sent for Reed Franken. Franken was a rather smallish man with eyes that seemed greatly enlarged by his glasses. When he came into the office, he was carrying a briefcase with him.

"It is good to see you back where you should be," Franken said. "The country has suffered greatly in your absence."

"Yes, but now we shall put it back together," Ohmshidi said. "Are you prepared to help?"

"Great Leader, I pledge my life to your service."

Ohmshidi nodded. "Good, good, that is good," he said. "When you were called, you were told that I wanted to speak to you about the State Protective Service?"

"Yes." Franken held up the briefcase. "It was fortuitous that you would send for me, because I have spent the last few months drawing up plans for a new SPS."

"Let's hear the plans," Ohmshidi said.

"I'll begin with the uniforms. A sharp looking uniform instills pride in the unit, and intimidates the citizens. We will continue to wear the forest-green uniforms. But if we are going to build a military force from the SPS it will take a lot of men. I think we will need as many as one million uniforms."

Ohmshidi smiled and nodded. "That is not a problem, and it will provide jobs for the people," he said.

"There will be no beards among the members of the SPS."

Ohmshidi's smile turned to a frown. "That cannot be. As Muslims, they must wear beards."

"Mr. President, if you will hear me out," Franken said. "The Prophet Muhammad, peace be on him, had reasons for a beard, so that the followers be easily identified from among the clean-shaven apostates. But it is not mandatory in the Koran, and only the Koran's laws are applicable at all times."

"But why would you not want your soldiers to wear beards?"

"I believe that a Muslim who is a holy man, in *dishdasha, taqiyah*, and wearing a beard, presents the image of peace. But as soldiers of the Prophet we must, at all times, present an appearance, not of peace, but of war, an image that is frightening enough to command the fear and respect of those who are subject to our laws. An imposing uniform with its military accouterments, and a clean-shaven face, will do this."

"I see."

"I intend to have an inner cadre that will be the most elite unit of the SPS. The men of this unit will be selected on the principles of loyalty to you, Mr. President, and they must prove that they have no Jewish ancestry. Also, no one under six feet tall will be permitted in this inner elite core."

Ohmshidi made no reference to the fact that Franken was considerably under six feet tall. "Have you a name for this elite corps?"

"We shall call them the Janissary Corps."

"Yes!" Ohmshidi said. "After the elite Turkish Guard that defeated the infidels at Constantinople! Janissary! Brilliant idea, Mr. Franken."

"Thank you, Great Leader."

"Tell me more about the Janissaries."

"Whereas the main body of the SPS will

wear forest green uniforms, the Janissaries will wear black with silver lapel pins depicting a scimitar and a severed head. No member of the Janissary Corps can be married, for they will have but one loyalty, and that is to you. They must take an oath of loyalty and obedience unto death."

"Yes, yes, that is as it should be. But of course, as they are my special guards, I will have an equal loyalty to them," Ohmshidi said. "Please, do continue."

"In order that the SPS be effective, it will be necessary for us to take over the administration of all police forces within the nation, city and state. Those organizations that we take over, and whom we deem worthy of the honor, will be incorporated within the SPS. Those who are not worthy to be incorporated will be dismissed. Those who refuse to be incorporated will be eliminated.

"In addition, all legal jurisdiction will be taken away from civilian courts, and turned over to the SPS. I have written a mission statement which I would like to read, for your approval."

"Yes, by all means, read the mission statement."

Reed cleared his throat, then began to read aloud. "We, the State Protective Service, shall unremittingly fulfill our task: to establish the security of our Islamic Republic, to maintain the safety of our Great Leader, Mehdi Ohmshidi, and to establish peace and stability. We will be the enemy to all Jews, Christians, and Muslims who do not show obedience to *Moqaddas Sirata*. And, without pity, we shall put the merciless sword of punishment to the neck of such infidels, today, tomorrow, and for centuries to come."

"Very good, Franken. Or, shall I call you General Franken?"

"With your permission, Great Leader, I would prefer the title of National Leader of the SPS."

"So be it. How soon can you put this organization together, National Leader?"

"I have the core of those who were members of the SPS in the before time. Those men whose loyalty I feel I can trust will be quickly assembled. And, because service in the SPS is to be much desired, I think that the ranks will be filled very quickly."

"Very well, National Leader Franken. Put your plan into operation."

There began, after that, a gradual improvement in day-to-day living conditions, but not without some unwelcome changes. Television and radio broadcasts were reestablished, but they were nothing but nonstop propaganda for *Moqaddas Sirata*, words that, the first time they were heard, meant absolutely nothing to the average American.

Every television and radio broadcast began with the same statement.

All praise be to Allah, the merciful.
Whomsoever Allah guides there is none to
misguide, and whomsoever Allah misguides
there is none to guide. You must live your
life in accordance with the Moqaddas Sirata,
the Holy Path. Those who do will be blessed.
Those who do not will be damned.

But these same television broadcasts brought
the citizens of the American Islamic Republic of
Enlightenment the welcome news that soon, a
new currency would be issued.

So that all may start equally, we will establish
distribution points where everyone will be given
enough money to provide yourself and your
family with the basic necessities of life. This we
do in praise to Allah the merciful.

Less than a month after his meeting with Reed
Franken, enough of the SPS had been reconstituted to make a show of strength in Muslimabad,
and, once again, Ohmshidi was summoned by
Rahimi. This time though, the meeting was not
in the White House, but in what had once been
the Harry S. Truman Federal Building, occupied
by the Secretary of State. Mohammad Akbar
Rahimi, the Minister of Culture for *Moqaddas
Sirata*, now occupied the executive office suite on

the fifth floor. In the "before time" the lobby of the executive office suite had been decorated with a mural by James McCreery, entitled *Liberty or Death: Don't Tread on Me.* The work depicted the founding of America, featuring maps, cannons, rifles, and flags of the era. Now, however, all the historical icons had been painted over by a dull green, in keeping with the elimination of images; for there is a *hadith* which states that one should not leave a picture without obliterating it. It was also a diminution of any history of what had been the United States.

"You sent for me, Imam?" Ohmshidi asked when he was shown into Rahimi's office.

"Yes. In one hour you will give a television address to the nation."

"But, what shall I say?"

"It has been written, and will appear on the teleprompter. All you have to do is read what it says."

"Where shall I give this speech?"

"You are the president; you will speak from your office."

"Yes, Imam. Thank you, for your mercy and kindness."

One hour later, cameras were brought into the Oval Office, teleprompters were put up, and a voice-over intoned:

All praise be to Allah, the merciful.
Whomsoever Allah guides there is none to
misguide, and whomsoever Allah misguides

*there is none to guide. You must live your
life in accordance with the* Moqaddas
Sirata, *the Holy Path. Those who do will
be blessed. Those who do not will be damned.*

*Ladies and Gentlemen, the President of the
American Islamic Republic of Enlightenment,
Mehdi Ohmshidi.*

CHAPTER THREE

Firebase Freedom, Fort Morgan, Alabama

"Look," Julie said, pointing to the TV screen. "It's President Ohmshidi."

"Ohmshidi? I thought that son of a bitch was dead," Willie Stark said.

The others who were present inside the fort at the moment gathered around the TV to see what Ohmshidi had to say.

Ohmshidi's appearance had changed drastically since he was first elected president of the United States. Now his hair was longer, he was wearing a beard, a *dishdasha* and a *taqiyah*. His desk was flanked, left and right, by two muscular and unsmiling men, both members of the elite Janissary Corps. They were wearing black uniforms with silver lapel pins of a scimitar and a severed head. Like the SPS, they wore the Ohmshidi "O" logo armbands around their left arms, and they stood at parade rest, staring unblinkingly straight ahead.

"My fellow citizens of the American Islamic Republic of Enlightenment, I am speaking to you from Muslimabad, a city you once knew as Washington. I greet you in the name of Moqaddas Sirata, *and swear my submission to this movement of enlightenment.*

"Since you elected me to this office we have suffered much, but much has been accomplished. And, as a woman must go through much pain to deliver a child, so too have we gone through pain, to deliver a new nation.

"Yes, my fellow citizens, we, you and I, have set forth upon this continent a new nation, conceived in obedience, and dedicated to the principle of holy submission. No longer are we a warlike nation imposing our will upon the rest of the world. No longer are we a society separated by a great gap between the wealthy and the poor. No longer are we a nation separated by apostates who practice heresy in the false religions of Christianity and Judaism, or even those misguided Muslims who have not yet found their way to enlightenment. For now, there is only Moqaddas Sirata . . . *the true religion of Enlightenment.*

"This wonderful change in our country was made possible by the brave jihadists who martyred themselves by detonating nuclear

*weapons to bring us into the light. Now we
are an Islamic nation obedient to* Moqaddas
Sirata, *and we are an equal partner in a
growing international caliphate that will one
day bring the entire world into holy submission.*

"*I am pleased to tell you that gradually our
country is recovering from the turmoil it went
through during its birth. We are printing new
currency, to be called Moqaddas, which will be
backed by our government, and accepted on the
international market. In many parts of our
country electricity has been restored, as you well
know since you are watching this very television
show.*

"*Fuel is again being delivered. Telephone
service has been restored, some television and
radio broadcasts have returned to the airwaves,
and soon, more programs will be available. I am
also pleased to report that distribution of food
and durable goods is under way. If distribution
has not reached your area yet, it soon will.*

"*You will also see that law and order is being
returned, as I am greatly increasing the size
and the scope of the State Protective Service.
Soon you will be able to enjoy the safety and
security of having men of the SPS patrolling
your neighborhood. You will find comfort in
knowing that the men who wear the forest green
and gold uniforms will maintain peace and
stability throughout the land.*

"*Now that I have told you of the wonderful*

things that are coming, I must tell you how you can enjoy the fruits of these developments. It is very simple, and it is something that I know most of you will want to do, because with your own eyes you have seen the benefits to be derived. So that you may take advantage of the newly emerging economy, I am asking you to denounce any former religion you may have practiced. It is an absolute requirement that you do this, and that you convert to Islam, and become obedient to Moqaddas Sirata.

"In order to do that, it will be necessary for you to appear before a government official where you will swear allegiance to me, to the American Islamic Republic of Enlightenment, and to Moqaddas Sirata, *the Holy Path. Once you are enrolled, you will be provided with identity passes which will allow you to be reconnected to electricity and running water, and will enable you to purchase gasoline, food, and everything that is necessary to help us establish our new nation.*

"In order to assure the peace and tranquility of our new nation, we will start by confiscating all privately owned guns, Bibles, Torahs, and any books deemed hostile to Islam. We will also carefully monitor all publications and speech in order to prevent the spread of anti-government propaganda that would do harm to our new order.

"And, so that we may bring this new nation

into its proper place in the world order, I cannot, and I will not, waste your valuable time in seeking re-election. Therefore, I am declaring myself as president for life.

"There are bound to be those who will neither understand nor appreciate the new direction I am taking this country, so I am announcing today new government measures to deal with anyone who refuses to swear obedience to me, as well as with those who would cling to their guns and Bibles. All true citizens can serve the American Islamic Republic of Enlightenment by careful observance of your family, friends, and neighbors, reporting to the nearest authority anyone who does not submit.

"I am issuing an order today, that requires the police force in every city and town to swear allegiance to me. Those who refuse to swear allegiance to me will be eliminated. Soon, I will be sending members of the SPS to cities and towns throughout the land, to make certain that the police are acting in compliance with my orders, and that they, and you, are living in compliance with Moqaddas Sirata. *Here is what you must do.*

"First, you must remove all pictures of animals and people from your walls. Destroy all statues, busts, and figurines.

"In your place of work, be diligent that there are no images. If you must decorate, do so with ribbons, or colored cotton.

"Take down any calendars that have pictures of animals of any kind.

"Do not allow your children to play with dolls, for they are Satan's playthings.

"Do not take, or display, any pictures of children.

"Satan sees through the eyes of dogs, and he hears through the ears of dogs. You may not have a dog as a family pet, and all dogs must be killed at once.

"Those who fail to do these things, will incur the wrath of Allah, and Allah's angels, in the form of the SPS. The punishment will be severe.

"Thank you, and may the peace of Moqaddas Sirata *be with you."*

"Turn that crap off, Willie," Deon said.

"I thought we might like to get a glimpse of what we are fighting," Willie replied.

"Do you think there is anyone living on this island who doesn't know what we are fighting?"

Bob Varney had been sitting in a chair, watching the news along with the others. Bob's wire-haired Jack Russell terrier, named Charley, was in Bob's lap and Bob was casually rubbing the animal behind his ears. It was a ritual they went through often, and Charley, to take advantage of it, would jump into Bob's lap anytime he had the opportunity to do so.

"Did you hear what that son of a bitch said?" Bob asked. "Excuse the vulgar language, ladies."

"Is it vulgar, if it is the truth?" Karin asked. "I mean, the man is a son of a bitch, there is no way of getting around it."

"He has just sentenced a million or more dogs to death. How could anyone do such a thing?"

"I don't think the people will do it," Marcus said.

"They won't have any choice," Willie said. "If someone is standing there pointing a gun at them, telling them either to kill their dog or get killed, what else can they do? If they refuse, they'll get killed, and so will their dog."

"And all this business about pictures," Cille Laney, James's wife, said. "Pictures are all I have left of my mama and daddy, and there's no way I'm going to destroy them."

"I can't believe we let our country get into such a mess," Willie said.

"What do you mean we *let* our country get into this mess?" Deon asked. "Hell, we not only let it happen, Willie, we caused it. Don't forget, Ohmshidi didn't take over by coup. We actually voted him into office."

"Not me. I didn't vote for the son of a bitch," Willie said.

Deon chuckled. "Since you can't find anyone who actually did vote for him, you have to wonder how he ever got elected, don't you?"

"Yeah, well, like I said, I didn't vote for the son of a bitch."

The core of Jake Lantz's team was made up of a group of soldiers, men and women. And while the United States Army was no longer in existence and there was no longer any rank, a natural hierarchy had developed within the team. As a result, Jake Lantz, though no longer a major, was still regarded as the commanding officer of the survival team.

Shortly after the team arrived, they rescued a young woman who had been raped. Her name was Becky Jackson, though now she called herself Becky Warner, because she and Marcus were married. There was no existing legal authority to bind the marriage by contract, but their marriage had been blessed by an Episcopal priest on the island, and they were bound by love. When the baby, who was a result of the rape, was born, Marcus treated it as if it were his own son.

There were three families who lived in a housing compound known as the Dunes, when Jake and the others arrived. They had since abandoned their beach houses, and moved into the fort with Jake Lantz and his team.

Bob Varney was, as he liked to say, "a fount of useless information," and before the Internet was restored, his knowledge was put to good use when he told the others the principle of wood gasification. By applying those principles, Marcus and James built a series of burners that would allow them to operate their vehicles without gasoline.

James's mechanical and construction skills had proved to be very valuable since the survivalist group had formed at Fort Morgan, and, with salvaged lumber and equipment, a complete village was taking shape within the walls of the fort.

First called "Mobile Point," a zealous chamber of commerce had changed the name of the barrier island to Pleasure Island. There were two towns on Pleasure Island: Gulf Shores, and Orange Beach. The combined permanent population of the two towns was less than 15,000, but because Pleasure Island had been a popular tourist destination in the "before time," at any time during the summer season the population could be as high as 250,000.

Although considerably fewer than 250,000 people were on the island now, the current population was significantly higher than 15,000, because many Americans, unwilling to submit to the dictates of *Moqaddas Sirata*, had come there. The island had no central source of electricity, nor did it have running water, but it did have a fairly stable supply of food from the many gardens, as well as unlimited seafood, ducks and geese, and a rather sizeable herd of goats. There were also enough freshwater wells and desalination units available, that the water supply was never critical.

So far the residents of the island had not been

bothered by any security forces from the American Islamic Republic of Enlightenment, primarily because the AIRE was just now beginning to get back on its feet, and Pleasure Island was so far out of the way that nobody was, as yet, paying any attention to them.

"Did that son of a bitch say he was going to be president for life? What the hell is that all about?" Deon asked. "This is like some third world country."

"Where have you been, Deon?" Jake asked. "This *is* a third world country. No, that's not right. We'd have to come up some to be a third world country."

"The way I see it," Bob said, "it doesn't matter what Ohmshidi, or anyone in Washington . . ."

"Muslimabad, remember?" Karin said.

"Yeah, Muslimabad," Bob said. "But what I'm saying is, it doesn't make any difference where he is, or what he says. We are off in our own world down here, and if we are lucky, they'll forget all about us."

"Yes, well, we can't be lucky forever," Jake said. "You know what I think we should do?"

"No, but I have a feeling you are going to tell us," Karin teased.

"I think the South should rise again. I say we secede from the union."

"Wait a minute," Marcus said. "I'm not from the South."

Chuckling, Bob Varney pointed south. "If you go two hundred yards that way, you'll get your feet wet in the Gulf," he said. "You can't get any farther south than that."

"Ha!" James said. "He got you on that one, didn't he, Yankee boy?" James had lived in Georgia before he and Cille moved down to the beach.

"I guess you're right," Marcus said. "Okay, let's secede. It might work for you this time, 'cause you got someone from the North with you."

"Hell, I thought we already had seceded," Willie Stark said.

"Well, in essence we have," Jake agreed. "But I think we should make it official."

"You mean make our own Declaration of Independence," Deon asked. "Just like George Washington and those guys did?"

"Yes, that's exactly what I mean," Jake said.

"If we do that, I think we should actually write out a document," Karin said.

"I think so too," Jake said. "Why not?"

"And do what with it?" Marcus asked. "It's not like we can print it up in a newspaper and circulate it around."

"I don't know. Post it somewhere, I suppose," Jake said.

"What if we called a meeting of everyone down here on the island, read it aloud, then got a vote on it? If everyone agrees, by vote, then we will be, officially, seceded," Bob said.

"Good idea," Jake said. "No, that's a damn fine idea. You're the writer, Bob. Will you write it?"

"Yeah," Bob said, smiling broadly. "You're damn right, I will."

"You write it, we'll get the word out to everyone else down here, and have a town hall meeting to make it official."

CHAPTER FOUR

Dallas, Texas

Sam Gelbman wasn't exactly sure how he had gotten here. Why had he turned down this dark alley? And why were his headlights not bright enough for him to even see where he was going? Where was he? And where was Sarah? When he left he thought Sarah was in the car with him, but she obviously was not.

Sam felt a sense of panic, and he stared through the windshield, trying to figure out where he was. The buildings on either side of the alley were getting closer, and if he were to meet a car coming in the opposite direction, there wouldn't be room for both of them to pass.

Rats darted out from behind a large trash receptacle and ran across the alley if front of him, their beady eyes shining bright red in the reflection of his headlights. The alley grew even narrower, and now he could barely proceed without scraping the sides of his car.

The engine died, and Sam tried to restart it, but the engine wouldn't turn over. The battery was dead. He tried to get out of his car but he couldn't, because the car was now so tightly squeezed in by the buildings on either side that he couldn't get the doors open.

Where was he? Where was Sarah?

Sam tried to make a call on his cell phone, but he couldn't. Every time he tried to dial, he got the numbers wrong.

"Sarah, where are you?" he asked aloud.

Sam woke up then, and found himself lying in his own bed, in his own bedroom. He was breathing hard, and he knew he had just had one of his recurring dreams, where he is lost and alone. He reached over to find his wife lying beside him, and he took her hand in his. He felt her squeeze his hand reassuringly, even though she was still asleep.

Sam lay in bed for a long moment until the beat of his heart slowed, and his breathing became more normal. Then he got out of bed and went to the bathroom. Turning on the bathroom light he stared at himself in the mirror. Sam was thirty-three years old with brown eyes, and hair that he kept short, because it had a tendency to curl.

This wasn't the first time he had had such a dream. At least twice a month, and sometimes even more often, he would be lost and separated from Sarah, not knowing where she was, knowing that she didn't know where he was, and unable to communicate with her. He had no idea what caused the dreams, but they were very disturbing, and each time the dream occurred he would wake up, highly agitated.

Oddly enough, when he had been in Afghanistan, and really was separated from Sarah, he had no such dreams. They had only started when he came back home, but they had been recurring now for almost ten years.

"Sam?"

Sam heard Sarah's call, and he turned the light off in the bathroom, then returned to bed.

"Sam, are you all right?"

"I'm fine."

She reached over to take his hand. "The dream?"

"Yeah."

"And I wasn't with you?"

"No."

"Well, I am now."

Sarah lifted his hand to her lips and kissed it.

"I don't know why I have that damn dream all the time," Sam said.

"Where were you lost this time?"

"I don't know," Sam said. He chuckled. "If I knew, I wouldn't have been lost."

Sarah chuckled as well.

"Well, you know where you are now. You are right here, in your own bed, with me. And I love you."

"I love you, too."

Sarah snuggled up closer to him. "Maybe if you feel me next to you, you won't dream that we are separated."

"Maybe," Sam agreed, reaching his arm out so she could lay her head on his shoulder.

When Sam went out to his car the next morning, he saw that, during the night, someone had put up a sign in his front yard. He went over to look at it, even though he knew what he was going to see.

**Get Out
Filthy Jew!**

Throughout most of his life, Sam had not had to deal with real ethnic prejudices. Oh, from time to time he might see a slight reaction in people when he was introduced to them, and he had heard a few off-color ethnic jokes. But shortly after the election of Ohmshidi, Jew-bashing became an official policy, and the anti-Semitic epithets were appearing more and more often. Last month someone had actually scratched a swastika into the paint on the side of his car.

He checked his car to see if it had suffered any further damage, and was glad to see that it had not. Walking over to the sign, he pulled it from the ground and tossed it into the back of his car before Sarah could see it. He knew that the growing mood of hostility disturbed her, and he wanted, as much as possible, to protect her from it.

As he drove out Interstate 635, however, he saw a big billboard which brought home the fact that he couldn't protect her from everything.

Jews
Are the Disciples of
Satan

St. Louis, Missouri

It very quickly became known that Reed Franken was the national leader of the SPS, because his pictures became as ubiquitous as those of Ohmshidi. And because the official policy of the *Moqaddas Sirata* forbade pictures, the fact that Ohmshidi and Franken were the only two photos on public display made them the two most recognized people in the entire nation.

There was a billboard on Lindbergh Boulevard, which had a picture of Franken, standing with his right arm folded across his chest, his hand clenched into a fist, staring out at the traffic which, because fuel was becoming increasingly available, was beginning to flow again, though not nearly with the intensity of the "before time."

The words, in big black letters alongside Franken's picture, read:

BE A GOOD CITIZEN
REPORT YOUR NEIGHBORS
WHO DO NOT FOLLOW
THE PATH OF MOQADDAS SIRATA
LET THIS BE YOUR GREETING
OBEY OHMSHIDI

Soon after Franken reconstituted the SPS, he sent his men out across the nation, confiscating guns, Bibles, and the Torah. They also began killing dogs, and enforcing the new law that required greetings be exchanged by making a fist of your right hand, holding it over your heart, and saying; "Obey Ohmshidi."

There were some who welcomed the invasion of the SPS because for the first few months after the total collapse, a wave of lawlessness had swept through the nation terrorizing the people. The SPS provided an element of security, albeit a security that deprived people of individual freedoms. Still, for the most part, it was within a person's power to avoid the wrath of the SPS, simply by following the rules, no matter how personally repugnant those rules might be.

The SPS men were immediately recognizable because of the forest green uniforms, and the gold SPS letters on their collar, the S's resembling two lightning bolts, separated by the letter P that looked like a hatchet. They wore the insignia of rank on the epaulets, and a red armband which had Ohmshidi's personal symbol, the letter "O." They greeted each other by making a fist of their right hand and clasping across their chest, while saying, "Obey Ohmshidi." What's more, they insisted that all citizens adopt that as a greeting.

The SPS seemed most zealous in enforcing the Religious Liberation Act which, contrary to its name, did not offer religious liberty, but outlawed all religion except for the *Moqaddas Sirata* of Islam.

In what everyone was now calling "the before time," Tom Jack had been a lieutenant commander in the U.S. Navy, a SEAL who had been involved in many combat operations. When the U.S. military disbanded, Tom, and tens of thousands of other career soldiers, sailors, and airmen, were forced out of service. Returning to his home town of St. Louis, he had earned a living by providing security for people, protecting them against roving bands of thieves. He also fished in the Mississippi, Missouri, and Merrimac rivers, and hunted deer and rabbit out in St. Louis County. And because in the beginning money was worthless, Tom supported himself and his wife, Sheri, on the barter system.

New money had now been introduced and it was gradually beginning to be a viable instrument of trade; though for gasoline, electricity, and water, money wasn't enough. An identity card was also necessary, and in order to obtain the card one had to swear personal allegiance to Ohmshidi—and that, Tom wouldn't do. Inevitably a black market developed, and it was through the black market that Tom was able to provide the necessities of life, though he hated assigning any value to a currency that had Ohmshidi's face on every denomination.

In addition, Tom's private security service was becoming more difficult to maintain, as the SPS was not only providing its own brand of security, but also closing down any private company they felt was in competition with them, including detective agencies, bodyguards, and security companies.

Despite the Religious Liberation Act, many

churches across the country continued to conduct regular services, doing so in open and defiant violation of that law. One such church was a Catholic church in St. Louis, and the announcement board in front of it read:

Congress shall make no law respecting an establishment of religion, or prohibiting the free exercise thereof.

The fact that there was no longer a constitution, or a congress, did nothing to lessen the impact of the statement, and on this particular Sunday morning, the priest, in liturgical garb, was standing in front of the church, welcoming the few parishioners who were brave enough to attend the service.

Tom and Sheri Jack were not parishioners, but by coincidence they were at this particular moment standing on the corner in front of the church, waiting at a bus stop.

Suddenly two motorcycles turned off the road and up onto the sidewalk.

"What are those crazy people doing up on the sidewalk?" Sheri asked. "That's not very smart."

The bikers were wearing the forest green uniforms of the State Protective Service.

"Look at their uniforms. They're SPS, that should answer your question," Tom replied.

"Nobody has ever accused any SPS person of being smart."

Suddenly the two riders opened their throttles to full and came roaring up the sidewalk toward the church.

"Tom!" Sheri shouted.

Tom grabbed Sheri and pulled her out into the street just in time to avoid being hit by the roaring motorcycles. They watched as the motorcycles headed for the church, then they heard the sound of gunfire, even above the noise of the engines.

Not only did the priest go down, but so did several of the parishioners who were standing nearby. The motorcyclists went to the far end of the block, then turned around and started back.

"They're coming back!" someone shouted.

Tom pulled a pistol from his pocket and aimed at the first biker, giving him a slight lead. Neither of the bikers realized they were in danger as they came back for a second pass. Tom pulled the trigger and the first rider lost control of his bike when he was hit. His bike fell over and the second biker, with no time to react, slammed into the first. The two bikes slid along the sidewalk, sending up a shower of sparks until they came to a stop, the two riders nothing but bloody pulps.

It was at that very moment that the bus approached, and Tom and Sheri boarded.

"What happened?" the driver asked.

"Motorcycle wreck," Tom replied.

"Hmmph. You'll never get me on one of those things." The driver closed the door and Tom and Sheri took their seats.

CHAPTER FIVE

Firebase Freedom

Although they still had the helicopter, fuel was now so short that neither Jake nor Bob, the only two pilots, were flying. In the eighteen months they had been here, though, Marcus still kept it in perfect flying condition, helped by both Willy and Deon. In the meantime they continued to make improvements inside the fort, which now had a large and productive garden with tomatoes, beans, peppers, cucumbers, lettuce, potatoes, cabbage, and carrots. Since they first arrived, they had managed to acquire some goats, which provided milk and goat cheese. Having made connections with others on the island, there was, through a system of barter and use of the Moqaddas money, a type of economy established, so that Pleasure Island, if not prospering, was surviving quite well.

It was night, and Jake was sitting on top of the

south wall of the fort, looking out over the water. Karin came to join him, and sitting beside him, handed him a glass of lemonade.

"I thought you might like this," she said.

"Thanks. But you know what I'd really like."

"I know. You want a root beer."

"Yeah. I don't know if anyone is even making root beer anymore. It kills me to think that I may never have another one."

"Ahh, you were too hooked on those things anyway," Karin said. "It'll do you good to go cold turkey."

"Whoa, cold turkey? We're not talking about drug withdrawal here."

"Why not? It's the same principle."

Jake chuckled, then took a swallow of his lemonade. "Yeah, maybe you're right." Lifting the glass, he pointed toward lights, out at sea. "I look at all those offshore rigs, and I wonder about them. Are they pumping oil? Oil and gas have started moving up on the mainland now."

"Yes, but it's not that available, it cost a ton of money, and you have to show an ID card. Do you want to get an ID card, swearing that you have converted?"

"No, but some of the people down here on the island have. I don't blame them, though. If we had no access of any kind, we wouldn't have any sugar, or coffee, or half a dozen other things that we aren't able to do for ourselves."

"That's true. But can you imagine what the

people on the mainland are having to go through, even for the simplest necessities of life? Destroy pictures, and kill their dogs."

"Ha, Bob wouldn't kill Charley if you pointed a gun at him and demanded it," Jake said.

"I was talking to Ellen Varney. Did you know this is the second dog they've named Charley? She says that Bob told her that if England could have eight kings named Henry, he could have two dogs names Charley."

"Bob is an interesting man," Jake said. "He told me a good story about the Battle of Mobile Bay. Except for four, all the Union ships involved were wooden ships, but they were protected by chain mail hanging over the sides, and the shot and shell from the fort just bounced off of them. One of them, the *Brooklyn*, was struck seventy times, and didn't sink."

"He knows a lot of history, doesn't he?"

"Ha! It's because he's so damn old that he's lived through it. Do you know he can remember, as a boy, knowing someone who actually fought in the Civil War? And he served in the army with someone who was the last World War I veteran to be on active duty. If we ever get bored, all we have to do is let him tell stories. Don't forget, that's what he did for a living."

"How is he coming along with the Declaration of Independence he's writing?" Karin asked.

"I don't know, he hasn't let me see it yet. But

I expect it'll be just about what we want, and need."

"Declaration of Independence. That's quite a thing. Do you really think we'll ever actually be an independent country?"

"Yes. How viable we will be as a country, I don't know. But that isn't our primary goal. Our primary goal is to throw Ohmshidi and those towel-headed sons of bitches the hell out of here, and take back America."

"You actually have confidence that we can do that?"

"I do. I mean, that's the whole point of this, isn't it? To take our country back?"

"How are we ever going to do that, Jake? You know as well as I do that Ohmshidi has access to every nuclear weapon this country had. I mean, if we started making too big of a problem for him, he could take care of us with just one nuke."

"You think we should just give up because he has nukes?"

"I think we should be realistic about our chances."

"What if someone had said that to George Washington? I mean, when you think about it, what chance did the Colonies have against England, in 1776?"

"Yeah? Well, England had to send troops 3,500 miles, and they didn't have a nuclear bomb," Karin said.

Jake took another swallow of his lemonade.

"Uh-huh, and the Colonies didn't have me to lead them," he teased.

Karin laughed, and punched him playfully on the shoulder. "You know what you remind me of? You remind me of a mouse, floating down the river on his back, with an erection, shouting 'Raise the draw bridge!'"

"Whoa now, that really hurts. Are you saying my pecker's the same size as a mouse's pecker?"

"Well, no, I do know better than that," Karin said, and she leaned over to kiss him.

"Want to play around?" Jake asked after the kiss.

"Up here, on top of the wall?"

"No. But we could walk up the beach for a way, nobody would see us in the dark. It might be fun."

"What would be fun about getting sand in the crack of your ass?"

"Wouldn't be my crack that got sand."

"Yeah, it would. If you really want to do this, we're goin' to roll through the sand like tumbleweed. It's both of us, or no go."

Jake chuckled, then stood up and reached down for her. "All right then, let's go. What's a little sand in your ass anyway?"

There was no moon, so it was quite dark on the beach, so dark that when then they were no more than a hundred yards away from the fort, it could no longer be seen. Jake stopped her, and they kissed again.

"This is far enough."

"How do you know?"

"Look behind us. If we can't see the fort, nobody there can see us."

"What if someone comes out for a moonlight stroll?"

"Haven't you noticed? There is no moon tonight. They would have to stumble over us to see us."

Jake sat down on the sand and pulled Karin down with him.

"It's time to get some sand in our ass," he said.

Karin laughed again. "I swear, Jake, you say the most romantic things."

They stretched out on the sand as the waves crashed ashore.

CHAPTER SIX

Dallas

Sam Gelbman stood at the window in his office, looking out onto the terminal lot at the two eighteen-wheelers that were parked there.

The two eighteen-wheelers were all that remained of what had once been a fleet of as many as fifty trucks. Mid-American Trucking, the company Sam owned, once hauled freight between Dallas and cities all over the country, from Spokane, Washington, to Miami, Florida, and from Portland, Maine, to San Diego, California, and from Canada to Mexico. That all ended shortly after Ohmshidi took office and decreed that fossil fuels could no longer be used. Mid-American, like every other freight and passenger line, went bankrupt.

Sam did manage to hang on to two trucks in the hope and belief that at some point Ohmshidi would see the error of his policies, and fossil fuels would once again be allowed. That did happen, but it was almost too late, and now businesses all over the country were struggling hard to make a comeback.

Because Sam had managed to hang on to the two trucks, he was slowly beginning to rebuild a successful business. He remembered reading something once which stated that, "if all the money in America were to be confiscated and redistributed evenly, within a year those who had been rich would again be rich and those who had been poor would again be poor."

Sam felt a sense of satisfaction in the belief that he was living proof of that declaration.

Recovery had not been easy, and it was still difficult. No matter how much money one had, the purchase of goods and services had to be accompanied by showing an ID card, proving that the customer had converted to Islam. But Sam and his wife were Jewish, and by decree of the government of the American Islamic Republic of Enlightenment, Jews were not allowed to convert to Islam. Instead, they were issued Jewish Infidel cards, which they had to show in order to buy anything. Once identified as such, they were charged a "Jewish Excise Tax" of one hundred percent, and that meant everything they bought cost twice as much for them as it did for other people.

That was not just for personal items, like food, clothing, and household appliances. It extended to his business as well, and Sam had to deal with crippling regulations and requirements.

He needed a Special Infidel Business License to do business. This cost three times as much as a business license did for non-Jews.

In addition to paying a one-hundred-percent Jewish Excise Tax on fuel for his personal vehicles, there was an additional hundred-percent tax on the fuel for his truck.

He was charged a commerce tax on everything that came through the store.

Despite all that, Sam's business was picking up, and he was thinking about adding another truck and another couple of employees. One of the drivers came into the office.

"Boss, we're pulling out now," the driver said. "I'm headed for Kansas City, Buck is goin' to Memphis."

"All right," Sam said. "You two drive safely."

"Hell, that's no problem," the driver said. "There ain't one tenth of the traffic on the road now that there used to be."

Sam stood in the window and watched as the two drivers climbed into the cabs and started the engines. The rumbling roar of the big diesel engines had a reassuring sound, a sound that connected him with the "before time." The trucks pulled out of the parking area, but almost immediately after they left, a car drove onto the lot. The car belonged not to the police, but to the SPS, and Sam felt a moment of apprehension.

His apprehension grew when the two men in the car got out and started toward the office.

These weren't just SPS men, they were Janissaries, and Sam knew that the Janissaries were particularly hostile to Jews. He watched them approach, wondering if he should try and leave through the back door so as to avoid them. He knew, though, that he couldn't avoid them forever, so he waited, nervously, until they came inside. Though they were wearing identical uniforms, the insignias on their epaulets were different, and Sam could only assume that meant that one was higher in rank than the other—though as he had purposely avoided any study of the SPS or the Janissaries, he had no idea what the ranks were.

The two men made fists of their right hands, and folded their arms across their chests, putting their fists over their hearts.

"Obey Ohmshidi," one of them said.

Awkwardly, self-consciously, Sam repeated the gesture. "Obey Ohmshidi," he said. "May I help you gentlemen?"

"We're looking for the Jew that owns this business," the taller of the two men said. He also seemed to have more hardware on his epaulets, so Sam decided he must be the higher rank.

"I'm Sam Gelbman."

"Gelbman, this is for you." The tall man handed him an envelope.

"What is it?" Sam asked.

"Read it, and comply." The two men left without a further word, and Sam pulled out the document to read. The first line he read caused him to get an empty sensation in the pit of his stomach, and he walked back over to his desk to sit down and read it more slowly.

Decree on the Registration of the Property of Jews

Effective immediately, all Jews are required to value their assets (foreign and domestic) and register them if their value is in excess of 500 Moqaddas. All real estate, to include houses, business buildings, and unimproved land holdings, will be confiscated without compensation. Effective this date, no Jew may enter into a sales contract for any property, as a means of avoiding the requirements of this document. The regulations adopted pursuant to this order shall prohibit all further economic activity of Jews except for such activity as is required to purchase food, those purchases to be made at Moqaddas Sirata–*compliant stores only.*

In addition, all Jewish businesses shall be put under government control with the goal of sale to Muslims with a substantial portion of the sale price going to the government.

Jews may be retained to work in their former businesses, but at a fixed salary, with no profit incentive.

If he were to be honest with himself, Sam would have to say that this decree didn't come as a great surprise. The sign in his yard, the graffiti scratched into the side of his car, and the fact that longtime friends, though they didn't join in with the harassment, were beginning to avoid him, told him all he needed to know about where things were going.

Sam's grandfather had been a survivor of the Nazi concentration camps, and Sam remembered, vividly, the ID number stenciled on his uncle's arm. The Nazis had turned an unreasonable hatred of Jews into their core principle. But Americans, he knew, had never had an official policy of anti-Semitism, and though there was a history of animosity between Muslims and Jews, he couldn't see that spreading into a national policy.

Neither one of Sam's drivers was Jewish, but he knew that they liked and respected him, and would do anything for him. And as long as there were men and women like that, he wasn't going to let this flare-up of anti-Jewish activity bother him. He was sure that goodness would prevail, and this would pass.

He looked again at the decree that had been given him.

But until it did pass, he knew that he, and all the other Jews in the country, were going to be in for a rough time.

Boston, Massachusetts

A sign in front of the building announced, proudly, that this was one of the oldest Christian churches in America. It was a Sunday morning, and several determined souls were walking to the morning worship service, walking instead of driving, for not one of them had made the conversion necessary to allow them the privilege of buying fuel. The reverend Al Stokes stood in front of the church, welcoming his parishioners as they arrived.

"Brother David, Sister Elizabeth, welcome," Stokes said.

"Good morning, Pastor. Beautiful morning, isn't it?"

"Yes, it is a manifestation of the glory of God."

"Have Elmer and Ann arrived yet?" David asked.

"Indeed they have, they are already inside."

"Good. They promised to sing in the choir today and I just wanted to make certain that Elmer didn't back out."

Stokes chuckled. "You be sure and hang on to them. We need all the singers we can get."

At that moment the friendly conversation between the pastor, David, and Elizabeth was interrupted as three vans drove up, screeching to a stop in front of the church. The other arriving parishioners were startled by the intrusion of the vans and they looked toward them in surprise and apprehension. The doors opened and a dozen armed men, wearing the uniforms of the State Protective Service, poured out.

"Here, what is this? What are you men . . ." one of the worshipers called out to the SPS but he was unable to finish the question because he was shot down.

There were screams after the first shot, and the

screams and shouts grew louder as the men in uniform continued shooting indiscriminately, their weapons on full automatic, into the crowd of churchgoers. Several went down with bleeding wounds, including women and children.

"Here!" the pastor shouted, not running from the armed men, but toward them. "What are you doing? This is a house of God!"

"This is a house of heresy," the leader of the attack squad shouted back.

"How dare you?" the pastor said, angrily.

"Grab him," the chief of the SPS group shouted, and two men grabbed the minister.

Other SPS officers approached the church then, and, directing flame throwers toward the building, quickly had it enveloped in flames.

"No!" the pastor called. "There are people in there!"

A television crew had arrived with the SPS squad, and they were filming the church as it was consumed by flames. From inside the church people could be heard screaming in terror. As the people in the church ran outside to escape the flames, they were shot down by the SPS troopers. A crowd of citizens had also gathered to watch, and they were almost evenly divided between those who shouted for the destruction of the church, and those who were lamenting the deed.

As the flames leaped higher into the air, the

leader of the SPS group signaled to have the pastor brought to him.

"Put him on his knees," the leader ordered, and the two men who were holding him forced him down.

"Renounce your heretical religion and pay homage to Allah," the leader demanded.

"Jesus Christ is my Lord and Savior," Stokes said.

The leader took a long bladed knife from his belt, then proceeded to cut off the preacher's head. It wasn't a clean, brisk stroke, but a series of sawing actions which spewed blood, and elicited shouts of horror from the onlookers. Finally the head was severed from the body and, smiling, the SPS leader held it up by the hair. Bone and gristle protruded down from the neck, dripping blood in an almost solid stream.

"Death to all who would violate the new order!" the SPS leader shouted.

Much later that same day, on TV receivers all across the country, the evening news started. The program began with a full-screen shot of the new national flag, White, with a wide red bar running from the top of the banner to the bottom. There was a white circle in the middle of the red bar, and in the middle of that white circle, a green letter "O" enclosing wavy blue lines which represented clean water, over which was imposed a stylized green plant.

The words Ameʀican Enlightened Tʀuth Television were keyed onto the screen, replaced by the words Obey Ohmshidi, then a reverent voiceover intoned the opening lines.

> *"All praise be to Allah, the merciful.*
> *Whomsoever Allah guides there is none to*
> *misguide, and whomsoever Allah misguides*
> *there is none to guide. You must live your life in*
> *accordance with the Moqaddas Sirata, the Holy*
> *Path. Those who do will be blessed. Those who*
> *do not will be damned.*
>
> *"You are watching the American Enlightened*
> *Truth Television network. And now, our*
> *National Anthem."*

As the music played, the national flag of the AIRE fluttered in the background, but superimposed over the letter "O" was Ohmshidi's face. It remained prominent as the music began to play, the words sung by an all-male chorus.

> *American Islamic Republic of Enlightenment*
> *Our people loyal and true*
> *To Ohmshidi our leader*
> *We give all honor to you.*
> *Glory to our great leader*
> *May he remain right and strong*
> *The party of the faithful*
> *Ohmshidi to lead us on!*

In Moqaddas Sirata
We see the future of our dear land
And to the Ohmshidi banner,
In obedience shall we stand!
Glory to our great leader
May he remain right and strong
The party of the faithful
Ohmshidi to lead us on

When the anthem ended, the scene returned to the studio where a young woman was sitting behind a news desk. She was wearing a burqa and her face was covered so that only her eyes could be seen.

"Yesterday, in our nation's capital of Muslimabad, a thief was captured, stealing a loaf of bread. The thief was only eight years old, so his life was spared, but as you can see from this video he did not escape punishment.

On screen a uniformed officer of the SPS was squatting down beside the front wheel of a car. Lying on the ground beside him, his arm wrapped in a towel, his eyes filled with terror and tears, was a small boy. The SPS officer was holding the boy's arm in front of the car wheel with one hand, while with the other hand he was speaking into a microphone to all those who were gathered around to watch the show.

"What you are about to see is just punishment for the sins of this boy" [the SPS officer said]. *"He violated* Moqaddas Sirata *by stealing from others. He took a loaf of bread from a store, and it wasn't just any store. He took a loaf of bread from the shelf of a store that is* Moqaddas Sirata*—compliant. In doing so, he committed a sin against our new republic, and our great leader. For that, he must be punished."*

"No, please," the boy begged, crying. "I won't do it again. I promise, I won't do it again."

The boy jerked his arm back, but the SPS officer punched him hard in the temple with his fist, driving the boy's face onto the pavement so hard that it knocked him out. With the boy unconscious, the SPS officer put the boy's arm under the front of the car wheel again.

"All right driver, come ahead slowly."

The car moved forward, the wheel passing over and crushing the boy's arm. There were gasps of shock, horror, and even morbid excitement from the crowd.

"A blight in Boston was eliminated yesterday by the good work of the State Protective Service. A church which proudly, and profanely, advertised itself as one of the oldest Christian churches in America. This church continued,

*despite many warnings, to lead poor souls to
hell by its heretical teachings. This sinful
practice left a tolerant government with no
choice but to act for the good of the people. As
you will see here, the church was eliminated."*

On screen could be seen forest-green uniformed men gunning down the worshipers as
they ran. Soon the church was in flames, those
inside shot as they tried to escape the blaze.

*"It is perhaps fitting that, for many of the
infidels who were inside the building as it
burned, their last memory on earth will be
of fire. For surely they have been cast into
the fiery furnaces of hell by their sinful
denial of* Moqaddas Sirata."

The last picture was of the pastor's head being
sawed from his body, then held up for all to see.
The camera moved in for a long, lingering view
of the severed head, one eye half closed, the
other wide open, still reflecting the terror of the
moment.

"Behold the severed head of the sinner," the news-
woman said. *"Allahu Akbar."*

The broadcast continued, intermixing scenes
of burning churches and strict punishments,
with scenes of smiling drivers filling their cars
with fuel, and shoppers selecting food from
filled shelves.

"*Mr. Jones, what do you have to say about the new order?*" a reporter asked, sticking his microphone in the face of a shopper.

"*I say we live in exciting times. We are here at the birth of a new nation, led by the father of the new nation, the Great Leader, President for Life Ohmshidi. And it is good to know that, for the first time in my life, we are not threatening any other nation with aggression, as we have in all our sordid history.*"

The broadcast closed with an earnest appeal from the news anchor.

"*My fellow citizens, as you can see by the images we have shown you tonight, our country has recovered, stronger, and better than it ever was. But, as you have also seen, there are still examples of misguided people who are doing the work of Satan by not complying with the order of* Moqaddas Sirata.

"*This television station urges each of you to do your part in serving our beloved Great Leader, President for Life, Mehdi Ohmshidi, by reporting to the authorities anyone who would violate the laws of* Moqaddas Sirata."

The broadcast closed with a full-screen, stylized portrait of Ohmshidi in a pensive pose, looking slightly up and to his left. The rendering was in red, beige, and blue, with the words *Obey Ohmshidi* underneath. The letter "O" in "Obey" duplicated the new national symbol.

CHAPTER SEVEN

Geneva, Switzerland—United Nations Headquarters

The United Nations had moved from New York to Geneva in the "before time" within the first year of Ohmshidi's presidency. They did so, declaring that conditions in the United States were no longer stable enough for the UN. For a while, the United States continued to be a member of the United Nations, and to hold on to their position as a permanent member of the Security Council. However, shortly after the three nuclear detonations in America, resulting in the total collapse of the country, the United States no longer had a seat on the Security Council, nor even a place in the General Assembly.

The American Islamic Republic of Enlightenment tried to reclaim the seat once held by the United States, but they were denied membership. The American Islamic Republic of Enlightenment was, however, granted a seat as a nonvoting observer in the General Assembly. And today, Barrack Azid Hussein, who was Ohmshidi's observer to the United Nations (he did not merit the title "Ambassador"), had to listen as country after country condemned AIRE for its human rights violations.

"Christian worshipers slaughtered, a young boy's arm crushed under the wheel of a car—and these are not isolated incidents, but are the policy of the government in Washington."

"A point of order, Ambassador, the name of the city is Muslimabad," Hussein said.

Hussein was gaveled by the Secretary General.

"The gentleman is not recognized, and will not interrupt again."

The ambassador from England continued. "It is, indeed, a sad commentary on the times, when the country that was once looked up to by the rest of the world, the country of tolerance, the country of good will, the country who held up a light of liberty for the rest of the world, has now become a pariah among nations. I weep for the hundreds of thousands of young Americans who, throughout the history of that once, great nation, gave their lives for the peace of the world. Great Britain supports the resolution condemning the—so called—American Islamic Republic of Enlightenment."

Hamid Karim Rahman, ambassador from Pakistan, defended the American Islamic Republic.

"For many years, the United States of America conducted war against Islam, and, with bribes, encouraged Muslim to fight Muslim. Now, they are no longer a threat to peace in the Middle East. Pakistan, and the fifty-five other Muslim nations who are members of the United Nations, protest this proposed resolution, and join with the Organization of Islamic Cooperation in praising AIRE for its awakening. We are proud to say that the American Islamic Republic of Enlightenment is a valued member of the OIC."

Despite the protest of all fifty-six Muslim members of the United Nations, the resolution of condemnation for violation of human rights passed, and a formal censure was issued.

Resolution 3817 is hereby issued by the United Nations in assembly in Geneva, Switzerland:

1. *Expressing grave concern at the deteriorating situation, the escalation of violence, and the disregard of human life by the entity identifying itself as the American Islamic Republic of Enlightenment, formerly the United States of America.*

2. *Reiterating the responsibility of the AIRE authorities to protect their people and reaffirming that armed representatives of the government bear the primary responsibility to*

> *take all feasible steps to ensure the protection of its citizens.*
>
> 3. *Condemning the gross and systematic violation of human rights, including arbitrary detentions, torture, and summary executions.*
>
> 4. *Further condemning acts of violence and intimidation committed by the authorities against independent journalists, media professionals, and associated personnel, and urging these authorities to comply with their obligations under international humanitarian law as outlined in previous resolutions issued by this body.*
>
> 5. *Warning the authorities of the American Islamic Republic of Enlightenment (formerly the United States of America), that continued crimes against the civilian population may amount to crimes against humanity.*

This resolution of condemnation was the first ever passed against the United States, though the resolution itself was quick to point out that the AIRE was no longer the U.S.A.

Nevertheless, news of the resolution appeared in newspapers and on radio and television around the world. The irony was that all the Western nations that used to be the allies of the U.S., such as Canada, Great Britain, France, Germany, Spain, Israel, and Japan, were in support of the resolution. So too were Russia and China.

Those nations that once condemned the United States were quick to issue statements of support for the American Islamic Republic of Enlightenment. In fact, the fifty-six member nations of the Organization of Islamic Cooperation issued two strongly worded resolutions, one condemning the UN resolution, and one offering support for AIRE.

Muslimabad

When Mohammad Akbar Rahimi sent for Ohmshidi, the president, who owed his position to Rahimi, responded as if he were an obedient student called to the principal's office. Without entourage or bodyguards, Ohmshidi went to Rahimi.

"You have seen the United Nation's resolution?" Rahimi asked.

"I have, Imam. I'm sorry if I have brought disgrace to the country."

"It is not the country who is disgraced," Rahimi said. "It is the United Nations. When we establish the World Caliphate, bringing everyone into Islam, we will replace the United Nations with the Organization of Islamic Cooperation. And we will use the old UN building in New York as our headquarters."

Ohmshidi smiled. "Yes, Imam, that is a wonderful idea."

"I have a new program I want you to establish across the land," Rahimi said. He slid a manila folder across the desk toward Ohmshidi. "Put it into effect at once."

"Yes, Imam."

One hour later, after having read the document Rahimi had given him, Ohmshidi called out to his chief of staff.

"Hassan?"

"Yes, Great Leader?" Raj Hassan answered, hurrying to respond to the president's call.

"You have read the resolution passed by the United Nations?"

"I have, Great Leader."

"I know it is because of the incident of the young boy having his arm crushed for stealing."

"Yes, Your Excellency, I believe that is so."

"It was televised for the whole world to see," Ohmshidi said. "I'm sure that there will be many who don't understand the necessity of such stern treatment. But if we are truly to create a new world, an Islamic world of *Moqaddas Sirata*, then we can make no exceptions."

"Oh, I quite agree, Great Leader."

"That's why I have conceived of Operation Blooming Flowers. If this young man had been part of Blooming Flowers, there would not have been the necessity of crushing his arm."

"Blooming Flowers, Great Leader?"

"Yes. If we are to have a country united in *Moqaddas Sirata*, we must take steps so that the next generation will be united in service to Allah. We will accomplish that by intensive schooling of the young people."

Ohmshidi, having revised the document given him by Rahimi so that it would appear to be his own idea, handed it to Hassan.

Hassan read the document, then nodded. "Yes, this is good. The entire country will bless you for your wisdom and compassion in establishing such a benevolent policy."

"How soon can we start?"

"I will have to arrange for the learning centers, but I will get started right away, Great Leader."

"Very good. Tell me now, where do we stand with the Jewish problem?"

"We have begun Operation Ultimate Resolution," Rahimi said. "Already we are confiscating Jewish property and wealth, and soon the relocation will take effect."

"Good. I want to be kept informed of the progress of both Ultimate Resolution and Blooming Flowers."

"I will do so, Great Leader."

Dallas

Sam Gelbman stood in the alley behind his house on Davenport Court and looked out across the railroad track and the creek that ran parallel with the track. For the first few months after the country had collapsed, and during that time when there was neither water nor electricity, this creek had been the sole source of water. They purified it by boiling it over a charcoal grill, though as charcoal was not readily available, they had used scavenged wood.

Sam and Sarah had already been gardeners, and canners, so they fared better than many others, not only having a supply of food, but using it as a form of barter for other necessities. Sam had a .22 rifle that his father had bought for him for his twelfth birthday. Initially he had kept it as a remembrance of his youth, but it quickly became one of his most valuable possessions during the hard times, because he was able to use it to kill squirrels, rabbits, a few doves, and even a beaver. Once the national confiscation of personal weapons began, he wrapped the rifle in oil cloth and buried it in his garden, rather than give it up.

Electricity and water were available again, as was food. However, because he and Sarah were Jewish and not authorized to convert to Islam—not that he would have—their struggle to survive was only marginally easier than it had been during the time of total collapse.

And now that struggle was going to be even more difficult because his business, his house, and all personal property were being taken away by the *Decree on the Registration of the Property of Jews*. Sam had not yet told Sarah of the decree, and as he stood out in his backyard now, he was trying to come up with a way of breaking the news to her.

Like Sam, Sarah's grandfather had survived the Nazi concentration camps, though his parents had not. While still young, Sarah's grandfather had been adopted by Major David Goren, an American officer of Jewish descent, when the camp where he had been held was liberated. Brought to America when he was nine years old, he had grown to adulthood in Dallas, though the horror of the concentration camps was never far from his mind.

When Ohmshidi was first elected, there had been an unexpected wave of anti-Jewish sentiment that began to emanate from his administration, manifested first by America turning its back on Israel, then spreading to include American Jews as well. That movement had frightened Sarah, and Sam tried to comfort her, assuring her that what happened in Germany decades ago would never happen in America.

"I fought in Afghanistan for this country," Sam told her. "I know America isn't going to turn its back on me."

Sam had, indeed, fought in Afghanistan, where he received the Silver Star. But, he realized, the America he had fought for was no more. And while the America he was born in, grew up in, and was proud to serve would not have turned its back on him, the American Islamic Republic of Enlightenment had done just that.

With a sigh, Sam went back into the house. There was a possible way out of all this. Along with the decree that had taken his business, was an offer that would allow Jews to relocate to an area where they could establish their own community.

Jews
Do You Wish to Relocate?
Land is being made available for you in West Texas.

Land and work are waiting for all Jews who would take advantage of this opportunity to relocate. You will be able to grow your own garden, raise your own poultry, and engage in productive labor which will be personally rewarding. If you refuse to take advantage of this opportunity you will see more and more of your freedoms taken from you, as good Muslims of faith will not stand by and watch our new society be corrupted by Jewish infidels.

Work shall make you free.

Of course, taking advantage of this opportunity meant that they would have to leave home, but the same decree that took his business was also taking his house, car, and all furnishings, so that was not even a consideration. When he asked how they were supposed to get to the new area without a car, he was told they would be transported, free of charge, by bus. Sam could see no alternative but to take the offer.

Sarah had been born and raised in Dallas, and Sam knew that it was going to be difficult for her to leave. They had met in college during a production of *Fiddler on the Roof*, Sam playing the role of Motel, and Sarah as Tzeitel. The stage romance developed into a real romance and the two planned to be married as soon as they got out of school. Upon graduation, however, Sam had to fulfill an ROTC obligation with the army. He went to Afghanistan, and they put the wedding off until he got back. Postponing the marriage had been Sam's idea, because he didn't want to leave a wife behind in case something happened to him. They were married as soon as he returned from Afghanistan twelve years ago.

Sam began working for Sarah's father, Nat Goren, at Mid-American Trucking. He worked first as a driver, then as a manager, then he bought half the business, and when Nat Goren retired, Sam bought the entire business from him. It had been an extremely profitable operation until the total collapse of the nation, which closed banks and rendered money useless. The collapse had cost Sam over four million dollars.

When Sam went back inside he could smell the aroma of roast chicken with carrots and zucchini.

"Mmm, it smells delicious. What are we celebrating?"

Sarah chuckled. "We are celebrating that we have chicken," she said.

"Reason enough for celebration," Sam agreed.

"Does it look like rain?" Sarah asked.

"No."

"Too bad, the garden could use a little rain. Dinner's about ready."

"Good, I'm starved."

"Tell me when you aren't starved," Sarah teased.

Sarah filled two plates, then sat down to the table with her husband. He reached across the table and took her hand. "I love you," he said.

"I love you too."

"I can't imagine my life without you."

"Why would you have to imagine it? I haven't found any new boyfriends," Sarah teased.

"You just try, I'll tell them how much you snore," Sam said, smiling back at her.

"I do not snore."

"And lemons aren't sour."

They ate their dinner before Sam gathered enough nerve to tell her what had happened today.

"Sarah, I've something I want to talk to you about," he said.

"What?"

Sam showed Sarah the decree.

"What? What does this mean?" she asked, her voice weak.

"It means we no longer own the company," he said.

"They can't just make you sell out to them, can they?"

Again, Sam reached across the table to take Sarah's hand. "My love, I wish they were buying us out. They aren't. They're just taking the company, lock, stock, and barrel."

"No!" Sarah said, as her eyes welled with tears.

"There is an alternative," Sam suggested. "Another path we could take if you are willing to do it."

"What is that?"

Sam showed Sarah the relocation document. "I want you to read this, and tell me what you think of it."

She looked at it for a moment, then glanced up at him, her eyes showing some hope. "Sam, do you think this is for real? I mean is there really a place where we can go and start all over, away from . . . from all this?" She made a motion with her hand to encompass "all this."

"Yes, I do think it is for real."

"Well, what's the catch? There must be some catch to it."

"The only catch I've been able to learn about, is that we will be signing over not only our business, but all our property—house, furniture, and cars. Also, when we report for transport, we can each carry only one suitcase."

"Well, if we're leaving Dallas, what good is our property to us? We may as well sell it."

"Uh-uh," Sam said, shaking his head. "The truth is, Sarah, whether we take this offer or not, we are going to have to give up our house, and we won't be paid for it."

"You mean it's not just our business? They're going to take our home as well?"

Sam shook his head. "No, they are taking our house, not our home. We are our home."

Sarah paused for a moment, then nodded. "All right," she said. "Yes, let's do it."

"I'll go down and make the application tomorrow," Sam replied, relieved that it had gone easier than he thought it would.

"What do we have here, anyway?" Sarah asked. "A little bit of this, and a little bit of that?"

"A pot, a hat," Sam replied, smiling as he remembered the lines. Together, they began to sing.

"*Anatevka*."

CHAPTER EIGHT

Mobile, Alabama

The first casualties of all public schools were the extra-curricular activities such as band, orchestra, chorus, and drama. History books were changed as well, and the students were taught that there had never been the holocaust, and that the continued perpetuation of that lie would be a sin. *The country once known as the United States, was the most hated country in the world because of its sins against the Muslim people. It was by an act of Allah that the United States was destroyed.*

They were also taught that *life for non-Muslims, and for all women, even Muslim women, is worth but a fraction of that of a Muslim male. The greeting, "Peace be upon you," is specifically for Muslims, and cannot be spoken to infidels. Jihad in the path of Islam is the noblest of acts.*

Eddie Manning was a student at LeFlores High School in Mobile, Alabama. Eddie's father, Paul, had played football at the University of Alabama for Paul "Bear" Bryant, graduating in 1983, the year Bryant coached his last game. For his entire life, Eddie, who was sixteen years old, had dreamed of playing football for the Crimson Tide. He had been the backup quarterback for LeFlores High School during his sophomore year, and would have been the starting quarterback his junior year, but there would be no football at LeFlores High School this year. There would be no basketball, baseball, or track either. Eddie's girlfriend, Jane Poindexter, would have been a cheerleader this year, but of course, that program was also dropped.

The natural competitive spirit was such, however, that Eddie and many of his friends continued to play football in pickup games. But even these non-sanctioned games were banned, and one day twelve boys from the ages of fourteen to sixteen were gathered in an empty lot for a football game as two cars arrived. The cars were unmarked, and for a moment they just sat at the curb.

"Eddie, what do you think that is?" one of the boys asked.

"I don't know, but I don't like the looks of it," Eddie said. Eddie was sixteen, and a born leader, so it was natural that the others should defer to him.

"What do you think we should do?"

"I think we should get out of here."

"There's no markings on the cars," one of the other boys said. "Maybe they're just football fans, and they've come to watch us play."

"I don't think so," Eddie said. "I don't have a good feeling about this. I think we should . . ."

That was as far as Eddie got before eight bearded men, all wearing *dishdasha* and *taqiyah*, spilled out of the two cars and started toward them. All eight men were carrying automatic weapons.

"Run!" Eddie shouted when he saw what was happening.

All twelve boys were athletes, so they were able to outrun the men, but not the bullets from their weapons. The eight men opened fire, and three of the running boys were shot down. Eddie and the other eight got away.

Later that same day, the nine boys who had been playing in the open field gathered in the garage of one of the boys. Shortly after they gathered, they heard the *Adhan*, or Call to Prayer.

Allahu Akbar
Allahu Akbar

Ash hadu alla ilaha illallah
Ash hadu alla ilaha illallah

The boys had left the door open to the garage and all of them got down on their knees, bowing toward Mecca. But this was just for show, because they knew that there were patrols through the neighborhoods, checking to see if the people were obeying the call to prayer.

In fact, though from some distance it looked as if they were being reverential, they were anything but, because they carried on a conversation throughout the ten minutes of "prayer."

"Eddie, Keith's mama asked me if I knew where he was," a boy named Timmy said.

Keith Leslie was one of the three boys who had been killed that morning. All three bodies had been picked up and taken away. As a result, none of the families of those who had been killed knew what had happened to them.

"What did you tell them?"

"I said I didn't know.

"That's good. Don't tell them anything."

"Don't you think their own parents should know what happened to them?" Carl, one of the other boys asked.

"You think they aren't going to find out? They just don't need to find out from us," Eddie said.

All the time the boys were talking, they were bowing repeatedly.

"That don't seem right," Carl said.

"Listen guys, you can't tell anyone that we know about this, not your brother, sister, parents, or best friend."

"You think they'll tell on us? My mom or dad would never tell on me," another said.

"That's not the point, Burt," Eddie said. "Anyone we tell is going to be involved, and then they'll be in danger. Do you want the police to come looking for your mother and father?"

"No."

"Then do like I say, and don't say a word about this to anyone."

The "prayers" were just finishing when a car stopped out front.

"Eddie, what do you think this means?" Burt asked.

"Nothing," Eddie said. "Everyone, sit down and be holding a Koran. I'll talk to them."

Two bearded men, each of them wearing *dishdasha*, walked up to the garage where, by now, the boys were all sitting on the floor, each of them holding a copy of the Koran.

"*Salaam*," Eddie greeted the two men. He saluted them. "Obey Ohmshidi."

"*Alaykum*," one of the two answered. "Obey Ohmshidi."

"We have just finished with the prayers," Eddie said. "Now we are reading the Koran. Would you like to join us?"

"You are Eddie Manning, aren't you?"

Eddie felt his blood run cold. "Yes, sir."

"You played something called 'quarterback' last year. I am told this is an important position in the infidel game of football."

"I was backup quarterback."

"I am also told you would have been starting quarterback this year. This, too, is said to be important."

"It was important before I learned better. Now I have learned that football is evil and a sin against Allah, so I have no wish to play the game. I don't want to sin against Allah."

"Suppose a group of young men gathered to play the game, not for a school and before large crowds, but on an empty lot somewhere? Would that be a sin?"

"I don't know, I've never thought about it like that."

"There were some boys playing football on an empty lot this morning. When some of Allah's warriors went to arrest them, they ran. They all got away."

When the man said "they all got away," he stared closely at Eddie to gauge his reaction. Eddie knew that three of the boys had not gotten away, but he gave no indication of that knowledge.

The two men stood there for a moment longer, then they started back to their car.

"Peace be upon you," Eddie called, but neither of the two men looked back.

"And may a pig shit on your next meal," Eddie added under his breath. The other boys snickered, but didn't laugh out loud for fear of being heard.

"They know it was us," Carl said. "They know we were the ones playing football."

"They don't know anything," Eddie said. "They were just fishing. Did you see the way he looked at me when he said that everyone got away? He was waiting for me to say something about the three who didn't."

"I'm scared," Tim said. Tim O'Leary was the youngest one of the group.

"Everyone, just keep your wits about you," Eddie said. "If you do that, I think we'll all be all right."

"You *think*."

"Yeah, I think."

"Where did all these people come from? I mean, how did the whole country turn Muslim all of a sudden?" Burt asked.

"I doubt that most of them are really Muslims," Eddie said. "I expect most of 'em are like my mom and dad. They turned Muslim to get the ID cards."

"That's what my mom and dad did," Carl Edwards said. "My dad said he had to do that to keep his job, and be able to buy food and gas."

"I'm not ever goin' to turn Muslim," Burt said.

"We may not have any choice. I mean, I don't want to be Muslim either, but if it's 'turn Muslim or don't eat,' I'll turn Muslim," Eddie said.

"Turn Muslim and have some barbequed ribs," Burt Rowe said, and all laughed.

* * *

The next morning the residents of Mobile woke up to loudspeaker-equipped trucks driving through all the residential areas of the city. On both sides of the truck, so that it could be seen from either side of the street, was a single command, written in large letters:

OBEY OHMSHIDI

The letter "O" in the word Obey, duplicated the national symbol.

"Attention, parents of children from six to seventeen. All children from six to seventeen must be brought to Ladd Stadium by four o'clock today. They must be registered in order for your identity card to be valid."

The residents of the city asked each other what that meant, and if they had heard anything about it. A few went into the street to try and stop the trucks to inquire as to what that meant, but the trucks refused to stop. They continued cruising throughout the city for the entire morning, repeating the same message.

"Attention, parents of children from six to seventeen. All children from six to seventeen must be brought to Ladd Stadium by four o'clock today. They must be registered in order for your identity card to be valid."

In addition to the loudspeaker-equipped truck, flyers were posted about town.

ATTENTION PARENTS
ALL CHILDREN FROM SIX TO SEVENTEEN
MUST BE BROUGHT TO LADD STADIUM BY
FOUR O'CLOCK TODAY
FOR IDENTITY REGISTRATION
THOSE WHO REFUSE
WILL BE SEVERELY PUNISHED

"Are you going to take Eddie to Ladd Stadium?" Clara Poindexter asked Edna Manning.

"It looks like we don't have any choice, so, yes, I will be taking him. Aren't you going to take Jane?"

"I suppose so. But what is it about, do you know?"

"It says for identity registration. I fear if we don't, we may lose our ID cards, then what would we do for food, electricity, water, and gasoline? You can't even work without identity cards."

"That's probably true. But I don't mind telling you, this bothers me," Clara said.

"What bothers me more is the warning that anyone who refuses will be severely punished. We've seen some of the severe punishment, and I've no wish to have anything to do with it, thank you very much."

"You're right, we don't have any choice. Would it be all right if Jane and I ride with you, when you take Eddie down today?"

"Of course," Edna said.

"Oh, we'd better not go without this," Clara said, and she held her hand over the bottom half of her face, indicating that they should wear a veil over their faces.

"Don't worry," Edna replied. "I've already received one warning for not wearing a veil. I don't want to risk a second."

When Paul and Edna Manning, along with their son, Eddie, and Clara Poindexter, with her daughter, Jane, arrived at Ladd Stadium, they saw posted on every lamppost in the parking lot:

OBEY OHMSHIDI

Again, with the stylized "O" in the word "Obey," on every other post, they saw the drawing of Ohmshidi's head, the ever-present portrait in red, beige, and blue, looking slightly up and to his left with his pensive, "I am so much better than you" look.

Here too, they were met by several dozen local policemen as well as several SPS men. It was a policeman, and not one of the SPS officers, who stepped up to the car.

"Obey Ohmshidi," Paul greeted.

The policeman returned the greeting, then asked, "How many children do you have?" He was holding a clipboard.

"There are two in the car," Paul Manning answered.

"Their ages?"

"My son is sixteen."

"And my daughter is fifteen," Clara spoke up from the backseat.

"Quiet, woman. You do not have permission to speak," the police officer said.

"But I thought you wanted . . ."

"I said QUIET, WOMAN!"

"Mama," Jane whispered.

"The girl is fifteen," Paul said. "But she isn't my daughter, she is the daughter of the lady in the backseat, my next-door neighbor."

"It is not permissible for a woman to ride in the car with a man who is not her husband or her relative."

"She is my sister," Paul said quickly. It was a lie, and Paul took a chance, but it was either that, or see Clara punished.

"And this woman?"

"Is my wife."

Both Clara and Edna were wearing scarves and veils, though Jane was not.

The policeman stood there for a moment as if he might challenge Paul to prove that Clara was his sister.

"Officer Carter! Move them out quickly!" one of the SPS men shouted to the policeman, and he nodded. Paul realized then, that any thought of challenge had passed.

"What are their names?" Officer Carter asked.

"Eddie is the sixteen year old. Jane is fifteen."

"Their full names," Carter demanded with a long suffering sigh.

"Jack Edward Manning, and Jane," he turned in the seat and, quietly, Eddie supplied Jane's middle name.

"Ann."

"Jane Ann Poindexter," Paul said.

Officer Carter wrote something in a notebook.

"Is this all there is to it?" Edna asked. "Are the children registered now? Will you be sending the identity cards to the house?"

"If either of your women speak again, without being spoken to, I will have all three of you whipped!" Carter said, gruffly.

"Then I shall ask the question," Paul said. "Are we free to return home now?"

"You two," Carter said to Eddie and Jane. "Out of the car."

"Out of the car? What for? We gave you their names and addresses. What more do you want?" Paul asked.

Officer Carter drew his pistol and pointed it at Paul. "I want them out of the car," he demanded.

"We're coming," Eddie said, opening the door and stepping out. Jane slid across the seat, then stepped out behind him.

The policeman tore off the sheet of paper he had been writing on, and handed it to Eddie. "You two, on that bus over there," he said.

It wasn't until then that Eddie and the others in his family noticed that there were several buses, and that there were lines of children of all ages boarding them.

"What do you want us on the bus for? I thought we were just supposed to come here to get registered," Eddie said.

"Don't give me any backtalk, you little punk! Just climb on that bus like I told you," Carter hissed, angrily.

"Just a minute!" Paul said. "You can't talk to my kid like that!"

Carter turned toward the open car window, then hit Paul on the side of the head with his pistol.

"Pop!" Eddie screamed.

"Get on the bus now, or I will shoot your father for resisting orders," Carter said.

"Come on, Eddie, let's do like he says, please," Jane said, pulling on his arm.

Eddie looked back at his father, and saw that his mother was wiping blood from his lip.

"Pop, are you all right?"

"Please, Eddie," Edna called to him. "Do what the man says before you get hurt."

Eddie paused for another moment, then turned to go with Jane toward the bus. Halfway to the bus Eddie heard a pistol shot and turning quickly, saw that the SPS had shot a man who was protesting what they were doing with his children.

Jane had shut her eyes when she heard the gunshot.

"It wasn't pop, or your mom," Eddie said, comforting Jane.

"Eddie, will we ever see our families again?"

"Yeah, sure we will," Eddie said, though he wasn't sure he believed they would.

CHAPTER NINE

St. Louis

The TV screen opened with the call letters AITV, then a full-screen picture of Ohmshidi over the words "Obey Ohmshidi" as a voice-over spoke the words

> *"All praise be to Allah, the merciful.*
> *Whomsoever Allah guides there is none to*
> *misguide, and whomsoever Allah misguides*
> *there is none to guide. You must live your life*
> *in accordance with the* Moqaddas Sirata,
> *the Holy Path. Those who do will be blessed.*
> *Those who do not will be damned.*
> *"This is American Islamic Enlightened*
> *Television."*

When Ohmshidi's picture went away, it was re-placed by a newscaster who stood facing the camera. He made a fist, and folded his right arm across his chest.

"Obey Ohmshidi!"

The newscaster then sat behind a desk, in front of the familiar portrait of Ohmshidi with the words Obey Ohmshidi underneath.

"And now, the news.
"Operation Blooming Flowers is nearly completed. Although it has been reported that some parents have protested the operation, the vast majority of our citizens welcome it and the positive effect it will have on raising a new generation, free from any corrupting influence from America's sordid past."

On screen a series of pictures showed young people in classrooms, in games, and at worship in *Moqaddas Sirata*–compliant mosques.

"Here you see some of the children at an Enlightenment Center at an undisclosed location. And as you can see, everything is being provided for them, from their studies, to their physical needs, to their religious training. It has been decided to allow no visitation between parents and children until they reach the age of eighteen, when the young people will

leave the Enlightenment Centers, well prepared
to become productive citizens in our new society.
  "As of now, every young person between the
ages of six and seventeen has been enrolled in
these Enlightenment Centers. Should anyone
be found in noncompliance of the Blooming
Flowers order, the entire family will be executed."

The picture returned to the studio, where the
stern-looking male newscaster continued with his
report.

  "It was announced in Muslimabad today,
that ninety-nine percent of the country has
embraced, with great enthusiasm, the progress
toward peace and prosperity offered by our Great
Leader, President for Life, Mehdi Ohmshidi. The
only dissension seems to be coming from an
insignificant island that acts as a barrier
between the Gulf of Mexico and Mobile Bay.
  "Reed Franken, who is the National Leader
of the State Protective Service had this to say."

The picture on the screen switched to a rather
small man, wearing rimless glasses over beady
eyes. He smoothed his close-cropped moustache
with the end of his finger as he stared into the
camera. Off camera could be heard the words,
"You are on, National Leader."
Franklin looked toward the sound of the words,

then back into the camera. As the newscaster had done before him, he gave the clenched fist salute to the camera.

"Obey Ohmshidi. My fellow citizens of the American Islamic Republic of Enlightenment, may the peace of Moqaddas Sirata *guide you in your service to our Great Leader, President for Life Ohmshidi.*

"As you may have heard, there is a group of misguided apostates who have refused to accept the order of Moqaddas Sirata, *and who have taken refuge on an island off the coast of Alabama, once known as Pleasure Island.*

"Although we have the military might to erase the island, and everyone on it, from the face of the earth, our Great Leader, President for Life Ohmshidi, is as merciful as he is powerful. And, in his great wisdom and benevolence, he has made the decision to take no action against them at this time. It is his belief that if we wait them out, they will eventually see the error of their ways, and will accept the new order, as so many million others have done."

The picture returned to the TV studio.

"A restaurant in Chesterfield was closed yesterday, when it was discovered that they were serving pork. The restaurant owner, two waitresses, and four diners were arrested and

*will be tried and executed. The public is invited
to the beheading, which will take place in Forest
Park, in front of the Jewel Box."*

Tom Jack turned off the television, and shook
his head.

"How the hell did we let this happen?"

"We elected him, remember?"

"Yeah, I remember. Look Sheri, we can't stay
here."

"Where will we go?"

"To Gulf Shores. We went there for vacation a
couple of years ago, remember?"

"You want to know what I remember? You
made me go deep sea fishing, and I got as sick as
a dog. That's what I remember."

"Well, yeah, but other than that, you liked it
there, didn't you?"

"Yes, but how will we get there? We don't even
have a car anymore."

"We'll ride our bicycles."

"Ride our bicycles? That's over 700 miles."

"I promise you, we won't try to make it in
one day."

"That won't work. SPS agents are everywhere.
They'll be checking us for ID cards, and when we
can't produce one, they'll arrest us."

"We'll go downtown tomorrow and get ID
cards."

"We can't get ID cards without swearing allegiance to Ohmshidi. Are you ready to do that?"

"We are going to have to do that," Tom said. "It's the only way we are going to get out of here."

"All right, but I'm going to cross my fingers," Sheri said.

"Nah, they'll see that. Stand there with your legs crossed, like you've got to pee," Tom suggested.

Sheri laughed. "What are you going to cross?"

"I'll reach down to scratch myself, and I'll cross the boys," Tom suggested, eliciting another laugh from Sheri.

"All right, let's go get our ID cards."

The ID cards were issued from the City Hall on Market Street. Tom and Sheri rode bicycles down to the City Hall, then Tom chained the two of them to a steel banister, before they walked up the steps. Just inside, they were greeted by a huge flag of the American Islamic Republic of Enlightenment, which hung down from the ceiling. On the wall behind the desk was a huge picture of Ohmshidi, and there were signs everywhere. A huge banner was spread across the outside of the building.

ONE PEOPLE, ONE COUNTRY, ONE RELIGION

Over the door, as they went in, they saw another sign.

*A GOOD CITIZEN REPORTS NEIGHBORS
WHO ARE APOSTATES*

Then, just inside the entrance hall,

SUBMIT TO MOQADAS SIRATA

At the opposite end of the hall just before they stepped into the main room, they saw

*BLESSING BE UPON OUR GREAT LEADER
PRESIDENT FOR LIFE OHMSHIDI*

In the main room, over the desk where they had to report, was the sign

*YOUR POLICE AND THE SPS
ARE FOR YOUR PROTECTION*

Tom and Sheri stepped up to a desk where a sign, much smaller than the others, read, "Start here." Sitting behind the desk was a rather large man with a bald head and a full beard. Although the room was full of the green and gold uniformed SPS troopers, this man was a civilian, and he was wearing a dishdasha.

"Obey Ohmshidi," the civilian said.

"Yeah," Tom replied, and when the man glared at him, Tom returned the salute. "Obey Ohmshidi."

"Why are you here?"

"To, uh, swear allegiance, and get ID cards," Tom answered.

"Where were you born?" the bald-headed man asked.

"Kotzebue, Alaska."

The official looked up in surprise. "What were you doing up in Alaska?"

"I was getting born."

He went through the same thing with Sheri, then had both of them sign a document swearing allegiance to the Great Leader, President for Life Mehdi Ohmshidi.

As the official filled out the paperwork, Tom looked around the room. In addition to the other signs, there were at least a dozen of the now ubiquitous stylized drawings of Ohmshidi, all of them over the words "Obey Ohmshidi."

"What do we do now?" Sheri asked as they went back outside to their bikes.

Tom unlocked the padlock. "We start getting things together for the trip. Food, water, clothes, matches, sleeping bags, a small tent. Things we will need for camping."

"How are we going to carry all that on a bicycle?"

"I'll make us a little trailer that I can pull behind the bike."

Over the next few days Sheri did some shopping, buying tins of sardines, coffee, cans of beans, and hard rolls. Tom bought a couple of sleeping bags, some camp cooking utensils, and a canteen. He also bought a used baby stroller, and using the wheels, attached them to a trailer he made from plywood. The last thing he did was put a false bottom on his bicycle seat, creating a small pocket where he could keep his pistol and the two boxes of ammunition he still had.

Packing the trailer required some very careful folding and placement, but he managed to get everything in. The last thing he put in the trailer was a copy of the Koran, placing it on the very top so it would be the first thing anyone would see when the trailer was searched. And Tom had no doubt but that the trailer would be searched.

They left St. Louis in the pre-dawn darkness, and encountered their first roadblock on Highway 61 just north of Ste. Genevieve.

"Tom?" Sheri said anxiously.

"I see them, just keep your cool, they're not SPS, they're highway patrolmen."

As Tom and Sheri approached, one of the five highway patrolmen held up his hand.

Tom got off his bike and gave them the closed fist across his chest salute. "Obey Ohmshidi," he said.

"Obey Ohmshidi," the state policeman replied. "Where are you going?"

"We're going south," Tom replied.

"Don't be a wiseass," the patrolman said. "I didn't ask which direction you were going, I can see you're going south. I asked *where* you were going."

"We have relatives down in Sikeston. We're going down there to see if I can find work."

"Let me see your papers."

Tom and Sheri showed their papers to the man who examined them carefully. One of the patrolmen stepped back to the homemade trailer.

"Did you build this?"

"Yes."

"What's in it?"

"Just things we need for the trip. Food, clothes, that sort of thing."

"It's locked."

"Yes. We can't afford to lose what's in there."

"Open it up."

Tom unlocked the padlock, then lifted the lid. The first thing the patrolman saw was the Koran. He reached for it.

"Please treat the Koran with respect," Tom said.

The patrolman nodded, and handed it to Tom. "You hold it while I go through the trailer."

Tom held the book with both hands, keeping it close to his chest as if it were his most important possession. He watched as the patrolman unloaded his trailer, tossing everything aside until he reached the bottom.

Fortunately, none of the patrolmen made a very close examination of Tom's bicycle. If they had, and they had discovered the false bottom, they would have found his pistol, a Beretta Px4 Storm Type F Sub-Compact pistol taped up under the seat.

"All right, you can go," the patrolman said when the trailer had been thoroughly checked.

It took a few minutes for Tom and Sheri to refold everything compactly enough to repack the trailer. Then, making a point of "reverently" putting the Koran back, he mounted his bike, and he and Sheri rode on.

CHAPTER TEN

Firebase Freedom

One of the things Bob Varney was most pleased with was the fact that the electricity provided by the solar panels that James and Marcus had installed allowed him to use the computer again. And though he knew there were no longer any publishers for his books, he was back writing again. Some of the others wondered why he spent several hours each day writing, and they asked Ellen about it.

"You don't understand," Ellen said. "Bob doesn't write just to be published. Bob writes because he must write. It is a part of his DNA." She chuckled. "Believe me, you don't want to be around him if he has to go for an extended period of time without writing."

Bob smiled as he thought about the conversation he had overheard. Ellen was right, of course, and back in the "before time," when Bob went all over the country giving writing seminars, he always told his students that he and they were just alike. Maybe he had been published, and they had not, but they all shared what he called a "divine discontent to write." He told them that, even if he had never been published, he would still write.

There were times when he thought that perhaps he was being a little disingenuous by making such a comment. But in the time since the collapse of the U.S., and the disappearance of the publishing houses, he had proven to himself that he meant what he said.

Of course, there was another reason that he wrote every day. Every time he sat down to the computer, his dog, Charley, would lie under his desk, just as he had done for the last six years. For Charley, the world had not changed, and Bob leaned on that bit of continuity to keep himself from falling into a deep and unrecoverable depression.

The problem now was that it was difficult to find a theme for his books. He had written mostly Westerns, mysteries, and thrillers, but in order to write that kind of book, the characters and story had to be laid against a matrix of reason and normalcy. Only against such a background could you develop conflict and drama. But there was absolutely nothing reasonable or normal about the country that had once been the United States.

In the "before time" there had been many post-apocalyptic novels and movies, not one of which had created a world more bizarre than the one they were living in now. Perhaps Bob should be writing an apocalyptic novel now, but he was writing about the Old West, finding escape in his novel of stoic and decent men and women carving out a nation where good triumphed over evil.

After a full day of writing, he checked his word count, 57,524, which meant he had written three thousand words today, a good day. He shut down, then walked out into the quadrangle of the fort where Deon, Marcus, and Willy were tossing a baseball back and forth.

"Finished with your book?" Deon asked, catching the ball, then throwing it over to Willy.

"For the day."

"Hey, Bob, when you finish that book, will you print it out and let the rest of us read it?" Willy asked.

"Yeah," Deon said. "I'd like that too."

"A good book is always welcome," Marcus said.

"Who says it'll be a good book?" Willy teased.

"Willy! What a thing to say!" Becky scolded.

"Don't mind him, Becky," Marcus said. "I don't think he's ever had a book where you couldn't color the pictures."

The others laughed as Bob took Charley out of the fort and down onto the beach, where he began digging for crabs.

Alexandria, Virginia

When Chris Carmack got home from the store, he was in a good mood. He had been able to buy a steak at the market, and he intended to cook it out on the patio of his Jordan Street apartment. The steak and a baked potato would make a fine meal for him and his fiancée, and though it was a bit extravagant, he figured it was worth it.

Margaret had finally agreed to a wedding date. Raised a Roman Catholic, she had not wanted a civil wedding, but Christian weddings were no longer allowed, and neither she nor Chris wanted a Muslim ceremony. So Margaret finally agreed to a civil ceremony, and the steak, potato, and bottle of wine—which, because all liquor was outlawed, had cost him more dearly than he was willing to say—was for the celebration.

It was costing Chris Carmack and Margaret Malcolm twice as much to live as other couples, because they had to maintain separate apartments, though both apartments were in the same building on Jordan Street in Alexandria, which allowed them easy access to each other. Neither Margaret nor Chris had converted to Islam—and merely converting to Islam wasn't enough; it was necessary to convert to the *Moqaddas Sirata* branch of Islam—but neither were they active in any other religion. They thought this would be the best arrangement, because, for the time being, the war being carried on against Christians,

Jews, and noncompliant Muslims was even more intense than the war against nonbelievers.

In the "before time," Chris had been a "non-affiliated contract source" for Homeland Security. On the surface, Chris was a research analyst. But secretly, so secretly that no more than three other people ever knew exactly what he did, Chris was euphemistically known as an adjuster, someone who settled accounts for Homeland Security, doing so "with extreme prejudice." There was not one person still alive who knew of Chris's particular occupation. His last contract had involved Ali Bin Jabril, who proudly identified himself as "Jabril the American."

Jabril had been born Adam Jason Clark in San Francisco to parents whose American roots went back several generations. Clark converted to Islam while attending college, then declared himself to be allied with Al Qaeda. He bragged that he had provided shelter for the "heroic hero martyrs of 9/11" and made a DVD which he sent to all the TV networks.

On the DVD he was sitting in a chair, wearing a full face mask, dressed in black, and holding an AK-47.

"No, my fellow countrymen, you are guilty, guilty, guilty, guilty," he said in the tape. He went on:

> *"After decades of American tyranny and oppression, now it's your turn to die. Allah willing, the streets of America will run red*

*with blood matching drop for drop the blood of
America's victims.*

*"You see here the fate that awaits you all,
if you do not convert. This was the McKenzie
family: father, mother, son, and daughter.
Only the father sinned in that, while he was
interrogating a brother Muslim, he put the
Koran on a table where lay a bacon and tomato
sandwich. Putting the Holy Koran next to pork
defiled the Holy Word. McKenzie paid for this
heresy, not only with his own life, but with the
life of his wife and children."*

The picture on the screen showed the masked
man murdering the family. Homeland Security
used voice analysis to identify Jabril as Adam
Clark. Already, many on the left were defending
Jabril's "freedom of speech," and the ACCR, the
American Commission for Civil Rights, had declared publicly that if Clark/Jabril was found and
arrested, they would defend him in court.

Homeland Security located Jabril in Spring-
field, Oregon, but they had no intention of
arresting him. Instead they issued a contract to
Chris Carmack giving him information as to how
to find Ali Bin Jabril, and authorizing him to
handle the American Al Qaeda "with extreme
prejudice."

Clark/Jabril worked in a health food store and
was going by the name of Benjamin Cowell. He
kept his Al Qaeda affiliation secret from the other

citizens of the small town. Chris had arrived in town driving a ten-year-old pickup truck, its bed filled with firewood. He parked on the street just in front of "Health Alternatives." Wearing coveralls, a Los Angeles Dodger baseball cap, and a week's growth of beard, he got out of the truck, then walked to the back to adjust the ropes that held the wood in place.

When Clark/Jabril came out of the store a few moments later, Chris reached down between two stacks of wood, grasped a CO_2 pellet pistol, and aimed it kinesthetically at him. Pulling the trigger made a sound no louder than a quiet sneeze, propelling a curare-tipped pellet into Clark's neck.

Clark/Jabril slapped at his neck, took about three more steps, staggered, then fell. Chris had parked the truck over a storm drain, and, unobserved, he now quietly dropped the pellet pistol down the drain. Then, tying off the rope, he got in the truck and pulled out into the street, driving off slowly.

That had been a little over two years ago, just before Ohmshidi was elected. When the ACCR learned that Clark/Jabril had been killed, they began a Freedom of Information search to find out who had ordered the killing, and who had actually carried out the operation. Ironically, the American Commission for Civil Rights, which had been ardent supporters of Ohmshidi, quickly became one of the first casualties of the new Ohmshidi administration.

Because both his handler, the FBI director, and the Secretary of Homeland Security had all been executed by Ohmshidi, there was no one left, except Chris, who knew the truth about the Clark/Jabril case.

Chris checked the steak, wondering if he should move it away from the heat so he didn't finish it before Margaret got back.

Margaret was on her way to a friend's house to invite her to the wedding. Just because it was going to be a civil ceremony was no reason why friends couldn't come. She would have invited relatives as well, but she had no relatives remaining. Her older brother had been on United Airlines Flight 93 on 9/11, when it crashed in a field in Pennsylvania. Her parents, and all her remaining relatives, had been killed during the nuclear attack on Baltimore.

Before Ohmshidi, Margaret had been a civilian data-systems analyst at Fort McNair. She lost her job when the military ceased to be. Now, jobs for women were so restricted that her only source of income was as a private contractor, and even then, her jobs had to come through Chris.

Margaret was wearing a dress which was modest by any description in the "before time." Her skirt came to just below her knees. Her neck and arms were bare, but the dress was not particularly low-cut. Nevertheless, she tended to stand out, because she was a very attractive young woman, and most women were now wearing veils or burqas. She was walking down Massey Lane, just at Huntington Creek, when suddenly a man jumped out from behind a building, grabbed her, and dragged her back into an alley.

Margaret screamed, but the man hit her so hard that it nearly knocked her out. Her head was spinning, and she was only partially aware of what was happening to her. She was dragged behind a Dumpster, then her dress was torn from her. The man seemed young, late teens or early twenties at best.

"No, please, you don't want to do this!" Margaret pleaded.

"Shut up, whore!" the young man said. He smiled manically at her, and, pushing her up against the brick wall, dropped his pants, and moved against her.

"No!" Margaret pleaded as she felt the forced entry. "Please, don't!"

The young man didn't reply. Instead he continued to use her until, with a few grunts, he finished. Then, spent and satiated, he stepped back from her and pulled his pants back up.

"I'm finished with you, whore," he said. "You can go on to wherever you were going," he added with an unsettling cackle.

As best she could, Margaret put her dress back

on, but it was so badly torn that one of her breasts remained exposed all the way to the nipple. Covering herself as best she could with folded arms, Margaret staggered back out onto the sidewalk. As she did so, she saw a car with SPS markings, and she called out.

"Help me! Please, help me!"

The car stopped, and two men, in SPS uniforms, got out. They weren't just SPS, they were wearing the black uniforms of the elite Janissaries.

"What are you doing on the street like this?" one of them demanded, his voice angry and condemning.

"I've been raped," she said.

"Where did it happen?"

Margaret looked around, intending to point out to the officers where the rape happened. To her amazement she saw that the rapist had made no attempt to flee. Instead, he was insolently leaning back against the building with his arms folded across his chest, looking on in bemusement.

"There!" she said, pointing to the young man. "He's the one who raped me!"

One of the two Janissaries walked over to the man that had just raped Margaret. The man rendered the proper salute. "Obey Ohmshidi."

The Janissary returned the salute. "Is what she is saying true? Did you have sex with this woman?"

"Yeah, I had sex with her."

"What kind of question is that? What do you mean, did he have sex with me?" Margaret called out to him. "Don't you understand what I'm saying? He didn't have sex with me! He raped me!"

"Then, you admit that you had sex with him?"

"What's the matter with you?"

"Madam, did you, or did you not have sex with this man?"

"He raped me. By definition, that means we had sex. But it isn't like that, it's . . ."

"Get in the car, Miss," the other black uniformed officer said. This was the first time he had spoken.

"Well, thank you, finally you understand."

As Margaret sat in the backseat of the car, trying unsuccessfully to keep herself covered, she saw the two Janissaries go over to talk to the man who had raped her. At first she thought they were going to arrest him, but they seemed to be involved in nothing more than casual conversation.

Then the man who raped her nodded and, amazingly, walked away. Why didn't they arrest him?

The two Janissaries got back into the car.

"I live on North Jordan," she said.

Neither of the men answered, but a moment later the driver turned in a direction that was totally opposite of the way he should go to take her home.

"This is the wrong way," she said. "I told you, I live on North Jordan."

"Shut up, whore," the one who wasn't driving said.

Margaret Malcolm was taken across the river into Muslimabad, and into a police station. The desk sergeant, seeing two Janissaries come into the station, jumped up quickly, and saluted.

"Obey Ohmshidi!"

Only one of the two Janissaries returned the salute. "Obey Ohmshidi," he said.

"What have we here?" the desk sergeant asked.

"We found this woman . . . "

"Thank you, I'll take it from here," Margaret said. "Sergeant, I've been trying to explain to these . . ."

"Madam, you will speak only when you are spoken to," the desk sergeant said. He turned to the two men who had brought her in. "Please forgive the interruption."

"We found this woman in an alley where, but moments before, by her own admission, she had been engaging in sexual activity with a man who was not her husband."

"Then I take it you will be filing a charge of adultery?"

"Yes."

"What?" Margaret shouted at the top of her voice, unable to believe what she had just been told. "What are you talking about? I did *not* commit adultery! I was *raped*! What part of rape do you not understand?"

"You will be able to tell your story at your trial," the desk sergeant said.

"What trial? When?"

"Soon."

"Well, thank you very much for that. At least we'll get this crazy charge dismissed. I want to make a telephone call."

"You are not authorized to use the telephone."

"What are you talking about? I have the right to make a telephone call."

"The only rights you have are those that have been granted you by the Great Leader, and he grants no rights to adulteresses," the desk sergeant reminded her. He handed her a couple of safety pins. "Please pin your dress closed. I find your nudity offensive."

After Margaret pinned the top part of her dress together, the desk sergeant took a camera from his desk drawer and told Margaret to stand against the wall. He took several pictures of her, then ordered her to sit in a chair.

"Are you going to take my statement?" she asked.

"In due time. Just sit there for a moment."

After the two men who had brought her in left, Margaret remained seated in the chair, wondering what was going to happen to her. It sounded like the police sergeant was saying she was going to be tried, but as she thought about it, she realized that when he said "your" trial, he was probably referring to the trial of the rapist, and it was "hers" only in that it pertained to her. She took some comfort from that.

She sat in the chair for nearly an hour, worrying now about Chris, knowing she should be home by now, and knowing he would be worried about her.

A man, wearing a western suit, and a woman in a burqa, head scarf, and veil came into the station then. They stopped at the desk, spoke a moment, then came over to her.

"I'll be prosecuting your case," he said. "Go with this woman."

Margaret followed the woman into another room and there, the woman opened a closet and pulled out a burqa, scarf, and veil. She pointed to them.

Within half an hour, Margaret was dressed the same as the woman who was with her. Not once during that time did Margaret see the woman's face, or even hear her speak.

CHAPTER ELEVEN

Back in the apartment on Jordan Street Chris Carmack was beginning to get a little concerned. He had been sure that Margaret would be home by now. But as he thought about it, he had a pretty good idea of what must have happened. She had gone to invite Kathy, Margaret's closest friend, to come to the wedding. No doubt they were planning the wedding right now.

"What's there to plan?" Chris had asked. "We just go see the civil servant, sign the papers, and we are married."

"If you don't know, I can't explain it to you," Margaret said with a little laugh. "You just don't worry about it. I'll take care of everything."

Chris smiled as he recalled that conversation. He was sure that Margaret and Kathy were planning everything down to the last, tiny detail. He was getting concerned about the steak, though.

It cost too much to ruin by letting it sit too long after being cooked.

Margaret's trial was being held in what had, in the "before time," been the Supreme Court building. The historic bas-relief features of Moses and the Ten Commandments had been removed. The nine justices of the Supreme Court had long ago been replaced by one *Moqaddas Sirata* judge, who had been born as Arnold Tate, but who now called himself Sulymam Ayambuie.

It didn't take Margaret long to realize that when the prosecutor called it "her trial," he really meant her trial. As bizarre as it might seem, Margaret Malcolm was being charged with adultery. She was on the verge of panic, and though she had begged the prosecutor and the burqa-clad woman to let her get in touch with Chris, or to contact him on her behalf, they refused to do so.

Margaret Malcolm was going through a trial for her very life, and without so much as one friend or advocate in the court.

She sat at a table with her hands cuffed in front of her, wearing a gray burqa which covered her head and face, leaving only her eyes visible.

"Your Holiness, prosecution calls its first and only witness," the prosecutor said.

The judge, if that was what he could rightly be called, nodded and lifted a finger. The court gallery was full, and they all turned as a young man wearing a dishdasha started toward the front of the courtroom.

"That's him!" she called out. "That's the man who raped me!"

The judge pounded his gavel and glared at Margaret. "The defendant will keep quiet. You will speak only when you are spoken to."

Margaret wanted to call out again, but she held her tongue.

The prosecutor began interrogating the young man, who was now sitting in the witness chair.

"Is it true that you had sexual contact with this woman?"

"Yes."

"Why did you have sex with her?"

"I couldn't help myself. It was the way she was dressed. It provoked me into committing the act."

The prosecutor looked over at the prisoner.

"Was she dressed like that?"

"Oh, no sir. If she had been dressed like that, I would have known that she was a good woman."

"How was she dressed?"

"She was dressed like a whore. She was wearing a short skirt. Her neck and arms were bare. She had no head covering, and she was wearing lipstick."

"Is this how she looked?" The prosecutor held up the photo he had taken of Margaret in his office, before he made her change clothes.

"Yes."

"Would you say that you were incited into this act?"

"What?"

"When you saw her dressed like a whore, did it make you lose your sense of propriety?"

"Yes."

"Would you have had sex with her if she had been dressed properly? The way she is dressed now?"

"No. As I said, if she had been dressed the way she is now, I would never have approached her. But the way she was dressed, it was the same as if she was asking me to do it. I didn't want to, but she, be . . . be . . . that word you told me to say."

"You mean she beguiled you?"

"Yeah. That."

"I have no further questions."

The judge looked at Margaret. "Do you have anything to say in your defense?"

"Don't I get a lawyer to defend me?"

"No."

"But, I'm entitled to a lawyer. Everyone gets a lawyer, even if they can't afford one. That's the rule."

"That is not the rule of *Moqaddas Sirata*. I cannot, and I will not ask a man to put his soul at risk by defending a whore," the judge replied. "You must defend yourself."

"I am not a whore. And I was raped. I was not a willing participant."

"Have you four male witnesses who will testify that you were raped?"

"No, there was nobody there but me, and the man who raped me. If there were four male witnesses, don't you think if they were decent men, that they would have stepped in and stopped it? The very concept of four male witnesses to a rape is ridiculous. What makes you think there would be four witnesses to something like that?"

"The Koran, chapter twenty-four, verse thirteen, clearly states," the judge said, then he read from the book. "Why did they not bring four witnesses of it? But as they have not brought witnesses, they are liars before Allah."

"I am not lying! I was raped!"

"The law is quite clear. You cannot prove rape unless you have four male witnesses. And even if you were raped, it is a condition that you brought on yourself. That, you cannot deny, for this court has photographic evidence of the way you were dressed. Prosecution may give his summation."

The prosecutor again held up the photograph of Margaret Malcolm, showed it to the gallery, then showed it to the judge.

"Your Holiness, I show this picture with great reticence, for I know its very licentiousness is an affront to all decency, and I beg your forgiveness, but I do so, only to make a point."

The prosecutor looked over the defendant, the expression on his face one of utter contempt. He pointed at the picture, then toward Margaret.

"This is how this whore was dressed!" he shouted loudly.

"This jezebel, for there is no other way to describe her, went out into the public dressed in the most beguiling way. And, I submit, she went that way for one reason, and one reason only. She was on the prowl, seeking sex from whomever she could entice."

"No, that isn't true!" Margaret shouted.

Imam Ayambuie pounded his gavel upon the bench. "Be silent, whore, while the prosecutor is making his case!"

"But what he is saying isn't true!"

"Gag this defendant," Ayambuie ordered. Uniformed SPS troopers stepped up behind her and tied a gag around the lower part of her face, drawing the veil into her nostrils, making it difficult for her to breathe.

"Prosecutor may continue with the summation," Ayambuie said.

"Thank you, Your Holiness. As I was saying, the defendant, in violation of the dress code, presented herself in a most lewd and vile way, little caring that she was endangering the souls of all who gazed upon her impurity. And one innocent young man, who had left home only to go to the store to buy milk for his mother, a young man whose life up until that time had been pure and unstained, did gaze upon her, and was so seduced by her wantonness, that he could no longer restrain himself.

"With Satan acting as her partner, this slut, Margaret Malcolm, enticed this poor, innocent young man to lose control of himself, and engage in sex with her. That this woman engaged in sex with this man is not denied, for by her own words has she confessed.

"There can be but one verdict, and that is to find Margaret Malcolm guilty of adultery, and of corruption of the soul of this poor, innocent man."

Ayambuie looked over toward Margaret, whose eyes were wide in fright.

"If you had held your tongue, you would be able to speak now, in your defense," he said. "But it doesn't matter, for no lying words you may speak can alter the truth. Therefore, I find you guilty of adultery. It is a *hudud* crime, and therefore I condemn you to death. Your temporal punishment is death by stoning. Your eternal punishment will be to writhe in the fires of hell forever.

"Sentence is to be carried out immediately. Remove the gag."

The same SPS man who had gagged her now removed the gag.

"No!" Margaret shouted as soon as she could draw a breath. "No, you can't do this! I did nothing wrong!"

"Take her to her punishment," the judge said with a dismissive wave of his hand.

Margaret Malcolm was tied to a lamppost on a street corner, and hundreds of people who were merely passing by were forced into participating in the stoning. Most of them did it with a sense of horror, but nearly as many took a perverse glee in throwing the rocks. Margaret remained conscious, and crying, for the first five minutes; then she grew quiet. The stoning continued for an entire hour, even though there was nothing left but a bloody pulp on the ground.

A TV camera moved in to get pictures of her, and of the judge, Imam Sulymam Ayambuie. A reporter began to interview him.

It was now past six o'clock, and Margaret still wasn't home. It wasn't like her to be this late, not even if she was visiting with a friend. Chris couldn't call, because Kathy didn't have a telephone. If she hadn't returned home by seven, Chris would walk over there and get her. He smiled as he thought of how embarrassed she would be, at having spent the entire day just talking.

To calm himself somewhat, he turned on the TV.

*". . . claimed she was raped this morning, but
that claim was dismissed in court. The woman
had to be forcibly restrained, and at one time,
was gagged because of repeated interruptions
to the lawful proceedings of the court."*

The picture on the screen was of the defendant, but because she was totally covered by a burqa, he had no idea what she looked like.

The picture returned to the male newscaster who was giving the news, with just the proper amount of condemnation in his voice. He held the microphone out toward a bearded man, dressed in black, and wearing a *taqiyah*.

*"We have much work to do in this county
to educate women, and bring them into the
righteousness of Moqaddas Sirata, due to the
sinful way American females have been raised.
This will be a lesson to all women."*

The camera returned to a shot of the reporter.

*"That was Imam Sulymam Ayambuie,
the Supreme Justice of the American Islamic
Republic of Enlightenment, who took such
an interest in this case that he handled it
personally.*

*"The whore, who had incited an innocent
young man to have sex with her, was, rightfully,*

tried, found guilty, convicted, and condemned. She paid for her sin by being stoned to death in front of the court. It is not known if the woman, Margaret Malcolm, had any relatives. But of course, even if she did, no one would claim her, for fear of being tainted by her heinous crime.

"The body was cremated."

Once, when Chris had been a young man, he fell from a tree and had the breath knocked from him. It had been a terrible moment, lying on the ground, unable to breathe, and not knowing if he would ever breathe again.

Chris felt like that now, and he put his hand to his head as tears sprang to his eyes.

"Nooooooo!" he shouted, his agonized cry heard by passersby in the street.

Fighting back the tears, Chris went into his bedroom and, unscrewing the cap at the top of the bedpost, reached down inside to pull out a bottle of whiskey. As in the days of prohibition, all whiskey now was bootleg whiskey, and had to be kept hidden.

Generally when Chris would take a drink, he would make certain that the window blinds were closed so that he couldn't be seen. But today, he made no attempt to close the blinds, because he didn't care whether he was seen or not. If ever he needed a drink—and these days it seemed that he was increasingly in need of a drink—it was now.

He tossed the first shot down, feeling the burn in his throat, and the warmth in his belly. But it would take several more drinks before the pain in his heart would be dulled. As he worked his way toward that glorious drunk, Chris made a silent vow that, somehow, he would avenge this young woman.

CHAPTER TWELVE

Near Vaughan, Mississippi

Vaughan, Mississippi is noted for being the site of Casey Jones's famous train wreck, and in the "before time," there had been a Casey Jones Museum there. On the evening of the sixth day after Tom and Sheri left St. Louis, they were making camp about five miles north of Vaughan, when they encountered their first trouble. Tom was standing by his bicycle, and Sheri was about to spread out their sleeping bags when someone suddenly leaped out from behind a tree and grabbed her.

"Tom!" Sheri shouted.

Tom reached under the bicycle seat and got his pistol.

The man who had grabbed Sheri had one arm around her waist, while in his other hand he was holding a knife to her throat. Tom raised his pistol and pointed it at the intruder.

"Let her go," Tom said.

"You better put that little popgun down, mister, before I cut your woman's throat."

"Why would you do that? If you kill her, I'll kill you."

"Didn't you hear what I said? Put that gun down, or I'll cut her up bad."

"Do the Bud, Sheri," Tom said calmly.

Bud was the parrot Tom's parents had once owned, and Sheri knew exactly what he was talking about, because when Bud wanted attention, he would sometimes bob his head back and forth.

Sheri leaned her head to the right, and the punk who was holding her, caught by surprise, suddenly had one half of his head exposed. Without a moment's hesitation, Tom pulled the trigger. His bullet struck the would-be mugger just above his left eye. He went down, dead before he hit the ground.

"Are you all right?" Tom asked, holding the smoking pistol in his hand.

"Well, I'm glad to know that you would have killed him if he had killed me," Sheri said.

"It's the least I could do for the woman I love," Tom said.

Sheri laughed. "I don't know why I'm laughing. Maybe it's to keep from screaming."

"Nah, you did very well, you did exactly what you had to do," Tom said.

"Damn, did he ever have a bad case of body odor," Sheri said. "What will we do with him?"

"I'll drag his sorry ass out into the woods so we don't have to see him tonight," Tom said. "Why don't you open us a can of sardines?"

"Last night was sardines," Sheri said. "Tonight it's kippers."

"They're coming out of the same can, aren't they?"

"Oh but Tom, my sweet. It's all a matter of perception, don't you know?"

Tom chuckled. "Then kippers it is."

SPS Headquarters, Arlington, Virginia

The two Janissaries who had arrested Margaret Malcolm were Americans by birth, having been born Clint Anderson and Keith Darrow. In order to join the SPS they had converted to *Moqaddas Sirata* Islam, and had taken the Muslim names of Husni Mawsil and Shurayh Amaar. Shortly after joining the SPS, they were selected by Reed Franken to be members of the elite Janissary Corps.

On the day after the arrest, trial, and execution of Margaret Malcolm, the Janissaries held an award ceremony. With every member of the elite force present, the Janissary commander, Omar

Faquar, called his troops to attention, then asked Mawsil and Amaar to step forward.

Mawsil and Amaar moved to the front of the formation, then stood at attention. Faquar lifted a paper and began to read.

"With the blessings of Allah, the all powerful, Husni Mawsil and Shurayh Amaar are here to be cited for meritorious service.

"Officers Mawsil and Amaar, while on patrol, did find a woman whose name is not worthy of mention, dressed as the whore she was. Further investigation by Mawsil and Amaar determined that the whore had but recently seduced an innocent young man. Acting upon this information, Mawsil and Amaar arrested the woman, who was subsequently tried, convicted, and executed for adultery.

"For their meritorious service, Officers Mawsil and Amaar are awarded, by order of the Great Leader, President for Life Mehdi Ohmshidi, the Crescent for Bravery, Third Class."

Mawsil and Amaar stood proudly as the medals were pinned to their tunics. Their fellow officers applauded, and congratulated them.

Muslimabad

The "innocent young man" who had been beguiled by Margaret's provocative attire was named Billy Donner. It was easy to find out about him, because he had given several interviews in which he discussed how the wanton woman had seduced him.

> *"It was my fault"* [Donner said]. *"As soon as I saw her dressed like she was, I should have turned my back on her."*
>
> *"It wasn't your fault, Mr. Donner"* [the interviewer said]. *"It is a well-known fact that Satan works his way on men and boys by residing in the souls of women, all women. It is for that reason that women must wear the burqa, so that Satan be contained. Margaret Malcolm, by refusing to wear the burqa, released Satan to ply his ways."*

From the interview Chris learned that Donner worked in a convenience store less than one block away from where Margaret had been raped. He waited one month, then, to make certain that he still worked there, Chris went to the store to buy a can of coffee.

"Say, haven't I seen you on television?" Chris asked Donner.

Donner smiled. "Yes. I'm the one who was seduced by the woman they stoned."

"How did that happen?"

"I had just gone out back to empty some trash in the container when I saw her. And, well, like they said, it was the way she was dressed. Satan took hold of me."

"Pretty, was she?"

"Oh, yeah!" Donner said with a smirk. "Only, she was pretty like a whore, if you know what I mean."

"I'm sure I do. So after you raped her . . ."

"The law says it wasn't rape."

"Really? Because from what I read, you forced yourself on her."

"Yes, but that's a mere technicality, don't you see? I told you, it was the way she was dressed. The two SPS who come along seen that right off. Why, they didn't do nothin' to me, but they sure hauled her off to jail."

"Were you surprised they didn't do anything to you?"

"Well, yeah, I was at first. But then when they told me that it wasn't my fault, I understood." Donner laughed, then reached down to grab himself. "That kind of makes any woman who ain't wearin' a burqa fair game, if you know what I mean."

"If it means what I think it means, you'll be doing it again."

"You better believe it. Next time I see a woman who ain't wearin' one of them burqas, well, it's Katie bar the door. 'Cause I aim to get me some of it."

"I guess the new *Moqaddas Sirata* law authorizes that, all right," Chris said.

"Yeah. You know, at first," Donner looked around the store to make certain he wouldn't be overheard, "At first, I didn't like the way things was. I mean, take for example no beer, no football or basketball or baseball. But it's turned out real good. You might not believe this, but in the before time I wasn't all that lucky around women. Seemed they didn't like me for some reason. But now it don't matter whether they like me or not. If I see one I like, why hell, I'll just take her."

"Rape her, you mean?"

"No, no, like I told you, it ain't rape. If they ain't wearin' one of them pup tent things, why, what they're doin' is seducin' me." Donner grabbed himself. "And poor ole' me, I just can't help it, when I'm seduced." He laughed.

"I know it's asking a lot," Chris said to Kathy York, the young woman who had been Margaret's best friend. Kathy was the one Margaret had been on the way to see, on the day she was raped. "And I can understand if you don't want to do it."

"I'll do it," Kathy said.

"I want you to know what you are getting yourself into. This is the son of a bitch who raped Margaret, and I intend to kill him. That means if you help me, you'll be an accessory to the murder."

Kathy shook her head. "It won't be murder, it will be justice."

"You're a good woman. No wonder you were Margaret's best friend."

That same day, at closing time, Kathy was standing by the trash container that was behind the convenience store where Donner worked. In these hard times, it wasn't that unusual for people to go through trash containers, especially behind stores, to see what they could salvage. What made this a little different, is the way Kathy was dressed. She was a beautiful girl, with long dark hair, and big brown eyes. Her face was visible because it wasn't behind a veil. Her voluptuous shape was clearly evident by her short skirt which showed a long stretch of legs, and she wore a very low-cut blouse.

The back door opened and Chris, who was concealed behind the trash container, saw Donner coming out back with a bag of trash.

"Here he comes," Chris hissed.

Kathy bent over toward the Dumpster, causing her skirt to rise up some, and cling tightly enough to her as to outline her derrière, just as Donner came through the back door of the store.

"Well now," Donner said. "What have we here?"

"Please, sir," Kathy said. "I'm not doing anything wrong, I'm just looking to see if I can find something to sell for food."

"If you're going to look through my trash

container, you're going to have to pay for it," Donner said as he began to unzip his trousers.

"No," Kathy said. "Never mind, I'll find another container to look through."

"Too late, whore." Donner chuckled. "I've done had me one woman, and guess what. She's the one that got arrested. Maybe you heard about it. They stoned her 'cause of the way she was dressed. And it wasn't as bad as the way you're dressed now. I tell you what a nice guy I am. After we have our fun, you can go on your way, and I won't even report you for seducing me."

Donner reached out to grab the front of her blouse. He jerked it down, and her breasts spilled out.

"Oh, yeah, I'm goin' to like this."

"I don't think you will," Chris said, stepping up behind Donner. Reaching around with his knife, he sliced through Donner's carotid artery. Donner put his hand to his neck, as the blood literally spurted through his fingers.

Chris stepped around in front of him, then pulled a silver flask of whiskey from his pocket. He took a drink, then raised the flask toward Donner in a macabre salute.

"I was in love with the woman you raped, you sorry son of a bitch. And I want my face to be the last thing you see before you go to hell."

Kathy had brought a burqa with her and now she stepped around behind the Dumpster and slipped it on over her clothes. Leaving the alley, they walked back to Chris's apartment building. Then, making certain no one saw her, Kathy went into the apartment.

Kathy took the burqa off, with a sigh of contentment.

"Who the hell came up with this monstrosity?" she asked, tossing the burqa into the corner, then sitting on the sofa.

"Don't you know? It is the dress of the enlightened."

"Enlightened, my ass."

"Would you like to engage in a little sin?" Chris asked.

"What?"

Chris laughed, then poured two glasses of whiskey before he came back to sit on the sofa beside Kathy. He gave one to her.

"Oh, you meant this kind of sin," Kathy said with a chuckle. She took a sip of the whiskey. "Sure, I'll sin. But I thought you meant something else."

"And if I did?"

Kathy took another swallow of her drink, and stared at Chris through smoky eyes.

"*Do* you mean something else?"

Chris put his drink down, then pulled Kathy into his arms, kissing her deeply.

"I'm sorry," Chris said. "I had no right to do that."

Kathy touched his cheek and held her fingers there for a long moment as she looked at him with a small smile playing across her lips.

"You shouldn't apologize for doing something that we both wanted," Kathy said.

"It's just that Margaret . . ."

"Has been dead for a month," Kathy said. "And I have a strong feeling that she would approve."

Chris smiled back at her. "You know what? I do too." His right arm was on the back of the sofa. With his left hand, he brushed her hair back, then he put his thumb and forefinger at the tip of her chin and leaned toward her. She came to him with her lips already parted so that their second kiss picked up at exactly the place where the first had left off.

At last they came up for breath, and when she looked at him, her eyes were deep and diaphanous and he could see all the way to the bottom, to the Kathy that was inside . . . elementary, hopeful, and very vulnerable.

"Chris?" she said. Her voice sounded small, and far away. "I don't think Margaret would mind, now."

Chris's heart raced and he had to take a gasping breath of air. He felt light-headed, then emboldened by the fact that she had just placed herself in his charge. Kathy rose at his bidding, then, without protest, let him lead her into his bedroom.

An airliner just taking off from Muslimabad International, perhaps heading for New York, or Mexico City, or London, roared overhead, but Chris and Kathy were oblivious to its passing. There were only the two of them, alone in their private cocoon.

CHAPTER THIRTEEN

Weeks Bay, Alabama

At one time the campground had been known as Camp Beckwith, a camp and conference center of the Episcopal Diocese of the Central Gulf Coast, located on Weeks Bay in South Baldwin County, Alabama. It set on eighty-two acres of tall pines and landscaped open spaces and served guests of all denominations, races, and national origins. But Camp Beckwith was no more. In its place today was something called the YCEC 251. That stood for Youth Confinement and Enlightenment Center Number 251.

The eighty-two acres was surrounded by ten-foot-high chain-link fences, topped by razor wire. Concertina wire also formed a barrier before even reaching the fence. Every 250 yards around the compound, there was a manned guard tower with inward-facing machine guns. In addition, floodlights were placed at intervals along the fence, their brilliant beams illuminating the grounds at night, as bright as midday.

Eddie Manning was seated at his desk in the classroom. On the wall in front of the classroom was the stylized, blue, red, and beige portrait of Ohmshidi over the words "Obey Ohmshidi."

Eddie looked through the widow as the girls were marched to their own classes. None of the girls were being taught to read, or do math. Their education was limited to household chores: laundry, dishes, scrubbing floors, and other such tasks.

Eddie had not seen Jane since they were brought to YCEC 251, or, just "the 251" as the boys were now calling the camp. Of course, he didn't really know whether he had seen her or not. Every girl, regardless of age, had been put in a full-body burqa so that nothing could be seen of them from head to toe. Since they all looked like walking pup tents, it was impossible for him to know which one was his sister. At no time since coming into the camp had he seen the face of any of the girl inmates.

"Students! They are students!" Imam Hudhafa corrected him, when he heard Eddie use the word inmates. "You are all students for the preservation of *Moqaddas Sirata,* and the glorification of our Great Leader, President Mehdi Ohmshidi."

Eddie had just come into the morning class with the others, coming from morning prayer.

"And now, let us say together, the pledge of allegiance to the Great Leader," Imam Hudhafa said.

Eddie stood with the others, and they recited together:

> *"Obey Ohmshidi*
> *I pledge allegiance to Mehdi Ohmshidi,*
> *Our Great Leader*
> *Islam is our faith*
> Moqaddas Sirata *is our law*
> *Jihad is our way*
> *Dying as a martyr*
> *Is our highest hope."*

Eddie mouthed the words along with everyone else in the class, but in his mind, he always replaced "dying as a martyr" with "getting out of here," as his highest hope.

With the pledge stated, the class was told to sit, so their lessons could begin.

Imam Hudhafa was a Saudi who had come to the United States twenty years ago. When he learned of the three nuclear bombs that had been detonated by martyrs in Norfolk, Virginia, Baltimore, Maryland, and Boston, Massachusetts, he dropped to his knees, faced Mecca, and gave thanks and praise to Allah, that America was being subjugated by Islam.

Afterward, proudly wearing the dishdasha, he applied and was accepted as a teacher in the Youth Enlightenment Centers. It was his belief that with the youth lay a future in which all the world would be subjected to Islam. And not just the Christians, Jews, and Hindus, but misguided Muslims as well, for there were many Muslims who did not follow the precepts of *Moqaddas Sirata*, the Holy Path. Hudhafa considered it a sacred honor to be among those who had been chosen for this holy task.

"Remember," Imam Hudhafa said, "as a martyr, you will be alive in Heaven. Martyred jihad fighters are the most honored people, after the Prophet, and, as suicide bombers, you will ascend to a paradise of luxury staffed by seventy-two virgins waiting to gratify the martyrs as you arrive.

"Ha, what do I want virgins for?" one seventeen-year-old joked right after they first arrived at the camp. "I don't want no virgins. Hell, I want some-one who knows what it's all about. I'm still young, I need to learn from an experienced woman."

The seventeen-year-old boy, whose name was Jarvis Morris, was deemed an apostate, then taken out to the middle of the camp and laid on the ground. Chains were attached to his arms and legs, then connected to four tractors. At a signal from the camp commandant, the four tractors started in opposite directions from each other, literally pulling him apart into four large pieces so that he was drawn and quartered, leaving a cross of blood and entrails. Every "student" of the camp, including the girls, was made to watch.

It was an object lesson that Eddie had taken to heart, so now, no matter how much he might despise the "re-education," he was always very careful to check any remarks, or outward display of disapproval.

He sat in the classroom, keeping his face as impassive as possible, while the instructor continued with the day's lessons.

"And now, repeat after me, our sworn objective. *Moqaddas Sirata* is the ultimate goal for the entire world. We have to fight all the enemies of our religion so that one day, the whole world will be united and enlightened. Allah promises us heaven if we fight and even embrace death in this holy task."

Eddie, and the other boys in his classroom, repeated the sworn objective.

Eddie had never been particularly religious, but had become so since coming to YCEC 251. He prayed every day, bowing and scraping, and facing Mecca as he was instructed. But regardless of what it looked like on the outside, on the inside his prayers were all Christian prayers.

Alexandria

From the *Moqaddas Sirata News Journal:*

Two Janissary Officers Decorated for Meritorious Service

Husni Mawsil and Shurayh Amaar of the Arlington SPS Brigade were recently awarded the Crescent for Bravery Third Class. The two men, said by their commanders and peers to be outstanding officers of the Janissary, were the ones whose thorough police work was responsible for bringing the whore, Margaret Malcolm, to justice.

Observant readers may recognize the woman's name, for after a trial and conviction, she paid for her sin by being stoned until death. This is in accordance with Islamic law (Sharia), which requires that adulterers be put to death, since it was the example set by Muhammad. In practice, it is the women who are executed far more often, since they are presumed to bear the burden of sexual responsibility. Rape victims are also guilty of adultery under Sharia law if four male witnesses cannot be found to confirm the victim's claim.

The newspaper report told Chris who the two men were, and it didn't take long after that to discover where they lived. Mawsil's apartment was just two blocks from the apartment building where Chris lived, and Amaar was only two miles away. It figured they were fairly close, because they were the ones who happened onto the scene, right after Margaret had committed the "crime of adultery."

It was three o'clock in the morning when Husni Mawsil was awakened by a pin prick in his arm. When his eyes opened, he saw a man sitting on the edge of his bed.

"Who are you? How did you get in here?" Mawsil asked.

"I picked the lock."

Mawsil put his hand on the sore spot on his arm.

"In case you are wondering about that pin prick you felt, I just gave you an injection of Batrachotoxin. You'll be dead in less than a minute."

Mawsil's eye's grew large in terror.

"And just so you know? Margaret Malcolm wasn't a whore."

Chris pulled a flask of whiskey from his pocket and took a drink as he stared at the dying Mawsil. Mawsil tried to talk, but already his nervous system was shutting down and the only thing he could do is make a squeaking sound.

"Oh, by the way, I'm pretty sure there aren't going to be seventy-two virgins to welcome you," Chris said. "Because in about thirty seconds now, you'll be in hell. Obey Ohmshidi, you son of a bitch."

Mawsil's eyes opened wider, the only part of his body he could still move, and they reflected his terror. Chris took another swallow of his whiskey as he watched the life go out of those eyes.

Just after dawn, Shurayh Amaar came out of his apartment building and started toward his car. He had left it parked on the street, clearly marked as an SPS vehicle, and not only SPS, a vehicle that belonged to the elite Janissary Corps. It would be the height of foolishness for someone to bother it.

And yet, this morning, someone clearly had.

Amaar gasped as he approached the car. Painted on the side of the car were the words:

"Take Back America!" An American flag fluttered from the radio antenna.

"Who did this? *Who did this?*" Amaar shouted.

Chris, who had been squatting down just on the opposite side of the car, stood up.

"I did it."

"Why you . . ." Amaar shouted in anger as he reached for his pistol.

"With a draw like that, you wouldn't live a day in the Old West," Chris said easily.

"We'll see about that, you son of a bitch!" Amaar shouted, pulling his pistol and bringing it to bear.

Not until then did Chris raise his own weapon, a Glock 19, with a suppressor. When he fired, it sounded no louder than a trigger being pulled on an empty chamber. His bullet hit Amaar in the middle of his forehead, and he fell back, his arms flung out to either side, the pistol lying loose in his right hand.

Chris pulled the whiskey flask from his pocket, took a mouthful, then spit it out on Amaar's body. Then he took a second drink, and turned to walk away.

Lower Alabama

Twenty-one days after they left St. Louis, Tom and Sheri Jack reached the Intracoastal Waterway in Southern Alabama. The bridge that led over the waterway to the island was down.

"Is there any other bridge across this water?" Sheri asked someone who was fishing.

"Nope."

"Is there a way around it?"

"Nope. That's why they call it an island."

"Come on," Tom said. "We'll find a way across."

"Have you got any money?" the fisherman asked.

"We have a little," Tom said. "Why do you ask?"

"I've got a boat. I'll take both of you across."

It cost twenty Moqaddas in AIRE currency to persuade the boat owner to take them across. Once they reached the other side, they stopped at what used to be a McDonald's. They could smell fish being cooked, and because they had last eaten yesterday morning when Tom killed a rabbit and cooked it in the woods, the aroma of fried fish made them both hungry. They parked their bikes and went inside.

A young black woman greeted them from behind the serving counter.

"I'm not sure how to pay for this," Tom said. "I don't know what you are using for money."

"Do you have any money?"

"All I have are Moqaddas. I have a feeling that isn't too welcome here."

"We use it," the woman said. "We don't like it, but we use it."

"Then we'll have two orders of fish," Tom said, smiling at the prospect.

When they took their food to the table, a man at the next table spoke to them.

"Just arrive on the island, did you?"

"How can you tell?"

The man chuckled. "I heard you ask what we use for money. My name is Heckemeyer. Tony Heckemeyer."

"I'm Tom Jack, this is my wife, Sheri."

"Where did you come from, Tom?" "St. Louis. But before the collapse of the military, I was in the Navy in Coronado. I must say, I was little surprised to hear that you are using AIRE money. I thought you folks were sort of off by yourselves down here."

"We are, and for the time being we are using Moqaddas as a matter of exchange for expediency. Our island is pretty self-sufficient, but not entirely so. From time to time we have to go over onto the mainland to buy supplies, and whenever we do that, we have to use AIRE money."

"How do you buy supplies without identity cards?"

"Some of us have ID cards," Heckemeyer said. "It's not anything we are proud of, it's merely a matter of expediency."

"I know what you mean. We have ID cards for the same reason. Tell me, what are people using to pay rent down here? Will Moqaddas work?"

"Ha! Rent? Nobody pays rent. We have twice as many places to live as we have people. All you have to do is find one that is empty, and move in."

"What if the real owner shows up?" Tom asked.

"Easy enough. Just find another one. I'll give you a hint, though. If you go to one of the high-rise condos, you'll find a lot of empty apartments up on the top floors. There's no electricity for the elevators, and nobody wants to climb up all those stairs."

"Thanks."

"What brings you to our island?"

"You aren't an undercover SPS agent, are you?" Tom asked suspiciously.

Heckemeyer laughed. "Lord, no!" he said. "There's not one SPS person on the entire island. In fact, we don't have any police force at all, though as the population of the island increases, it is becoming more likely that we're going to have to have some kind of police. Actually, I was a lawyer before the nation collapsed."

"I'll answer your question, but it might sound a little hokey," Tom said.

"Try me."

"We heard about this place on the news, and we came here to find freedom."

Heckemeyer smiled. "There's not a thing

hokey about that." He extended his hand. "Oh, and you might be interested in coming to a meeting we will be having tomorrow afternoon."

"Who is we?"

"We is all of us. Everyone on the island. As I understand it, we are going to be discussing future plans for the island. If you are at the meeting tomorrow, you'll be in on the beginning."

"That sounds good. If I'm going to live here, I think that is a meeting we should attend. Where will it be?"

"It'll be at Holy Spirit Episcopal Church, on Fort Morgan Road. And, I understand they will be furnishing a free meal to all who show up."

Tom smiled. "Then I know damned well we will attend."

CHAPTER FOURTEEN

Pleasure Island

There was no central supply of electricity on the island, but there were many buildings that had their own supply of electricity, drawn from solar panels. Holy Spirit Episcopal Church was one such place, and it was for that reason that on this sunny afternoon Karin Dawes, Julie Norton, Ellen Varney, Becky Warner, Cille Laney, Gaye Cornett and a few other women were cooking a large meal in the kitchen of the church. Jake Lantz had called a meeting of all interested parties on the island, the stated purpose of which was to "chart the course from here forward for the residents and patriots of Pleasure Island."

Jake was pleased to see that the turnout for the meeting was even larger than he had expected. Most had walked to the meeting, some had ridden bicycles, and others were driving cars, or pickup trucks, that worked by wood gasification.

Bob Varney, who was a rather large man, with silver hair and beard, had come to the meeting wearing a ball cap that said "Vietnam Veteran," and a red T-shirt with the words "Alabama Crimson Tide" on the front. Earlier, there had been some good-natured ribbing between Bob and another citizen who was wearing an Auburn T-shirt. But then they became melancholy as they realized that the storied college football teams of the past—Alabama, Auburn, LSU, Ohio State, Michigan, Notre Dame, Nebraska, Oklahoma, and USC—were no more, because the universities and their athletic programs no longer existed.

The group had managed to put together a very good dinner, consisting of barbequed goat, fried fish, coleslaw, and fried potatoes, every morsel of it drawn from resources available on the island. For most of those who came, it was their first gala gathering since the collapse of the republic, and despite the serious intent of the meeting, everyone was genuinely enjoying it. When all had been served, and while they were still eating, Jake stood up and tapped a spoon against his glass, causing it to ring out. Conversations at all the tables stopped as everyone turned their attention toward Jake.

"First, I would like to thank all of those people who made this absolutely delicious food available for our gathering, and, I want to thank the ladies for preparing it," he said.

There was a round of applause.

"And now, if you will allow me, I would like to get right into the cause of our gathering.

"The America we were born into, the America that we all loved, and the America that many of us fought for, is no more.

"But we here, on this island, are prepared to make a new beginning. And I am sure that you know we are not alone. There are several other freedom groups around the country, and though we are in contact with them by radio, unfortunately we are so separated by distance that as yet we are not able to form one contiguous body. I do believe, however, that in time, we will be able to do just that. But in the meantime, we must all exist as separate, but cooperating, entities.

"We called this meeting because it is time that we organized ourselves, and to that end, I asked Bob Varney, our resident writer, to draw up for us a Declaration of Independence. He did, and I think it's a damn good one. I'm pretty sure that all of you will think so as well. Bob, would you read it for us, please?"

Bob stood up and held out a sheet of paper.

"I've printed out several copies and they will be available to anyone who wants them. But I will read it to you," Bob said. He cleared his throat, and began to read:

"Resolved by the people of Pleasure Island here assembled, that whenever any government becomes destructive of the inalienable rights of its citizens it is the right of the people to dissolve any connection with that government and establish a new government. It was those principles that emboldened our forefathers to declare American Independence from Great Britain in 1776, and it is those same principles which guide us today.

"Be it now declared and ordained that all powers over the residents of Pleasure Island heretofore delegated to the Government of the United States, and usurped by the American Islamic Republic of Enlightenment, and they are hereby irrevocably withdrawn from said Government, and are vested in the people of Pleasure Island. And it is the desire and purpose of the people of Pleasure Island to ally ourselves with other groups of patriots who at their core, as do we, continue allegiance to the United States of America as it was before the election of Mehdi Ohmshidi, and in cooperation with said group coordinate a plan of action by which we will take back America.

"Signed and agreed to by officers elected

in convention on this day, July 4th, in
the time since the collapse of the United
States, one year and six months."

"Excellent!" someone shouted, and the audience applauded.

"As I am sure you can guess, our choosing this
day, the fourth of July, to declare our independence, wasn't just a coincidence," Jake said.

"What are we goin' to call ourselves, Jake?"
someone called up from the audience.

"We've been calling ourselves Firebase Freedom," Jake said.

"That was all right when we were just getting
started," Bob said. "But a firebase is temporary.
We need to move into something more solid. I
think we should declare ourselves to be a state.
We should write a constitution, we should establish military defense and law enforcement, we
should elect a congress and a president, and we
should take on a name that is fitting to our
plans."

"Do you have a suggestion for a name?"

"I think we should call ourselves the UFA,"
Bob said.

"UFA?"

"United Free America."

"I second!" someone shouted, and by unanimous vote, the fledgling nation of United Free
America was born.

One of the people in the audience raised his hand and Bob called on him.

"My name is Tony Heckemeyer," the speaker said. "It's my opinion that we aren't going to be all that successful as a state if we don't have electricity and water."

"I agree that is going to give us problems," Bob said. "But without fuel, we can neither generate electricity nor pump water. And even with the few ID cards we have on the island, there's no way we can get enough gasoline to make any difference."

"We don't have to worry about ID cards, or rationed gasoline. We have a nearly limitless supply of fuel."

Heckemeyer's comment got everyone's attention.

"Oh? And just where is the limitless supply of fuel?"

"I'm a lawyer," Heckemeyer said. "And for the past several years, or at least until Ohmshidi shut them down, I represented the Alabama Gulf Coast Platform Company. There are twenty-three drilling rigs within eyesight, just off our beach."

"Yes," Bob said. "I can see them from my house. I can also see that they are still well illuminated at night."

"The drilling crews have all been taken off the platforms, but many of those who worked on the rigs are still here on the island." Heckemeyer looked around the room for a few seconds before he continued. "In fact, I see Don Webb here right now. Don, why don't you tell us a little about the rigs?"

"I was the drilling chief for AGCP 98-1," Don said. "The wells didn't run dry. We were ordered to shut down in mid cycle and evacuate the platform."

"And you say there is still recoverable oil?" Jake asked.

"Not oil, better than oil. Oil has to be refined. This is natural gas, and it doesn't have to be refined. All that has to be done to it is to process it, to get rid of water and some of the heavy particulates. And that's a much easier thing to do. In fact, we can get it into a useable state right there on the platform, before we even pipe it ashore."

"So what you are saying, Mr. Webb, is if we put you and your crew on the platform, that will take care of our energy problem?" Jake said.

"Well, yes sir, if you can actually get us on the platform. But that's where the problem is. Unfortunately, it isn't just a matter of going out there and getting on the platforms," Webb said.

"Why not?"

"When we were evacuated we were replaced by security teams from the State Protective Service."

Jake smiled. "No sweat. We'll just ask them to leave."

The next item on the agenda was to elect officers for the new country of United Free America. Jake's name was the first one to be put up for president.

"Ladies and gentlemen, I thank you for this honor, I truly do," Jake said. "But I am going to quote General Sherman, when he was asked to run for president. Sherman said, 'If nominated I will not run, if elected, I will not serve.' That, I'm sure you will agree, is the most definitive refusal ever offered with regard to running for president.

"And while being president of United Free America doesn't rise to that level, I'm going to turn it down because I believe that if I remain independent of any specific office, I can do my job much more effectively. I would, however, like to nominate Bob Varney."

Bob's nomination was seconded, and he was elected by unanimous consent. Karin Dawes was elected as vice -president, Julie Norton as Secretary of State, and Tony Heckemeyer as Attorney General. Jake Lantz was Secretary of Defense, and all of them signed the Declaration of Independence.

After that they began to discuss plans to take over one of the offshore drilling rigs.

A young dark-haired man came up then. "Mr. Lantz, I wonder if I could join your team."

"Well you have, haven't you?" Jake replied. "As far as I'm concerned, everyone who was here today is now a part of the team."

"No, I mean specifically, as when you take over the drilling rig. That is going to require a strike team, and I've had some experience in that sort of thing."

"What sort of experience?"

"My name is Tom Jack and I am . . . that is, I was a SEAL, a lieutenant commander in the Navy. I understand you were a major in the army."

"Yes, I was." Jake stuck out his hand. "It's good to have you aboard, Tom. And you are absolutely welcome to be a part of our strike team."

Tom took his hand, smiling broadly. "I'm glad to be with you. And this won't be the first time I've worked with the army."

"Where are you staying?"

"My wife, Sheri, and I have taken an apartment in a beach condo. It's nice enough, but we have no electricity. We're also on the fifth floor, with no elevator."

"If you are going to be part of our assault team, it would be best if we all stayed together. Why don't you and Sheri move out to the fort?" Jake invited. "We've got power, water, and a spare cabin."

"Thanks!"

"Have you got a way out there?"

"We have bicycles."

"Good. It's about a twenty-three-mile ride."

Tom chuckled. "We've just come 750 miles, what's another twenty-three?"

"When can you come?"

"Is this afternoon too soon?"

"We'll be looking for you."

"You don't have to ride out there. Throw your bikes in the back of my pickup truck, I'll take you," James Laney offered, having overheard the conversation.

"You've got gasoline?"

"No. I've got it rigged to run on wood gas. But if you folks are able to take the gas platform, it won't take long to convert it to running on natural gas."

"When that happens, I'll have to get a car."

"There are plenty cars, minivans, pickup trucks, and SUVs available," James said. "You can just about have your pick."

The drive out took a little over half an hour, then James turned off the road and drove toward a large, gray, stone wall.

"Here it is," James said. "Home sweet home."

"You live here?" Sheri asked.

"Yes. Well, just inside the walls. Wait until you see it. We've got a regular little village in there."

James stopped near the wall, then the three of them exited the truck. Tom handed the two bicycles down and he and Sheri pushed their bikes as they followed James inside the walls.

"Wow!" Sheri said when she looked around. There was a long row of connected units on one side of the fort grounds, but around the other four sides were scattered houses, from one-room cabins to rather substantial looking four-, five-, and six-room houses.

"That's what we started with when we first got here," James said, pointing to the row of connected units. "But over the last eighteen months, we've added a few more people, and a few more buildings. The last three units of the motel have doors interconnecting them, and no one is living there now. You're welcome to it."

"What do people do here to make a living? I mean, how will I pay my way?"

"You're too young to remember the hippie communes of the sixties, aren't you?"

"I've heard about them," Tom said. He laughed. "My dad said he joined one for a little while after he came back from Vietnam."

"Well, that's sort of what we have here. Everybody pitches in to do what they can. We've got people who garden, people who fish and hunt, people who build. You'll find your niche."

"I'm afraid I don't fit in to any of those niches."

"You're goin' to be one of the fellas to go out to the gas rig, aren't you?"

"Yes."

James chuckled. "All right, you do that for me, I'll take care of carpentry and the like for you."

Tom smiled, and extended his hand. "You've got a deal."

Chapter Fifteen

Atlanta, Georgia

Raj Hassan, who was Mehdi Ohmshidi's chief of staff, had taken over an entire hotel in Atlanta in order to give a party. Security was extremely tight and uniformed SPS officers were carefully monitoring all the vehicles arriving on the premises. Only those from the top echelon of the AIRE government had been invited, and even those who were granted entry from the street were limited from further access according to their pecking order among the guests. As a result, each arriving automobile, whether it was a chauffeur-driven stretch limousine, or an individually driven luxury sedan or sports car, had to negotiate a phalanx of SPS guards before reaching its final destination.

One vehicle that was allowed in from the street was a van, sporting a painted sign that read "Crystal Creations, by Andre." When it arrived at the portico of the hotel, a security officer motioned for it to stop. The driver complied, then let his window down. His blond hair was perfectly coiffed, his narrow moustache was well trimmed, his fingernails neatly manicured, and a diamond earring glistened from the lobe of his right ear.

"Now, what is wrong?" he asked, irritably. "I was cleared to the portico. Oh, I suppose I should say Obey Ohmshidi."

The guard looked at the clipboard he was holding, but didn't respond.

"Aren't you supposed to say that back to me?"

"Obey Ohmshidi," the security officer said. "You're Andre?"

"No, I'm Rambo."

"What?"

"Of course, I'm Andre, you silly goose."

"Open up the back of the van," the security officer replied.

"Is that really necessary? I assure you, sir, there is nothing back there but an exquisite ice sculpture of Venus de Milo," the driver insisted, somewhat mincing his words.

"Open up," the guard said again.

Andre got out and pranced to the back of the van to open the doors. He showed his chagrin by putting his hands on his hips, and tapping his foot.

"You are the third person to stop me. Should this lovely piece melt, I assure you, sir, that you and these other uniformed Spartans who are guarding this place shall answer to Mr. Hassan."

The guard looked into the back of the truck, saw the ice sculpture, then snorted. "Damn, she ain't got no arms."

"Oh, you are a cretin, aren't you?"

The guard closed the back doors. "Okay, drive on."

"Thank you."

As Andre pulled away, the guard raised his two-way radio. There was a pop of squelch as he pushed the talk button. "Marty, there's a van coming through with an ice sculpture or some damn thing. Let the faggot through without stopping him anymore. Otherwise he may hit you with his purse."

"Copy," Marty answered, chuckling over the rush of static.

With no further interference, Andre drove to the kitchen entrance of the hotel, then backed the van up to the loading dock. Hopping up onto the dock, he pushed the bell button alongside the door. While he waited, he checked his watch. The watch was digital, and counting down. The numbers read 06:27, meaning that he had six minutes and twenty-seven seconds remaining.

There was a rattle of a chain pulley as the door was raised. When the door opened, it revealed one of the hotel kitchen employees as well as a narrow-faced, hawk-nosed man with beady eyes and narrow lips. Even in a tuxedo, the beady-eyed one looked exactly like what he was, a goon for Raj Hassan. A slight bulge in his jacket disclosed that he was wearing a shoulder holster.

"I shall require a cart of some sort," Andre said.

The kitchen employee nodded, then came back a moment later with a small, four-wheeled dolly. Andre pushed the dolly into the back of the van, carefully moved the ice sculpture onto the dolly, then placed a thermal blanket around it. He pushed the dolly out of the van and into the kitchen.

"Hold it," the goon said, raising his hand. "What's that?"

"It's a thermal blanket to keep the ice from melting," Andre explained, pulling the blanket aside enough for the goon to see.

"Okay. You can go."

"Well, I should hope I can go," Andre minced. "Heavens, give a brute like you some authority and it goes right to your head."

Andre pushed the sculpture through the kitchen and into the large reception room. The reception room was already filling with guests, and as the thermal blanket was removed, revealing Venus de Milo, there were many "oohs" and "ahhs" of appreciation.

As he walked away from the display carrying the thermal blanket, Andre checked his watch again. He was now down to less than two minutes.

When he reached the kitchen, he stepped into the walk-in freezer to store the blanket.

Once inside, though, he locked the door. Quickly, he began stripping out of the white pants and shirt he was wearing. After that he took off the blond toupee, stripped off the moustache, and removed the clip-on earring. Then he put on the tuxedo he had carried in, concealed in the thermal blanket. After the transformation, there was nothing left of the man who had passed himself off as Andre.

This was Michael Moran. No longer the effeminate and mincing ice sculptor, he now resembled the self-confident, solidly built, former police lieutenant and ex–Green Beret that he really was. Moran looked at his watch as it counted down to zero. At zero, he opened the door.

From all around the hotel, he could hear the sirens of approaching police cars, followed by the bark of machine-gun fire, then the announcement from an outside bullhorn.

"This is a police raid! Everyone stay where you are! No one will be allowed to leave the building!"

From inside the hotel there were shouts of anger and alarm.

"What is this?" Hassan asked a senior SPS officer. "Don't the local police know who I am?"

"I swear, I don't know anything about this!" the

SPS officer replied earnestly. "I thought we had everything coordinated!"

"Do something. Find out what this is all about!"

"I'm checking on it," the State Protective Service officer promised, pulling out his cell phone.

As the turmoil continued outside the hotel, Moran hurried up to the second floor. There, behind a closed door, was the hotel office, where two men were guarding a briefcase which contained nearly three million Moqaddas in the new AIRE currency. From his planning, Moran knew that the impending transfer of money was payoff money from drug dealers to Hassan.

Moran knocked on the door of the hotel office. The door opened slightly, and someone peered through the crack.

"Yeah?" the man inside said.

"Mr. Hassan is leaving. He wants you to take the money to him," Moran answered.

The guard stepped back from the door, allowing Moran inside. Then he called to the other guard. "Len, Mr. Hassan is leaving. Bring the money."

Len started to comply, then, perhaps realizing how much money he was responsible for, decided to double check. He began punching numbers into a cell phone.

The first guard had turned toward Len, which meant his back was to Moran. That was the opening Moran needed. He brought the knife-edge of his hand down hard, on the side of the man's neck, and he went down. Len looked up in surprise, then, dropping the cell phone, reached for his pistol. That action left him wide open, and, using the heel of his hand, Moran drove a smashing blow onto the point of Ernesto's chin. Like his partner, Len went down.

While they were still down, dazed, but not unconscious, Moran grabbed the briefcase and ran back out into the hall. Instead of turning toward the elevator or stairway, though, he went the other way, stepping into one of the housekeeping rooms. There, he slipped into the laundry chute, then fell two stories into the basement, landing in a large bin of sheets, pillowcases, and towels.

In the basement, Moran changed jackets, taking off the tux jacket and replacing it with a chauffeur's jacket he had planted there. After that, he climbed through the basement window, then walked easily to a stretch limousine.

As previously arranged with the driver of the limo, the key was in the jacket pocket. It was a proximity key, so all Moran had to do was open the car, get behind the steering wheel, and drive off.

"There's nobody out there! It's nothing but a bunch of loudspeakers!" one of the SPS men said, reporting back to Hassan.

"What?" Hassan asked. "Is this some kind of joke?"

At that moment there was a pop, like a muffled gunshot, in the reception room. There were more screams, then gasps of amazement, and finally, laughter. The laughter built until it was an avalanche of sound, filling the reception room.

"What is it? What's going on?" Hassan demanded. "Why is everyone laughing?"

Hassan hurried into the reception room, then saw what everyone else had seen.

The beautiful ice sculpture of Venus de Milo had split exactly in half, one side falling to the left, the other to the right. Everyone could now see that this hadn't been an ice sculpture at all, but was clear plastic, covered with a patina of ice.

There was, however, a piece of ice sculpture inside Venus de Milo. This particular sculpture was of a hand, with all the fingers closed except the middle finger. The middle finger was sticking obscenely into the air. Propped up at the base of the hand was a neatly printed sign.

TAKE BACK AMERICA!

Muslimabad

Chris Carmack sat at a table in a sidewalk café, drinking coffee which he had, earlier, surreptitiously spiked with whiskey from the silver flask he was never without. As he was sitting there, a government car drove up and Judge Sulymam

Ayambuie and three *Moqaddas Sirata* clerics got out. They left their car parked on the sidewalk, evidence of their power and position within the government.

Barely paying attention to the supplications of the other patrons of the café, the four men chose a table under the awning, forcing the two men and two women who were already at the table to leave.

"You!" Ayambuie shouted, pointing at a young woman. "Cover your face, or be caned!"

The bottom of the woman's face was covered, but that wasn't enough, and Chris could see the fear in her eyes as she pulled the veil up even higher.

Chris got up from the table and went over to the cash register to pay for his coffee. The new money, issued by the AIRE, did make business transitions easier than they had been after the collapse of the dollar, but it disgusted him to have to use the bills decorated with Ohmshidi's face.

As Chris left the outdoor café, he was counting his change when he tripped over a table leg and nearly fell, dropping his money onto the sidewalk.

"Watch where you are going, you clumsy oaf!" someone said.

"I'm sorry," Chris said. Bending down he began gathering his coins until he saw one that had rolled under the edge of the car. He reached down to retrieve it, but as he did so, he placed a magnetic bomb underneath the car, and with a quick twist, armed it.

Getting up, he brushed himself off, then looked at the man sitting at the table over which he had tripped. It was this man who had called out to him.

"Allow me to buy you a fresh coffee, or a sweet roll," he said.

"Just get away from me, infidel," the customer said.

Chris nodded. "I'm sorry," he said again.

Chris climbed on his bicycle, then rode away, but he went no more than a block. Then he turned the corner and looked back toward the car. He waited for half an hour until Judge Ayambuie and the other three clerics got into the car and started driving away. He watched the car and waited until it was clear of anyone else. Then he set off the remote.

He saw a huge ball of fire suddenly blossom around the car, followed a full second later by the solid thump of the explosion.

The man who had raped Margaret, the two SPS officers who had arrested her, rather than the rapist, and now the judge who had sentenced her to die by stoning, were all dead. It didn't bring Margaret back, but it sure gave Chris a sense of satisfaction as he rode away.

CHAPTER SIXTEEN

Fort Morgan

Willy Stark got in touch, via shortwave radio, with a group that called themselves the Brotherhood of Loyalists. When he made contact he called Jake over.

"I've got the Loyalists," Willy said.

Jake took the microphone. "Loyalist, this is Firebase Freedom Six."

"Authenticate, Firebase Freedom Six."

Over the last several months the various groups had put together and exchanged an SOI, the *Signal Operating Instructions*, which had a daily authentication code. No conversation between the groups could be conducted without first authenticating the transmission.

Willie pointed out the sign and countersign authenticators.

"I authenticate Red dog," Jake said.

"Blitz," Loyalist replied.

"Loyalists, I am announcing today the birth of a new nation. We are calling ourselves United Free America, and we are prepared to work in alliance with our brother freedom fighters wherever they might be. Our call sign will still be Firebase Freedom, but that will be but the military arm of the new nation of United Free America."

"Roger, Firebase Freedom. And congratulations on your move. I think some of the others are contemplating the same kind of action. Watch the Gregoire broadcast tonight."

"Will do. Out."

"Out."

At five o'clock that evening, everyone at Fort Morgan gathered around the television to watch the broadcast from George Gregoire. Before the collapse of the United States, Gregoire had been one of the most popular conservative commentators on TV. But shortly after Ohmshidi was elected president of the U.S., he issued, by executive fiat, the "Fairness Act," which deemed Gregoire's broadcasts to be advocating revolution. He declared Gregoire to be a traitor, tried him in absentia, and sentenced him to death.

Gregoire had gone into hiding but continued to broadcast by pirating a signal off the satellite. That didn't last long before AIRE was able to interrupt it. But AIRE also reestablished the Internet, and Gregoire's technicians managed to put together an Internet operation which, while hiding the source from hackers, enabled Gregoire to continue his television operation via the World Wide Web.

Willie Stark devised a way to connect the computer feed to the television screen so that the broadcasts could be followed easily. The broadcast started with the red and white striped letters "GGTV" appearing against a blue background.

"*We are the truth!*" Gregoire's voice shouted over the screen.

The music for the intro was "The Battle Hymn of the Republic," and the picture was the Stars and Stripes, billowing in the wind. Then the image faded to images of Navy ships, U.S. Air Force planes, and Army tanks moving majestically across the screen.

When the intro was done, a short, rather stocky red-faced man with close-cropped, white hair appeared.

"Hello, America.
"And thank you for tuning in to GGTV. I will bring you up to date on the latest news we have been able to gather. Tonight, there is a new star in Freedom's firmament. A group of loyal patriots have issued a declaration of independence from the outlaw government that usurped power from the people of the United States. These patriots have formed the nation of United Free America, and declare in their

constitution to continue allegiance to the United States of America as it was before the election of Mehdi Ohmshidi. They also pledge to coordinate a plan of action by which we will take back America.

"Take back America. Let that be the rallying cry of true Americans of all stripes, regardless of race, religion, or ethnicity.

"And now for the news. The chief justice of the so-called American Islamic Republic of Enlightenment, Sulymam Ayambuie, was killed when a bomb destroyed his car. Authorities are saying that it was a random terrorist attack conducted by traitors to the new state. But, there is an interesting parallel to a few other recent killings.

"You may remember that on a previous broadcast, I told you about a young woman, Margaret Malcolm, who was raped in Arlington, Virginia, then taken to Washington, D.C., where she was brutally stoned to death. Yes, I call it Washington, because I refuse to refer to it by any other name.

"Margaret was raped, but her rapist, a man named Billy Donner, wasn't prosecuted. On the contrary, he became the witness for the prosecution, because the defendant in the case was not Billy Donner; it was, amazingly, Margaret Malcolm. Her crime was adultery. Now, I want you to think of that for a moment. Margaret Malcolm was raped, but she was tried

for adultery. She was tried, found guilty, and sentenced to death. The execution was carried out by stoning.

"There is a followup to that story. Since that happened, everyone involved in that case has died—or, I should say, has been killed. First, it was Billy Donner, found dead in the alley behind the convenience store where he worked. A few days later the two Janissaries who, rather than coming to Margaret's aid, delivered her to court for her trial, were also found dead. And now, Justice Sulymam Ayambuie.

"Do you want to know what I believe, ladies and gentlemen? I believe that justice has been served.

"Now, we have pictures for you, of a successful strike against an AIRE detention center."

Over the next few minutes fuzzy video on the screen showed an attack against a jail in an unidentified location. There was a brief firefight between the attackers and the defenders, culminating in the release of several happy prisoners, both men and women. After that, the picture returned to Gregoire.

"This wasn't your ordinary detention center. The prisoners held there had been given their choice of public conversion to Moqaddas Sirata, or public execution. They are now safe with their

*families in one of the many pockets of freedom
that are scattered around our country.*

*"Now, I want all of you to think about the
group of patriots I told you about at the
beginning of this broadcast. They are brave men
and women who have taken control of their own
lives, and they are but one of many such groups
around the nation.*

*"Ladies and gentlemen, patriots all, I want
you to consider doing the same thing. We have
all tasted freedom in the past, and once you get
a taste of freedom, you are loathe to give it up.
I believe that the day will come, and soon, when
there will be enough of us to coalesce into one
powerful nation, a nation that will possess
both the will and the means, to drive out our
oppressors.*

*"Thank you, good night, and God bless
America."*

"Tom, we'll get you and Sheri set up in your
cabin, then you can have dinner with us tonight,"
Jake said after the telecast that evening.

"I don't know, what are you serving?"

"Tom!" Sheri scolded.

"Road kill," Jake answered, without skipping
a beat.

"Sounds good, we'll be there," Tom said with
a chuckle.

* * *

After dinner Jake took Tom up onto the wall of the fort and pointed out to sea. From there, they could see nearly two dozen well-lit off-shore rigs, some very close, some so far away as to be barely visible.

"That's the one we're going to take first," Jake said, pointing to the closest one. "That is AGCP 98-1, the one where Webb was working, and he assures us that he can have it up and functioning in less than twenty-four hours."

"How are we going to approach it?" Tom asked.

"There's a fisherman, Gary Bryant, who lives out here . . . in fact, he supplies us with most of our fish. He has a boat that he, Marcus, and James converted to run off wood gasification. He has done a lot of fishing very close in to the rigs, so they are used to seeing him. He's agreed to sneak us out there."

"Sounds like a plan," Tom agreed. "How many on our strike team?"

"There will be a total of six, counting you, me, and Gary. But Gary won't do anything but drive the boat."

"If you don't mind, I'd like to meet the other team members," Tom said.

"No problem. Come on back down and I'll introduce you."

Tom followed Jake back down from the wall, then over to where a small group of men stood.

"Gentlemen, this is Tom Jack. Tom is a former

SEAL who has volunteered to help us take the gas platform. Tom, this is our team, Deon Pratt, Willie Stark, and Marcus Warner. And this is Gary Bryant, he'll be our boat captain."

Tom shook hands with the others, then they began making plans for the operation.

As they were talking, a small toddler started toward Marcus Warner, holding his arms out to be picked up.

"And who is this handsome little fellow?" Tom asked.

"This is John Clay Warner," Marcus said, picking the child up.

"John Clay. That's a good, solid-sounding name," Tom said.

"It comes from a couple of really good people, Sergeant Major Clay Matthews, and Sergeant John Deedle," Marcus said.

"They started out with us," Deon explained. "But both were killed."

"It looks like you've found a good way to honor them," Tom said.

"Yes, and when John Clay grows up, I'm going to make certain that he knows the significance, and the honor of having the name he has."

"All right, gentlemen, if there are no questions, I suggest you all get a good night's sleep," Jake said. "Tomorrow is going to be a busy day."

* * *

That night, after Tom and Sheri got into bed, Tom sensed a bit of uneasiness.

"I know this cabin is pretty rough, but we won't be here forever. We'll find some place a little nicer than this. It's just that I think we should be here now, as long as I'm going to be a part of Jake's strike force."

"It's not the cabin that's bothering me," Sheri said. "I'm okay no matter where we are, as long as we're together. It's tomorrow I'm worried about."

"Tomorrow? Why, what happens tomorrow?"

"What happens tomorrow? Have you forgotten? You and some others are going on a crazy mission to take over an oil platform."

"It's not oil, it's gas."

"You know what I mean," Sheri said in exasperation.

Tom reached over to take Sheri's hand. "Darlin', the advantage is all ours. When you think about it, how many people can they have out there on that rig? And they won't be expecting us. I wish you wouldn't worry about it."

"I have to worry about it," Sheri said. "You sure won't."

"Well, if I've got you to worry, then I don't have to, do I?"

Sheri chuckled. "You make me so angry sometimes."

"That's just to keep things fresh," Tom teased. "Hell, if you never got mad at me, how boring would that be?"

Sheri sighed. "There's no arguing with you," she said. "Just promise me that you will be careful tomorrow."

"I promise you, I'll be careful."

When the sun came up the next morning, the fishing boat *Red Eye* was within one hundred yards of AGCP 98-1. The trawling net was deployed, and the *Red Eye* was slowly closing the distance between itself and the gas-drilling rig. To the casual observer it appeared that two of the *Red Eye*'s crewmen were on deck, tending to the net.

But the two men on deck weren't crewmen, and they weren't tending to the net. Gary Bryant was on the flying bridge, Deon Pratt was on one side of the boat, and Tom Jack was on the other side. Jake Lantz, Willy Stark, and Marcus Warner were hiding in the boat's cabin.

High up on the deck of AGCP 98-1 there were nine State Protective Service men. Four were playing cards, three were kibitzing, and two were walking around the deck.

"What's that boat doing?" one of them asked, pointing to the *Red Eye*.

"Same thing he does ever' day. He's fishin'."

"Don't seem like he's ever come this close before."

"I've heard that the fish sort of like being around a rig like this. Maybe they're just taking advantage of it."

"Wonder if he's caught anything. I wouldn't mind a little fried snapper."

"Yeah, well, it don't matter none now, the boat's goin' away."

As the boat pulled away from AGCP 98-1, Jake, Tom, Deon, Willy and Marcus clung to the base of the rig. They started a climb to the top, a climb that would have been easy if they could have used the steps. But the steps were under continuous observation by those up on the deck, whereas the scaffolding could not be seen from above.

It was a long way up, and the ascent wasn't easy, as they had to depend upon braces and cross supports to pull their way up. It was particularly difficult for Jake, because he was afraid of heights.

"How can that be?" he once asked a flight surgeon. "I'm not at all frightened by height when I am flying. But when I am on top of something high, I get almost woozy."

The flight surgeon explained that it was quite common for aviators to be afraid of heights.

"You see, when you are flying you are in a totally different world . . . The aircraft is your world. Whereas when you are on top of some stable object, you have a spatial orientation toward the ground, and that spatial orientation is what makes you nervous."

Jake concentrated on looking up until, finally, all five of them were in position, just under the platform. Slowly, quietly, they moved from the supporting struts to a platform just below the work deck. There, the four men drew their weapons, and all looked toward Jake for guidance.

Jake sent Tom to one side of the platform and Deon to the other side. There, they waited until the two men who were pacing around on the deck reached a point right above them. When they did, Tom and Deon reached up simultaneously, grabbed them, and jerked them over the side.

Both men fell one hundred feet, face down, screaming all the way until they hit the water.

"What the hell?" one of the card players shouted, standing up. "What happened?"

Just below the deck Jake gave a signal, and the five of them rushed up the stairs and out onto the work deck.

"Son of a bitch! Where'd you come from?"

"Shoot 'em, shoot 'em!" One of the other security men shouted.

"No! Give it up!" Jake countered.

Jake's offer had no effect, as all seven men went for their guns. What followed was a short, but very brutal gunfight. Soon all seven SPS men lay dead on the deck of the giant drilling rig.

CHAPTER SEVENTEEN

Muslimabad

Mohammad Akbar Rahimi was angry, and he summoned Mehdi Ohmshidi to his office so he could express his anger. He was sipping tea when Ohmshidi was shown into his office. He did not offer tea to the president.

"You sent for me, O Merciful One?"

Rahimi glared at Ohmshidi without responding. It wasn't until then that Ohmshidi realized that Rahimi was waiting for him to pay the proper respects, and he wondered how far he should go. After all, he was the president for life. If he wanted to, he could have Rahimi arrested.

But no, for now, Rahimi was useful, so Ohmshidi decided that, for the time being, he would play the obsequious one. Ohmshidi got down on his knees, bowed so low that his forehead touched the floor, and extended his hands, palm down, also touching the floor.

"You may rise," Rahimi said.

Ohmshidi got up from the floor, and only after Rahimi's invitation did he take a seat.

"Where is this man George Gregoire?" Rahimi asked.

"I don't know, Imam," Ohmshidi said. "We have tried to track him, but he moves about, and he broadcasts by Internet."

"He must be found, and killed," Rahimi insisted. "It is people like him, revolutionaries, who are the greatest danger to our position. Offer a reward of one million Moqaddas for his capture. But I want him alive. We must make a public broadcast of his execution."

"Yes, Imam. I will make finding this infidel my top priority," Ohmshidi said.

Amish country, Pennsylvania

Solomon Lantz's buggy was but one of nearly two dozen horse-drawn vehicles going down a long, narrow dirt road that stretched out between flanking fields of corn. Ahead of Solomon, and slightly downhill, lay his farm. To the left was the house, a functional building two stories high, without cupolas or dormers, but with a chimney on each end. In the same compound was a large barn, and several other smaller buildings. There were also two silos. Behind the farm, and rising slightly, were more fields, then a great collection of trees.

Because of their style of living, the Amish society

had suffered the least from the total collapse of what had been the United States. So far, their communities had not been terribly bothered by the *Moqaddas Sirata*, primarily because they were self-contained, and absolutely nonconfrontational.

Riding in the buggy with Solomon was an old man with a wrinkled face, a white beard, and white hair. Like Solomon and the other Amish men he was wearing plain clothes, and a small, black hat. But unlike the other men, neither his beard, hair, nor wrinkles were authentic. This was George Gregoire, who, with the artistry of his makeup assistant and the help of Solomon Lantz, was now hiding out in Amish country.

Through his sources, Gregoire had learned that Jake Lantz, one of the founders and leaders of the new nation of United Free America, had been raised Amish. He had come to Amish country to see what he could learn about him from his father. Then, with Solomon's cooperation, he decided to hide out here. Only Solomon and Gregoire's technician and makeup woman knew who Gregoire was. To the other members of the community, he was Solomon's uncle Jacob Yoder from the Amish community of Arthur, Illinois.

Gregoire and Solomon had ridden together in total silence for the last thirty minutes.

"Mr. Lantz," Gregoire said. "Why is it that you are so quiet?"

"There is a reason God gave us two ears and

one mouth," Solomon said. "It is because we should listen twice and speak once."

Gregoire laughed out loud. "I shall have to remember that," he said.

Ahead of them, the buggies came to a complete stop. Beyond the most distant buggy was a rise in the road, and they couldn't see on the other side.

"I think there is a roadblock," Solomon said.

"I should get off here. I've no wish to get you in trouble."

Solomon put his hand on Gregoire's shoulder. "*Nein, bleib, ist es in Ordnung.*" Then, realizing that he had spoken in German, he translated. "No, stay, it will be all right."

When they reached the crest of the hill, they saw two cars with SPS markings, parked in such a way as to force any traffic through their check point. An SPS officer held up his hand to stop the buggy as they approached.

"*Ihren Namen?*" the SPS man said.

"*Ich bin Solomon Lantz.*"

"*Und Sie?*" the guard said to Gregoire.

"He is my uncle Jacob. Jacob Yoder."

"Why can't he speak for himself?"

Solomon pointed to his ears. "*Er kann nicht horen.* He is deaf."

The guard stared at Gregoire for a long moment, then stepped back and waved his hand.

"Go on through," he said.

"*Danke*," Solomon said, snapping the reins against the back of his horse. The buggy passed through the roadblock without further incident.

"My son warned me that this would happen," Solomon said as they drove off. "He came home to see his mother and me a year and a half ago, and he told me to be prepared. I paid no attention to him then. I should have, because he was right."

"Your son is a genuine American hero," Gregoire said.

"I think he would not be comfortable to have people call him a hero."

"Heroes, real heroes, never are comfortable with accolades," Gregoire said.

Late that afternoon, just before broadcast time, Gregoire was in Solomon's barn. Here, he had secreted a satellite receiver which would allow him to access the Internet. Here, too, hidden among the bales of hay, was a camera, microphone, and a laptop computer. That was all he needed for broadcast.

He had two assistants who, like him, were hiding out among the "plain people." Mark Riley was his cameraman, and Jennie Lea was his makeup artist. He didn't need any field reporters, because there were still citizens out there who were brave enough to cover events that were newsworthy and against the government, who would put video on the net, for Gregoire to use.

"We've got some good stuff today, George," Mark said. "Pictures of concentration camps for children."

"What? Concentration camps for children? Are you serious?" Gregoire was sitting in a chair as Jennie removed his "old man" makeup, to prepare him for his broadcast.

"Yeah, wait until you see the pictures," Mark said.

Muslimabad

"Great Leader, it is time for the Gregoire broadcast," Hassan said, coming into the Oval Office.

Although the broadcast was over the Internet, Ohmshidi had it linked to his TV, and he picked up the remote, turned on the TV, then leaned back with his feet propped up on the Resolute Desk to watch the broadcast.

The first thing to come onto the screen were the letters "GGTV."

"*We are the truth!*" Gregoire's voice shouted over the screen.

When the intro was done, Gregoire appeared.

"Hello, America.
Today I want to show you something that will disturb you to your very core. No, that's wrong, I

don't want to do this, but I feel I have to do it.
Every American needs to know what is
happening in this once great country."

The images on the screen were of a Youth Confinement and Enlightenment Center. After showing the barracks and the razor wire, the video switched to a figure in a burqa, whose age couldn't be determined, since all that could be seen was the burqa. The girl was led up to a post that stood in the middle of the camp. She was secured to the post by handcuffs. Then a man, wielding a bullwhip, gave her twenty lashes.

"We are told this is a twelve-year-old girl,"
Gregoire's voiceover explained. "You may
wonder what heinous crime this young girl
committed, that would subject her to such brutal
punishment."

The picture came back to Gregoire who stood there for a long moment, just staring at the camera as his eyes glistened with tears.

"Her crime," he started, then his voice broke,
and he had to start again. "Her crime was
reading a novel." Gregoire shook his head.
"What have we become?" he asked, as he dabbed
at his eyes. "What have we become?"

"How did he get those pictures?" Ohmshidi asked.

"I don't know, Great Leader."

"I want you to find that man," Ohmshidi ordered. "I don't care what it takes, I want him found, and I want him brought to me."

"Yes, Great Leader," Hassan replied. "I will give the order to National Leader Franken. I'm sure he will use the Janissaries for this."

Youth Confinement and Enlightenment Center 251

Eddie Manning and his girlfriend, Jane, had been at YCEC 251 six weeks, but he still had not been able to locate her. He took some comfort in realizing that, while he couldn't identify her because she was always totally covered from head to toe, she would be able to identify him.

Of course, even if she could identify him, she couldn't communicate with him, because they had been warned that communication of any kind between the boys and girls of the camp would result in punishment of the strictest kind. And of course they had already seen an example of punishment of the strictest kind, when Jarvis Morris's body was pulled apart.

Then one day as the girls were passing by, one of them stopped, and stared directly at Eddie. Neither she nor Eddie spoke a word, but Eddie knew that she had just made contact with him. He saw her waving her hand, slightly, and when he looked toward it, she had her hand formed into a fist except for the index and little fingers which were extended.

Eddie smiled, because he knew that she had just told him how she would identify herself from now on.

As Jane continued on toward the morning class, she was feeling good about the fact that she had finally been able to make contact with Eddie. She wished she could speak to him, but she was afraid that if they were caught speaking, Eddie might receive the same punishment they had given Jarvis Morris. She and several others, boys and girls, had thrown up in horror over the sight.

This morning the lesson they would be learning was entitled: "A woman's role in the Islam of *Moqaddas Sirata.*"

The teacher, a tall, bearded man, began to speak. "The Prophet has commanded that any statement made by a female can only be considered valid if it is the testimony of two women. That is so as to be sure that they remember, because it takes the mind and memory of two women to be equal to the mind and memory of one man.

"The Prophet has said, 'The righteous among the women of Quraish are those who are kind to their young ones and who look after their husband's property.' When you are married, you will be the property of your husband.

"You may legally belong to a man in one of two ways; by continuing marriage or temporary marriage. In the first, the duration of the marriage need not be specified; in the latter, it must be stipulated, for example, that it is for a period of an hour, a day, a month, a year, or more."

"Imam," one of the girls asked. "What if the woman does not want to be married for an hour, but wants a husband for life?"

"It is not the woman's prerogative," the imam replied. "For in each case, these arrangements are always made by the man, for the woman shall have no say in the matter."

"But Imam, if the woman is married but an hour, is she not committing the sin of adultery?"

"Yes, for it is adulterous for a woman to have sex with a man if she is not married to him."

"But you said it would be a marriage of one hour."

"It is only called a marriage so that the man does not commit adultery. But it is a marriage for the man only, not for the woman. He is innocent of any sin, but the woman is not."

"That doesn't seem right for the woman."

"It doesn't matter, for women have no rights, only obligations."

The expression in the imam's voice indicated that he was getting irritated by the repeated questions, and Jane wished that the girl who was asking the questions would stop.

Mercifully, she did stop, and the imam continued with his lesson.

"A man may marry a girl younger than nine years of age, even if the girl is still a baby being breast-fed. A man, however, is prohibited from having intercourse with a girl younger than nine, though other sexual acts such as foreplay, rubbing, kissing, and sodomy are allowed."

"Imam," another of the girls asked. "What is the punishment for a man who has intercourse with a girl younger than nine?"

"There is no punishment, for a man having intercourse with a girl younger than nine years of age has not committed a crime, but only an infraction. For that, he shall be verbally admonished.

"While you are here, you may be approached by one of the men who are on the staff. If he wishes to take you as a wife, whether by continuing or temporary marriage, you must obey."

"But, Imam, what if we don't wish to marry the man?" one of the older girls asked.

The instructor shook his head. "It does not matter what you wish. You will have no say. You are to be totally subservient to the man."

"But you said that to do so, would mean that we are committing adultery," the girl who had been questioning him earlier said.

"That is true."

"But, if we commit adultery, won't we be punished?"

"Severely."

"So, we are damned if we do, and damned if we don't," one of the oldest girls said.

The Imam looked at her with cold, hard, flinty eyes, then without saying a word he walked over to her and slapped her so hard that she was knocked out of the chair. The veil came off her face.

"Cover your face, harlot!" the imam said, angrily.

The girl was too shaken and frightened to cover her own face, so one of the other girls, who had been sitting close to her, put the veil back in place.

"I will not tolerate swearing," the imam said. "This harlot should praise Allah that I am in a benevolent mood. Had I not been, she would have been tied to the stake and beaten."

CHAPTER EIGHTEEN

Pleasure Island

By the time Mike Moran reached South Alabama, a pontoon bridge had been constructed across the canal, and over to the island. There was a huge sign just north of the canal, and Mike read it.

STOP!!!
If you have come to join us
you will be required to pull
your own weight. We can use
carpenters, electricians, plumbers
engine and vehicle mechanics,
as well as farmers, doctors, nurses,
and those with military experience.
If you meet that criteria and seek
freedom among us, you are welcome.
If you have come to live off the toil of
others, you are not welcome.
—Robert Varney, President

Mike had come to Gulf Shores because he knew about the movement here, having picked it up over shortwave radio broadcasts and Gregoire's Internet television shows. He had ditched the stretch limousine soon after he stole the three million Moqaddas, but the car he was in now, a 2011 Volvo, ran on gasoline, not wood gasification, so that alone would be enough to garner the attention of others as soon as he came on the island.

Mike had spent some time on Pleasure Island back before the collapse of the United States, so he knew the place fairly well. Assuming that governing offices of the island would be in the old police station building, he went there.

"No, if you are looking for Bob Varney, you are going to have to go all the way out to Fort Morgan. What used to be the fort museum is now the president's office," he was told.

"How far is that?"

"Twenty-three miles."

"I have enough fuel to drive out there, but won't have enough to drive back. I don't suppose there is any gasoline available on the island, is there?"

"No, but if you have enough to get out there, either James or Marcus can convert your car to take natural gas. We've got a lot of that."

"Really?" Mike replied with a smile. "Damn, that's great! I thought I was going to have to give up my car."

Mike knew exactly where the fort museum was, because the last time he had come down to the island, he and his wife had gone out to visit the fort. He recalled that visit now, remembering with sweet sadness the happier time, before Ohmshidi had brought about the collapse of the republic, and before his wife had been murdered.

Mike blamed Ohmshidi for her death, even though neither he, nor any of his State Police goons, were directly involved. She had been killed because she was carrying a loaf of bread. The fact that the world had so collapsed around them that a woman could be killed for a loaf of bread was, Mike believed, the cause and effect of Ohmshidi's disastrous policies. What Mike didn't know was whether the destruction of the greatest nation in the history of humankind was the result of Ohmshidi's incompetence, or if he had brought this about by some grand scheme.

When Mike pulled his Volvo to a stop in front of what had been the office and museum of Fort Morgan, there was someone standing out front, watching him. The man out front was wearing a shoulder holster, and Mike recognized the pistol as a P-38, nine millimeter.

"Can I help you, Mister?" the man asked.

"I'm here to see President Varney."

"He's inside."

Mike reached back into his car and pulled out a briefcase.

"Hold it. What have you got in there?" the armed man called.

Mike opened the briefcase, then turned it upside down over the hood of his car. What tumbled out from the case were several bound packets of Ohmshidi notes.

"Holy crap! What is that?"

"That, my friend, is three million Moqaddas in negotiable currency."

"What do you plan to do with it?"

"I plan to give it to the treasury of the new nation of United Free America."

The armed man came over to Mike then and extended his hand. "The name is Marcus Warner. Welcome to United Free America."

"You want to help me put this back in the case?" Mike asked as he started scooping up the money.

It took but a moment until all the money was back in the briefcase, then Marcus opened the door and led Mike inside.

Bob was sitting at a desk, tapping on a computer keyboard.

"Writin' another story?" Marcus asked.

"Yes."

"Well, if you can pull yourself away from it for a minute or two, I think this fella—"

Marcus realized then that he hadn't gotten the name and he turned toward him.

"Mike Moran."

"Mr. Moran, this is Bob Varney. He's our

president. Bob, I think Mr. Moran has something you will be interested in."

"All right," Bob said, looking expectantly toward Mike.

Again, Mike opened his valise and turned it upside down. This time the money tumbled down onto Bob's desk.

"There's three million Moqaddas here," Mike said. "Use it however you need it. I've come to join up."

Bob chuckled. "Well, I'd say you just bought your way into our little group."

"You know what we should do," Bob said later, as he, Jake, Tom, and some of the others were talking. "We should gather up every Moqaddas on the island, then use it to buy gold. If we have gold to back it, we can issue our own currency."

"Damn," Jake said. "That is a good idea."

"I've got a better idea," Tom said.

"What's that?"

"Instead of buying gold from Ohmshidi's government, why don't we just take it?"

"Take it from whom?"

"Take it from Ohmshidi."

"Hah. Yeah, right," Jake said. "We just go to Fort Knox and take it. Do you have any idea how that gold is stored?"

"Yes," Tom replied. "It's in a two-story building constructed of granite, steel, and concrete. Its exterior dimensions measure 105 feet by 121 feet. Its height is forty-two feet above ground level. Within the building is a two-level steel and concrete vault that is divided into compartments. The vault door weighs more than twenty tons. The vault casing is constructed of steel plates, steel I-beams, and steel cylinders laced with hoop bands and encased in concrete."

"What the hell?" Jake said. "How do you know all that?"

"When everything started going south, I was detailed by the U.S. Navy to take a shipment of gold there."

"How much gold did you take?" Bob asked.

"I took seventy-two bars."

"Whoa! Seventy-two bars? How much is that?"

"Two thousand pounds"

"Two thousand pounds, times sixteen ounces, that's what? Thirty-two thousand ounces?"

"No, it's times twelve," Tom said.

"What do you mean, times twelve? There's sixteen ounces in a pound."

"No, Tom's right," Bob said. "You measure precious metals in troy ounces, and that's twelve ounces to the pound."

"All right, so it's twenty-four thousand ounces. That's still a hell of a lot of ounces. How much money is that?"

"At the time I took the shipment, it was worth in the neighborhood of forty million."

Jake chuckled. "Yes, I'd say that forty million

was a pretty damn good neighborhood. But the gold is up at Fort Knox in that building you just described, so I don't see . . ."

Tom smiled, and held up a finger. "Ah, but you see, the gold I'm talking about isn't at Fort Knox."

"What? What do you mean, it isn't? You just said that you took it there."

"No, I said I was *detailed* to take it there. But before I even left San Diego, I saw the writing on the wall. I knew the country was going to hell in a basket, and I thought it might be nice to know how to get my hands on forty million dollars at some future time. So I didn't take it to Knox. I took it to Fort Campbell."

"Fort Campbell? What's at Fort Campbell?" Jake asked.

"Damn!" Bob said. "I know what's there. At least, I know what was there in 1963, when I was stationed there. There was a secret Navy weapons storage facility there . . . just south of the officers' club."

"You mean when there were still officers' clubs," Jake said. "They closed all the O clubs, even before Ohmshidi was elected."

Tom smiled. "I know the building he's talking about though. It's still there, even though it was no longer an officers' club. And you've got it. The gold is at that Navy facility in an empty weapons bunker."

"What makes you think it's still there?" Bob asked.

"Well, of course I don't know for sure, but I would be willing to bet it is. I pulled out a board at the top of the wall and dropped the bullion bars down in between the wall and the lead sheet that lines the bunker, and I replaced the board. It's not likely anyone would just stumble across it, unless they pulled the bunker apart. And there's no reason for anyone to do that. Except for the gold, there's absolutely nothing of value in any of the bunkers."

"I'm sure you didn't do that alone," Jake said. "What about the men who were with you? What makes you think they didn't go back for it?"

"There were only two with me that day, and they're both dead," Tom said. "One of them was killed in a car wreck. The other committed suicide."

"Why haven't you gone back for it?" Bob asked.

"It's not that easy for one person to get rid of a bullion bar. That's 27.5 pounds, which was worth about half a million dollars when we moved it. Then, right after the country collapsed, gold wasn't worth much. If you recall, for a while there, we were strictly on the barter system. To be honest with you, I don't know how much it would be worth for us to have it now."

"If we had gold here, we could issue our own currency, backed by the gold," Bob said. "And that gold would secure our currency in foreign exchange, and that would make our money viable. We wouldn't have to depend on Moqaddas anymore."

"Well then," Tom said, smiling, and rubbing his hands together. "What do you say we go get it?"

CHAPTER NINETEEN

Baltimore

Baltimore had been leveled by the nuclear bomb and was pretty much a wasteland, totally flattened for a distance of a mile in every direction from where the blast was detonated. The damage was severe for up to two miles away, and there was considerable damage for as far as five miles away.

Many of those who survived the initial blast subsequently died of radiation sickness, and those who were not, evacuated. As a result, there were many homes, otherwise totally intact, that were empty in the city.

There was no governmental control of Baltimore, because the SPS and other government officials feared the radiation, even though the amount of radiation had now dropped to below the danger level. That meant that the empty homes were quickly filling with those who were avoiding the government, from those who were here as an act of conscience, to the petty thief, to the murderer.

Technically, Chris assumed that he was in the latter category. He had just killed six people, including Justice Ayambuie and the two clerics who were with him in the car. But he didn't consider that murder, any more than he considered the "with extreme prejudice" jobs he had taken for the FBI or the CIA in the "before time" to have been murder.

Chris and Kathy had come to Baltimore shortly after he killed Ayambuie. As far as he knew, he wasn't a suspect for those murders, but caution seemed the best option. He brought Kathy with him because he didn't want what happened to Margaret to happen to her.

There had been enough canned and packaged food abandoned when Baltimore was evacuated to feed the few thousand who eventually found their way back into the city, so for a while, people subsisted on a "take what you need when you need it" basis. But as the supplies began to dwindle, a commerce system developed where some would leave Baltimore to make purchases out of the city, then bring their purchases back for barter, or sale.

The others in the city sort of naturally fell into occupations they had held before. Carpenters made a good living in refurbishing the houses, mechanics did just as well by putting cars and trucks back into service. Since pork was outlawed throughout the rest of the AIRE, some enterprising men and women were raising pigs . . . and finding a surprisingly large market for pork, which was always marketed as "goat" to customers outside of Baltimore.

There were also the black marketers who bought gasoline within the official economy, then brought it into Baltimore to be used by those who were outside the mainstream of things.

For the first few days after he arrived in Baltimore, Chris was unsure as to just what he would do. He wasn't a carpenter, or a mechanic. He didn't have a feel for merchandising, and he certainly wasn't a farmer. He was a man of action. But whereas the FBI and the CIA had paid him for his contract work, that kind of work was no longer available to him now.

Or was it?

There was no longer an agency around that would pay him for his rather unique work, but there was certainly no reason why he couldn't go into business for himself.

Not as a contract killer, but as a thief. Because of the new currency, shipments of the Moqaddas bills were being sent everywhere, and those money transfers, as well as the *Moqaddas Sirata*–compliant banks which controlled all the transactions, were ripe for the picking.

Willie Sutton once answered the question, "Why do you rob banks," by saying, "Because that's where the money is."

Chris chuckled as he thought about that. He had just hit upon how he was going to make a living.

He was going to rob banks.

With Jake Lantz

They left Gulf Shores in two vehicles, a Toyota minivan and a Ford two-ton pickup truck. James had put a false bottom in the bed of the truck, leaving just enough space between the false bottom and the real bottom to have a place to conceal the gold bars. For now, M-4 rifles were concealed in the false bottom. The truck was loaded with cut logs.

Mike Moran was driving the pickup, and Tom was with him. Deon was driving the minivan, and Jake was with him. There were saws and axes in the back of the minivan. Because I-65 was being patrolled, they went up the back roads: 59, then 21, finally joining I-65 at Montgomery. That was where they were stopped for the first time; but at least now, there was nothing to indicate they had come from the "land of the rebellion."

They were stopped by highway patrolmen, which was good because the highway patrolmen weren't as dogmatic as the SPS.

"Papers," one of the patrolmen asked.

Jake took some encouragement from the fact that the patrolman had not greeted him with the "Obey Ohmshidi" salute.

"I've got the papers for the two of us in this car, and the two men in the pickup behind me. They're workin' for me."

The patrolman took the papers from Jake's hand.

"Kind of hot to be standin' out here all day lookin' at people's papers, isn't it?" Jake asked.

"Yeah," the patrolman said.

Using Tom's papers and ID, Bob had duplicated them on the computer so that all four had the "proper credentials."

"St. Louis? All four of you are from St. Louis?"

"Yeah."

"What are you doing down here?"

"We came down here to cut wood for the paper mill up in Wickliffe, KY."

"This seems like a long way to come to get wood."

"The wood is cheaper down here."

The patrolman walked back to the truck and looked inside. It was filled with cut wood.

"All right, you can go," he said.

They were stopped six more times before they reached Fort Campbell, and their story and papers held up every time.

* * *

Because they weren't driving very fast, and because they were stopped so many times, they spent one night on the road, camping alongside their vehicles. They actually did go to Wickliffe, where they sold their logs.

"I'd like a paper that says you bought the wood from us," Jake said. "I'll need to show it to the police when we go back down to Alabama."

"Alabama? Why did you bring the wood all the way up here to us? You've got dozens of paper mills in Alabama. Birmingham, Tuscaloosa, Huntsville—they would have all been closer."

"I've got family in Paducah, thought this would pay for the trip up."

"All right," the manager of the paper mill said. "Say, didn't this used to be the New Page Corporation?"

"Yeah. But the government owns it now. You have a problem with that?"

"No, why should I? It's no sweat off my balls," Jake said. "Whether the government pays me, or New Page, it's all the same."

"I thought you might see it that way," the manager said. He counted out one thousand Moqaddas, then gave Jake a paper validating the sale.

"Thanks," Jake said. "This will pay for our trip."

* * *

They reached Fort Campbell, or what had been Fort Campbell, later that day, driving down Highway 41 from Hopkinsville, past all the businesses that had, at one time, catered to the soldiers of the 101st Airmobile Division. The businesses, like the fort, were now closed. All the gates into the fort were blocked off, but they were able to get around the barriers at gate 5, then drove onto the main section of the base.

Coming onto an army base again was a nostalgic thing for Jake, who had spent his entire adult life in the army. But there was a sadness in seeing abandoned buildings, weeds growing in areas that were once kept neatly trimmed, and the rusting hulks of military trucks and hummers.

A long, brick wall which once proudly proclaimed Fort Campbell as the home of the 101st Screaming Eagles now had only a few letters remaining.

F t CMP L H E F E O1S   E ING   GLES

The empty flagpole was rusting and the lanyard was slapping against it.

"Stop the car," Jake said, and Deon complied. Jake got out of the car and faced the flagpole. Deon, Tom, and Mike got out with him.

"Present arms!" Jake said, and all three men, former U.S. Military, snapped a salute. They held it for a long moment, then Jake said, "Order, arms!" And, with military precision, all four men brought the salute down.

"At ease," Jake said.

"Were you ever stationed here, Major?" Deon asked. It had been a while since he had called Jake "major," but it seemed appropriate for the moment.

"I was never stationed here, but I flew in and out of here a few times. What about you?"

"No, sir, I never was," Deon replied.

"Me neither," Mike said. "I was at Fort Bragg, but never here."

"Bob was here," Jake said.

Deon chuckled. "Yeah, in 1963. You know how long ago that was? That's over half a century ago."

"Don't sell that old man short," Jake said. "You haven't forgotten that nifty bit of flying he did back when we first got to Fort Morgan, when there was a group of outlaws who blocked the road, have you? They were going to kill us and take what we had, remember?"

"Yeah, I remember. I was riding door gun for that old man."

"What are you talking about?" Tom asked.

Jake told the story, telling it so vividly that Tom and Mike, who had not been there, could almost witness it.

* * *

"*Is that a helicopter I hear?*" *John asked.*

"*It is, yes,*" *Jake said.* "*I hear it, but I don't see it.*"

"*It's close,*" *John said.* "*Look, they hear it too.*" *John pointed to the men who were standing by the barricade. They could be seen searching the sky and talking to each other, obviously looking for the helicopter.*

Suddenly a Huey popped up just over the roof of the houses along the beach. "*Damn! That's our Huey!*" *John said.* "*Who the hell is flying it?*"

Jake laughed. "*It has to be Bob,*" *he said.*

The helicopter did a quick pass by the barricade, and Jake saw an arrow streaming down.

"*What the hell? He's shooting arrows at them?*"

There was a loud explosion where the arrow hit, the blast big enough to throw several of the refrigerators around.

Jake laughed out loud. "*C-4!*" *he said.* "*They've put C-4 on the arrows!*"

The helicopter made another pass. This time Jake and John could see tracer bullets coming from the cargo door. There was also a second arrow fired, and another explosion.

Some of the men at the refrigerator barricade started shooting back at the helicopter, but the M-240 in the cargo door of the Huey was too much for them, and those who weren't killed began running. The Huey chased down the runners, and fired again, until the area was completely cleared of any would-be bandits.

"*That old man can handle it, can't he?*" *John said.*

"*Patriots one, this is Goodnature, do you copy?*"

"Goodnature?" Jake replied.

"It was my call sign in Vietnam. I figured I may as well use it again," Bob said.[1]

"It had probably been forty years, at least, since he'd flown, but he handled that Huey like he had just stepped out of it the day before," Jake said, finishing the story.

"I'm not surprised at all," Tom said. "I've learned to take the measure of a man pretty quickly, and Bob Varney rates high in my book."

"This place is spooky," Deon said.

A freshening breeze blew up, and bits of trash, itself an incongruous sight on a military base, whipped by.

"Listen," Jake said. "Do you hear that? Sounds like a distant bugle."

The others listened, and sure enough, they could hear a high-pitched hum. It was Mike who pointed out that it was the wind passing through a gutter.

"All right, Tom, take us to the gold," Jake said, and the four men got back into the two vehicles, but this time Tom was driving the minivan, and Deon was following behind, in the truck.

They drove by the golf course, by the building that was, at one time, the Fort Campbell Officers'

---

1. From *Phoenix Rising*.

Open Mess, then down a narrow blacktop road until they reached a fenced-in area.

UNAUTHORIZED PERSONS
NOT ALLOWED
BEYOND THIS POINT

The sign was still legible, though kudzu vine had nearly taken it over, as it had taken over the high chain-link fence itself. The gate was open and off the top hinge, so that it was hanging at an angle. When they drove through they saw several bunkers, the mounds overgrown with weeds.

Jake had been concerned as to how hard it would be to get into the bunker when they got there, but he saw that the doors to all the bunkers were missing.

"That's good," Jake said. "We won't have any trouble getting in."

"I'm sure all the bunkers have been gone through, and cleaned out of anything they might have held," Tom said. "I just hope . . ."

Tom didn't have to finish his comment, because Jake knew exactly what he was about to say.

"Yeah, I know what you mean. I hope so as well."

"There it is," Tom said, pointing.

"You're sure that's the one? They all look alike to me."

Tom chuckled. "I'm not likely to forget where I hid forty million dollars, now, am I?"

They stopped in front, then got out of the car. Deon and Mike got out of the truck.

"Deon, you and Mike get your weapons and stand by. I haven't seen anyone, but it's better to be safe than sorry."

"Roger that," Deon said, and walking to the back of the truck, he opened the panel that let him reach between the floors, and pulled out a couple of M-4 rifles that had been secreted there.

"All right," Tom said. "Let's see if anyone has been here."

To provide light, Tom took a Coleman lantern inside, lit it, and set it on the side of the bunker opposite the wall where he had hid the gold. He and Jake then took axes into the bunker. Tom blew on his hands, rubbed them together, and swung the first blow.

Outside Deon and Mike could hear the steady thump of the axes from within the bunker.

"Damn, I hope this isn't all for nothing," Deon said.

"Yeah, you and me . . . Hold it," he said. He stuck his head in through the open door of the bunker. "Jake, someone's comin'!"

Tom and Jake started back outside, but Jake stopped him. "Wait," he said. "They're going to want to know what we're doing in here. Grab up some of that sheet lead we've pulled down, and take it outside.

Jake and Tom, each carrying a piece of sheet lead, stepped outside.

"Deon, Mike, get behind the bunker and keep them covered. I'll try and talk us out of it. If things start to go south, open up."

"Right," Deon said, and he and Mike moved quickly to get behind the bunker, managing to get out of sight before the car arrived. When the car stopped, four men got out. Jake was relieved to see that they weren't SPS, but were local police.

"What are you two doing here?" one of them asked.

"Obey Ohmshidi!" Jake said, and he and Tom gave the salute.

"Obey Ohmshidi," the policeman said. "I'm going to ask you again. What are you doing here?"

"We're stripping lead off the walls of the bunkers. We can get three Moqaddas per pound back in Nashville. And it doesn't take that much lead to make money. I figure, if we strip down all these bunkers, we'll likely come up with a thousand pounds. That's three thousand Moqaddas!"

"What makes you think you can just come in here and start stealing this lead?"

"Imam Malik gave us permission," Jake said.

The policeman had a look of confusion on his face. "Who is Imam Malik?"

"What? You don't know who the blessed Imam Malik is? He has been appointed by the Great

Leader as the caliph of all abandoned military bases. I can't believe you don't know who he is." Jake pulled out his cell phone, punched in a few numbers, then held it to his ear. He waited for a moment, then began talking.

"Obey Ohmshidi, oh noble Caliph. The peace of Allah be upon you. This is your humble servant, Jake Lantz. We are removing the lead as you requested, Imam, but some men have stopped us. I don't know, I'll ask."

"What is your authority for stopping us," Jake asked. Then, before the policeman could answer, he put the phone back to his ear. "What's that? You want to speak to their leader? I'll ask."

"Who is your leader? The Imam wants to talk to him."

"I . . . uh . . . that's all right," the policeman said, holding up his hand. "You go right ahead."

"Imam, they have said that we can continue to strip the lead. Oh, wait."

"The imam wants to know if he has to personally give you the order."

"No, no, that isn't necessary," the policeman said. "Tell the Imam, I wish Allah's blessings upon him, I don't wish to disturb someone as important as he is. We'll be going now."

"Obey Ohmshidi," Jake repeated, saluting again. This time all four police responded with the salute. Then, they got back into the car and drove away.

"Ha!" Tom said as they watched the dust swirl

up from behind the car as it headed, quickly, for the gate to the compound. "Who did you actually call?"

"Nobody," Jake replied with a chuckle. "I just poked in a few numbers. I didn't hit 'send.'"

"Remind me never to play poker with you. That's as cool a bluff as I've ever seen run."

Deon and Mike were laughing as well, when they came back around front.

"Okay, let's get the gold," he said.

It took another fifteen minutes of chopping before Tom let out a triumphant shout.

"There it is!" he said. "There's the first gold bar!"

Less than one hour after they found the first gold bar, they had every bar out, and safely tucked away between the floors of the truck. It was late afternoon when they drove back out through gate 5, then turned south on 41 for the long drive back home. This time, though, their cargo wasn't wood, it was gold. Tom and Deon were in the truck, Jake and Mike were following behind.

"I've been doing some figuring," Mike said. "As near as I can figure, we have about fifty five million Euros here."

"Fifty five million," Jake said. He nodded. "I think we'll be able to get our economy going with that."

Chapter Twenty

Fort Morgan

"For the time being, I don't think we should let anyone beyond out little group here know about the gold," Bob said when Jake and the others returned with the truck.

"Where will we keep it?" Deon asked.

"We'll make a vault here, in the fort, and keep it there," Bob said. "I'm sure James can build us a place for it."

"What we have to do now, is establish an exchange system, and issue our own currency," Jake said. "But I admit, I'm not sure how to go about that."

"I don't see it as any problem. We did it in the army with MPCs," Bob said. "We could use that as our guide."

"MPCs?" Jake asked.

"Military payment certificates. When we got paid in Vietnam, we weren't paid in dollars, we were paid in scrip—certificates that were good only on the military bases—but one dollar in MPC was equal to one dollar U.S. And, we could exchange them for Piasters. The MPCs were accepted by the soldiers, because they were backed by dollars. We can do the same thing here, but back our currency with gold."

"Yes," Jake said. "And I think we should call them dollars."

"How about, Freedom Dollars?" Bob suggested.

"Yeah, Freedom Dollars. I like that," Jake said.

Youth Confinement and Enlightenment Center 251

Jane Poindexter was sound asleep when she was awakened by her teacher, Miss Mugambwe.

"Come girl," Miss Mugambwe said. "Get dressed."

"Why?"

"Don't ask questions, just do as I say."

"Why aren't you waking the others?"

Miss Mugambwe slapped Jane hard.

"Ow! That hurt!"

"Then do as I say, and don't give me any back-talk."

Jane reached for her burqa.

"You won't be needing that," Miss Mugambwe said.

"What should I wear? All my clothes have been taken from me."

"You'll wear this." The woman handed Jane a

very sheer nightgown, so sheer that you could see through it.

"I don't understand."

"You don't need to understand. All you need to do, is do what I tell you to do."

Jane took off her sleeping gown, then reached for her bra and panties.

"You won't be needing that."

"Miss Mugambwe, I don't like this. I don't know what is going on, but I can't leave this barracks wearing only this, and nothing under it. Why, you can see right through it."

"This is your wedding night."

"What? Wedding night? I'm only fifteen years old! I don't want to get married!"

By now several of the other girls had been awakened, and although they overheard the conversation, they were too frightened to do anything, so they lay in their beds, quietly, praying that nobody came for them.

Except for one girl.

Barbara Carter was seventeen years old, the oldest girl in the barracks. She had been thrust into a position of leadership by virtue of her age, and had willingly taken on the responsibility. She lay quietly until Miss Mugambwe took Jane out. Then she got out of bed, put on her burqa, and slipped out of the barracks.

Hiding in the shadows, she watched the cabin into which Miss Mugambwe took Jane, then, when the coast was clear, she moved quickly to the boys' barracks.

Eddie was asleep when he felt someone pushing on his shoulder. "What?" he asked.

"Shhh."

In the dark over his bed, Eddie saw a burqa-clad figure, and he sat up quickly.

"Jane? What are you doing here?" he whispered harshly.

"I'm not Jane," Barbara said quietly. "But Jane is in trouble."

"What sort of trouble?"

"Shh. Come with me. Be quiet."

The air was rent with snoring and heavy breathing, and it didn't appear that anyone was awakened.

Eddie got up and quickly pulled on a pair of trousers, then put on his shoes. That done, he and Barbara left the barracks, walking as quietly as they could.

"What is it?" Eddie asked, once they were outside. "What's going on?"

"Jane has been selected to be a bride tonight."

"To be a bride? What are you talking about?"

"You haven't received any classes on the *Moqaddas Sirata* rites of marriage?"

"No, I don't know what you are talking about."

"What I'm talking about, is Jane is going to be

raped tonight, unless we can do something to stop it."

"What the hell! I'll kill any son of a bitch that tries."

"You may have to," Barbara said. "But whether you kill him or not, once you interfere, you won't be able to stay here. They'll punish you and Jane."

"Thanks for telling me. Who are you? No, wait," Eddie said. "Don't tell me. If I don't know who you are, I'll never be able to tell them who helped me, no matter what kind of torture they put me through."

"She's in that cabin," Barbara said.

"Thanks. Now, go, get out of here while you can," Eddie said.

"You are a good person, Eddie. God be with you," Barbara said as she turned and slipped back into the dark night, her black burqa making her invisible within a few steps.

Eddie moved up to the side of the cabin, then looked in through the window. He saw his girl-friend, her young, nude body, being tied hand and feet to a bed. The person tying her was obvi-ously a woman, as she was dressed head to toe in a burqa. A beardless man, dressed in the forest-green uniform of the SPS, was standing by the bed watching, his face contorted by lust.

"That's good enough. Leave her now. You can come back for her in about an hour."

The woman bowed, then started toward the door.

Eddie waited outside the cabin, behind a tree, and as the woman walked by, he stepped out in front of her and brought her down with a powerful roundhouse right to her head.

With the woman knocked out, Eddie quickly stripped her of her burqa, then he put it on, and went back to the cabin. Opening the door he stepped inside, just in time to see the man dropping his trousers.

"What are you doing here?" the man asked angrily as he saw, what he assumed to be Miss Mugambwe coming back into the cabin. "I told you to leave us now."

Eddie pointed toward the corner as if the woman had forgotten something, and when the man looked around to see what it was, Eddie picked up a chair and brought it crashing down over his head. The man went down, but Eddie didn't stop. He hit him several more times until he was sure he had killed him.

Jane had been looking on in frightened and confused silence.

Eddie pulled off the burqa.

"Eddie!" she said.

"Shh. We're getting out of here," Eddie said. "As soon as I get you untied, put this on."

Eddie worked quickly to undo the ropes at her hands and feet. Then, when she was free, she slipped into the burqa. As she was doing that, Eddie went through the pockets of the man he had just killed. His ID card identified him as Troy Dawson, Captain of the Mobile Branch of the SPS. He also found car keys, and that gave him an idea.

Quickly, Eddie stripped the man. Then, taking off his own trousers, he put on the SPS uniform. By the time he was finished dressing, Jane was sitting on the foot of the bed, now wearing the burqa, but not the scarf and veil.

"Eddie, what are we going to do?" Jane asked.

"He's got a car out there somewhere," Eddie said. "As soon as we find it, we're going to get out of here."

"Are we going home? Oh, I so much want to see mama again."

"I'm sorry, Jane, we can't go home. That'll be the first place they look for us."

Dawson had also been wearing a pistol, and Eddie strapped that on as well.

"Let's go," he said. "Be quiet. When we leave here, don't say a word."

Once outside, Eddie reached out for Jane's hand as they hurried through the night. At least twice during their move through the darkness, Eddie and Jane had to stop and get behind a tree or a shrub, to avoid detection by roving guards. Then, when they reached the parking lot, Eddie raised the remote key up and clicked it. He saw the lights flash on one of the cars.

"There is it," he said quietly.

Taking Jane by the hand, he guided her through the parking lot to the car, a black Buick. On the door were the letters SPS, above the stylized "O" that was now the national symbol. The doors had been unlocked by the remote, and he and Jane slipped into the car. Eddie started the car and drove toward the gate. To his pleasant surprise, the car had a remote device that opened the gate automatically as they approached.

"Where are we going?" Jane asked.

"We can't go to Mobile, but I have a place in mind that's not far."

"Where? No matter where we go, we'll be caught and brought back here."

"No we won't, not with what I have in mind. I overheard some of the SPS talking about a group of people down at Gulf Shores who have sort of broken away from the others. That's where we're going to go."

"If they've broken away from the others, you won't be welcome wearing that," Jane said.

Eddie chuckled. "If I take this off, I'll be in my underwear."

"Just take off the jacket," Jane suggested.

"Yeah, that's a good idea."

Stopping the car alongside the road, Eddie

pulled off the shirt. A couple of minutes later, when he drove onto the bridge across Weeks Bay, he tossed the uniform jacket into the water.

"I wish I had something else to wear," Jane said.

"We'll find something for you to wear when we get there," Eddie promised. "At least you won't have to wear that damn bee keeper's screen over your face."

Jane laughed. "Bee keeper's screen."

They made it from the confinement camp to the Intracoastal Canal on Highway 59 in just over half an hour. The permanent bridge had been destroyed, but had been replaced by a pontoon bridge. It was still dark as they approached, and Eddie stopped the car about one hundred yards short of the bridge.

"What are we stopping for?" Jane asked.

"I don't expect we'll get a very warm welcome in this car," he said. "We'd better walk the rest of the way."

"All right."

Leaving the car, Eddie and Jane walked toward the canal, but they were stopped about twenty-five yards short of the bridge by two armed men. One of them raised a bullhorn.

"Both of you, put your hands up."

"Eddie, I'm scared."

"This can't be any worse than what we've already

been through, can it? Put your hands up, like the man said."

"Yeah, I guess you're right."

"Advance slowly," the guard with the bullhorn ordered.

As Eddie and Jane got close enough, it was easy to see that they were both very young.

"Damn, they're just a couple of kids," one of the guards said.

"He's wearing a pistol," the other said.

"I'll take the pistol out," Eddie called to them.

"No, don't touch it. Just advance slowly."

Eddie and Jane walked on up to the gate.

"Who are you?" the other guard asked.

"My name is Eddie Manning. This is my friend, Jane Poindexter."

"What are you two doing here?"

"We escaped from YCEC 251," Eddie said.

"You escaped from what?"

"Youth Confinement and Enlightenment Center, number 251," Eddie explained.

"What is that? I've never heard of it."

"You haven't heard of the youth confinement centers?"

"No."

"Everyone between the ages of six and seventeen have been put in confinement camps. There's one at Camp Beckwith. That's where Jane and I were being held before we escaped."

"Are you serious? Everyone between six and seventeen has been rounded up?"

"Yes."

"And you say you escaped?"

"Yes. That's where I borrowed these pants. Actually, I borrowed the whole uniform, but I threw away the shirt. Then I borrowed this car," Eddie said, pointing to the vehicle they had come in.

The two guards laughed.

"You stole an SPS car?" one of them said. "Good for you, kid. I'll say this, you've got balls." Then realizing that he said that in front of a young girl he put his hand to his mouth. "I'm sorry, Miss, excuse the language."

"If that means Eddie has courage, then you are right," Jane said.

"That's exactly what it means. All right, come on across the bridge, we'll figure out what to do with you."

"What about the car?" the other guard said.

"What about it?"

"It's got SPS markings. You never can tell when it might come in handy."

"Yeah, you're right. Okay, go get it, bring it in."

"What do you want us to do?" Eddie asked.

"To tell the truth, kid, I don't have the slightest idea. But I guess the best thing would be to take you to the president, and let him figure it out."

CHAPTER TWENTY-ONE

"I had no idea that they were doing anything like that," Bob Varney said when Eddie and Jane were taken to meet the island's president. "How long has it been going on?"

"We've been there for two months," Eddie said. "The guards and teachers told us that this is going on all over the country."

"Teachers? You mean it's a school?"

"Yeah," Eddie said. "But they don't teach anything real there, like math or English or history or anything. It's just all stuff about Muslims, and how glorious it is to die for Islam."

"And you say they came to take you out of your parents' home?" Jake Lantz asked. Bob had invited Jake to come listen to the story of the two young people.

"They didn't exactly come take us from our homes. Everyone was told that they had to bring their children, between six and seventeen, for registration. I know that our parents thought they would be getting ID cards for us, so they could buy more things," Eddie said. "But it was a setup. As soon as all the parents of Mobile brought their kids to Ladd Stadium where we were supposed to be registered, the SPS put us all on buses and took us away."

"Away to where?"

"Camp Beckwith. Or at least, what used to be called Camp Beckwith."

"Oh, well, that's not so bad," Bob Varney said. "I'm Episcopalian, the camp is sponsored by the Gulf Coast Diocese. It's really quite a beautiful place."

"Not so pretty when it's surrounded by strands of razor wire and patrolled by guards," Eddie said. "It's like a concentration camp."

"But they don't let us call it that," Jane said, speaking up then. No longer in the burqa, Jane was now, quite happily, wearing a dress given her by one of the citizens of the island. "We're supposed to call it an educational camp."

"Do they feed you in the camp? Do they torture you?"

"They feed us, and no, they don't torture us," Eddie said. "But they do everything they can to make us conform. And it's worse for the girls than it is for the boys. At least the boys don't have to worry about getting raped."

"Are you saying the guards are raping the young girls?"

"Jane, you want to tell them what happened to you?"

"Good Heavens," Bob said. "Were you raped?"

"I would have been, if Eddie hadn't saved me," Jane said.

"Where are your parents?"

"My mom and dad are in Mobile," Eddie said. "Jane's mom is there as well. Her dad is dead. I was afraid to go there because I figured that would be the first place they looked. And, right now, I'm probably wanted for murder. I'm pretty sure I killed the son of a bitch who was about to rape Jane."

"Son, if the son of a bitch needed killing, it's not murder," Bob said. He smiled. "You and your friend are welcome additions to our group here."

Bel Air, Maryland

When Chris and Kathy first arrived in town, they drove up and down every street, checking them all out to make certain which routes were least likely to be blocked by the police, and which ones did not wind up as dead ends.

The bank they chose was on Main Street, occupying the same building that had once been the People's Bank, but now billed itself as "Bank of the Faithful." Kathy, who was wearing a *dishdasha* and *taqiyah*, as well as a false beard, was driving.

She had to be dressed that way, because it was illegal for a woman to drive, and they didn't want to get stopped. She parked in the bank parking lot, in a spot nearest the bank.

Right across the street from the bank was a huge billboard with the now-ubiquitous "Obey Ohmshidi" portrait.

"Keep the engine running," Chris said. Like Kathy, Chris was wearing the *dishdasha* and *taqiyah*.

When Chris went into the bank there was one customer standing at the teller's window. Walking around the bank he checked all the offices and found that only one was occupied.

Chris stepped into the office, uninvited. "Are you the bank president?"

"I am, but I don't see anyone without an appointment," he said.

"Oh, I think you'll see us."

"Who is 'us'?"

Chris raised his revolver and pointed it at the bank president. "Me, Mr. Smith, and Mr. Wesson."

"What? Are you robbing the bank?"

"Robbing is such a harsh word. I prefer to think of it as a redistribution of wealth. After all, wasn't that what Ohmshidi promised us, when we were foolish enough to vote the son of a bitch into office?"

"You're out of your mind, you'll never get away with it."

"Maybe not," Chris replied with a smile. "But I do think it will be fun to try. Come out into the bank with me. I think having you along will facilitate things."

"If you think I'm going to help you rob this bank, you're crazy," the bank president said. "I'm not moving from this desk."

"No problem, you can stay there until they come for your body. Because as I think about it, I don't really need you at all."

Chris cocked his pistol and aimed it at the bank president's head.

"No! No, wait!" the bank president said, sticking both hands out in front of him, as if holding Chris away. "I'll come with you."

Chris smiled. "Now, I do believe that's why you are the bank president. You do know how to make quick decisions when under pressure."

The customer who had been at the teller's window was just leaving as Chris and the bank president came back into the lobby.

"Teller," Chris said, throwing a cloth bag across the counter. "Would you be so kind as to fill that bag with money, then bring it to me?"

"What?"

"Please do as he says," the bank president said. "He is holding a gun on me."

"But there are no guns. They've all been confiscated," the teller insisted.

Chris smiled, and held the gun up for the

teller to see. "You mean I was supposed to turn this gun in? Hmm, I didn't. Do you think that means I'm in trouble?"

"I . . . I . . . Mr. Jones . . ."

"It is Rashad," the bank president corrected.

"Yes, Mr. Rashad, what should I do?"

"Do as I told you, man! Fill this gentleman's bag with money."

"Ah, you called me a gentleman. How nice of you," Chris said. He waved the gun toward the teller who was still just standing there. "Do hurry, won't you?"

"Yes, sir," the teller replied, as, with shaking hands, he began emptying the cash drawer.

"How much is there?" Chris asked.

"There's about fifteen thousand dolla . . . uh, I mean Moqaddas here," the teller said.

"Bless your heart, son, you are having a hard time getting into this American Islamic Republic thing too, aren't you? Fifteen thousand, huh? Well, I don't want to be greedy. That's plenty enough money for the moment. You two take care now, you hear?"

Clutching the bag of money, Chris went outside then hurried over to the car.

"Let's go," he said.

They drove the car, a yellow Ford, less than four blocks from the bank, then turned down an alley. They stopped behind a drugstore and parked the car between a Dumpster and the back wall. From there they walked out to the parking lot and got into a dark green Toyota, Chris getting behind the wheel this time. When they pulled back out onto Main Street, they encountered two police cars speeding to the bank, with lights flashing and sirens honking.

They drove out of Bel Air without being stopped.

Glenview, Illinois

Mustafa al Shammari had gathered ten of his closest and most trusted friends to a meeting at his house.

"I've asked you here for a very special reason, and, having spoken to all of you one on one, I think you already have an idea of what this meeting is about. Before I go on, I want to say that what I am about to propose is very dangerous, and if even one among us is not ready to commit with heart and soul to what I am about to propose, it could mean death to all of us."

Mustafa looked into the faces of everyone who had come to the meeting.

"If there be anyone among you who wishes to leave, do so now, for after this moment, we are all bound by blood."

Although the others looked at each other, not one person left.

"Good. Gentleman, I am proposing that we

form a group, which we will call American Scimitars."

"That sounds pretty militant, Mustafa," one of the others, Abdul, said.

"I intend for it to be militant. I don't intend to stand by and see the religion that I grew up with, the religion that I love and serve, be hijacked by Ohmshidi and the *Moqaddas Sirata*. They are not the true Muslim religion. They are apostates who pervert Islam."

"If you are making them our enemy, we are taking on quite a task. The last estimate I read was that more than seventy percent of America has converted," Abdul said.

"You and I both know those aren't legitimate conversions," Mustafa said. "They have converted only to survive, for without a *Moqaddas Sirata* ID card, you can't even buy food."

"Then who will our enemy be? Will they be the innocent who have been forced to convert in order to survive?"

"No," Mustafa replied. "There are enough who are profiting by this evil that we will have a target-rich environment."

"I'm ready," Raboud said. "When do we go?"

"Tonight. There is a meeting in Waukegan. We'll pay them a visit."

* * *

At the Waukegan Mosque of Holy Path, Imam Abdullah was speaking to his followers.

"There are still Christian churches and Jewish synagogues in Glenview, churches that, by their very existence, are an affront to our religion. I, here and now, issue a *fatwah* that all churches and synagogues be destroyed. And it is my suggestion that we strike some of the churches now, during Wednesday night prayer service, when the buildings are full of people, because only by inflicting the maximum damage to the apostates, will we be able to get our point across."

"But, Imam, before the Holy Path of Ohmshidi, many of us were Christians and we worshiped in those same churches. We have friends there."

"How can they be friends, if they have not converted?" Abdullah asked.

"The imam is right," one of the others said. "It is our duty to convert all to the holy path, and to kill those who do not convert."

Outside the mosque Mustafa and the others of the newly formed group, American Scimitars, waited quietly, with weapons in hand.

"Are we going to challenge them, Mustafa?" Raboud asked.

"No. Do you challenge a snake before you kill it? Or do you just kill it?"

"I understand."

"I know I am asking much of you. But to those upon whom it falls to defend the faith, much must be asked."

"I will serve the Prophet," Raboud said.

Inside the mosque, Abdullah now had his followers whipped into a killing frenzy. "All right," he said. "We start now. There are cans of gasoline and torches in the back of my pickup truck. We'll cover all the exits, set fire to the church, and shoot everyone who tries to escape the flames."

There were ten at the gathering, counting Imam Abdullah. When they all came out front of the mosque, they were confronted by Mustafa and four others, all of them armed. Abdullah's men had no time to respond, for as soon as they all exited the mosque, Mustafa and his men opened fire.

The shooting was loud and sustained as the five men under Mustafa continued shooting. Abdullah's men jerked and jumped about as the bullets slammed into them.

Those who lived in houses close to the mosque heard the shooting, loud and insistent, but none of them dared to look outside to see what was going on. Finally the last shot was fired, and the neighborhood grew quiet, save for the barking of a few dogs, and the crying of one or more very young children.

* * *

In the Waukegan Baptist Church the worshipers who were attending Wednesday night prayer service were irritated and concerned by the gunfire that interrupted the preacher's sermon. They tried to close their minds to it, telling themselves it had no bearing on their lives.

What they didn't realize is that the sound of shooting that they found irritating had, in all likelihood, just saved their lives.

From the *Moqaddas Sirata Enlightened Press:*

Bank Robberies

Two infidel outlaws have carved out a swath of bank robberies from Muslimabad to Philadelphia. One is an excellent shot and has demonstrated that talent on numerous occasions. The other drives the getaway car. So far every bank robbery has been earmarked by the superior gunmanship of the one and the skillful driving of the other.

Their identities are not known, though the SPS has promised to learn who they are, then to track them down and kill them on sight.

* * *

Imam Abdullah and Faithful Murdered

The peaceful town of Glenview, Illinois, a Chicago suburb, erupted with gunfire recently when the Imam and nine of his faithful followers were murdered. They had just completed a meeting on how to conduct an outreach program to minister to those who have not yet converted to *Moqaddas Sirata*. Their peaceful entreaties were met with callous brutality from a group of heretics who have yet to abandon their misguided Christian faith.

This newspaper advocates the conversion, by force if necessary, of all who have not yet seen the light.

CHAPTER TWENTY-TWO

Within two months after the first offshore rig was taken, every remaining rig off Alabama's coastline had been captured by Jake Lantz and his strike team. As soon as a rig was freed, a work detail was put on board and shortly thereafter a steady supply of natural gas had the electricity flowing and water running all over the island. In addition, automobiles, trucks, and boats on the island were converted to run on CNG, compressed natural gas, so that transportation from one end of the island to the other was no longer a problem.

Businesses all over the island were opening, and proudly posted signs reading:

Freedom Dollars Accepted Here

With fuel for their vehicles, Jake decided it was time to start expanding their base of operations beyond Pleasure Island. Jake, Tom, Deon, and Mike started north in a Dodge Ram extended cab on Highway 59 until they reached Interstate 10. There was very little traffic on I-10, though there were still abandoned cars and trucks along the route.

This wasn't just a random trip. Before leaving the island they had coordinated a meeting, by radio, with someone who identified himself as Charley Moore. By code, they chose a rendezvous point in Mobile.

"Jake, what if this is a setup?" Tom asked as they drove through the tunnel.

"Why do you ask? Do you have a gut feeling about it?"

"Not particularly, but I'd hate like hell for us to just drive right into a trap."

"What's your idea?"

"Drop me off about two blocks before we get there. I'll walk the rest of the way. If everything is all right, all I've done is miss a little conversation. If it is some sort of setup, I might be able to do something about it."

"All right. Sounds like a pretty good idea."

Jake stopped the truck and Tom got out, then started walking toward the rendezvous point. He saw an SPS car drive by, but the occupants of the car took no notice of him.

When he reached the meeting point, he saw Jake, Deon, and Mike in conversation with another man.

* * *

"Wait," Charley Moore said as he saw Tom approaching.

Jake looked around, then seeing that it was Tom, smiled. "It's okay," he said. "That's Tom Jack, he's one of us."

Moore nodded, and waited until Tom joined them. Introductions were made, then Moore continued. "We want to join you," Moore said.

"Who is we? And what do you mean, join us?"

"We are the people of Mobile. We would like for you to take Mobile and all of Mobile County into United Free America."

"How many SPS are here?"

"There are about forty of them," Moore said. "And of course, there are the local police, very damn few of whom were policemen in the before time. I'd say there are really no more than two hundred people who sort of lord it over the rest of us."

"What about the average citizen of Mobile?"

"Most of 'em have gone over, but it's just for the ID card so they can get fuel, and have electricity and water. I doubt there's one in a thousand that's really converted."

"Do any of them have weapons?"

"Very damn few," Moore said. "You folks down there on the island didn't have to go through it, but one of the very first things the new government did was gather up every gun they could find. There may have been a hundred or so who managed to hide their guns, but, for the most part, the population is completely unarmed."

"Yes, well, until we know where everyone stands, we are probably better off that way," Jake said.

"I can tell you where they stand. Once we get control back from the SPS and their constabulary, ninety-nine percent of the population will be with us."

"We will have to establish a military force immediately. I'm sure that AIRE will try and retake Mobile, but if we mount a strong enough defense to fight them off, they may leave us alone for a while."

"You know what? I think we could probably take everything south of I-10 from Pensacola to the Louisiana line. And maybe even push on across Louisiana to Texas," Moore said.

"I think you are right. But let's take Mobile first. Then we'll spread out."

"Roger."

The building at 850 Virginia Street had, at one time, housed the offices of the 1st Precinct of the Mobile police department. Today, it, and the other four precincts, had been taken over by the SPS, and all the original components of the station had been taken down. There was no Alabama state flag, nor was there a Stars and Stripes. Photographs of past chiefs and precinct captains had been removed, along with photographs of honored officers from the past. The flag that flew in front of the building was Ohmshidi's personal banner. The sign that once read "Mobile Police Department" had been replaced by the words "State Protective Service."

Jake and Willie Stark, wearing work coveralls and carrying toolboxes, pulled up in front of the station and went in.

"Here, what are you doing here?" one of the SPS men demanded.

Willie showed the man a work request. "Your telephones are out."

"What do you mean, our phones are out?"

"How long has it been since you received a call?"

"I don't know. But I can assure you . . ." the SPS man picked up the receiver. "Damn, no dial tone."

"Like I said, your phones are out."

"Well fix them."

"That's why we're here," Willie said. "Where's your main junction box?"

"How the hell do I know? You're the telephone repairman."

"Never mind, I'll find it."

Willie and Jake found the junction box, then Willie opened it, and started working with the wires. He worked for about half an hour, then one of the phones rang.

"SPS one, Mobile," one of the SPS officers said. "Yes, I know our phone has been out. But, evidently it is repaired now."

The SPS officer hung up, then looked over at Willie and Jake. "Looks like you got it fixed."

"I need you to sign the work order," Willie said.

"What for?"

"If you don't sign the work order, we don't get paid."

"All right." The officer signed the work order.

Fifteen minutes later Jake and Willie were with the ten men they had put together to form the strike team.

"Now, no matter who they dial, the call will come to this phone," Willie said. "And no matter who tries to call them, the call will come to this phone."

"What if they use a cell phone?"

"Same thing, I've got a translator outside that will pick up their signal and relay it to this phone."

"Good," Jake said. "That keeps them isolated. We'll take them down before anyone else in town knows what is going on."

Jake took an inventory of their equipment, saying out loud each item. "Two NFDD grenades, two M-249 machine guns, eight M-4 rifles, ten Glock 33, .357 pistols, two thousand rounds of 5.56 ammunition, one hundred rounds of .357."

"We're going with the noise flash diversionary devices first?" Deon asked.

"Yes. That should get them disoriented enough to give us an early advantage," Jake replied. "Anyone have any questions?"

No one responded.

"All right, men, saddle up," Jake said.

"Jake, I suggest that you and the others get as close to the building as you can without being seen. I'll go in through the front door, deploy the NFDDs, and as soon as they go off, the rest of you come in as fast as you can," Tom said.

"All right, but take Deon with you. That way you can get both of the devices deployed at the same time."

Deon nodded, then he and Tom stayed back while the men, one at a time, moved into positions behind a long row of shrubbery. When everyone was in position, Tom and Deon, each carrying a pistol in one hand and the NFDD in the other, walked right up to the front door, opened it, and tossed in the two noise flash grenades.

"What the hell?" one of the SPS men shouted.

The NFDDs went off immediately, making a huge noise and a bright flash of light, though as they weren't shrapnel producing grenades, the

assault team was able to follow up immediately.
Willie and Marcus had their M-4s on full automatic. Jake and the others were firing single
rounds, carefully selecting their targets.

There were several SPS inside the building and
they returned fire, though the shock and awe of
the unexpected attack left them disoriented, and
the return fire was ineffective. One by one the
SPS men went down, while not one of Jake's assault team was even hit.

From behind a desk, less than twenty feet
away, another SPS popped up, carrying an AK-47.
As he raised it to his shoulders, but before he
could shoot, Deon fired his pistol at the SPS. Jake
saw a spray of blood coming from the officer's
neck, and, with a surprised look on his face, he
dropped his weapon and clutched his throat.

Deon shot again, this time hitting him in the
chest, and the SPS officer went down.

All firing stopped when there were no more
targets. The entire operation was over within less
than a minute. The room smelled of gun smoke
and blood as at least twelve SPS men lay dead.

"Check everyone out," Jake ordered. "But be
careful."

Jake's men went from body to body confirm-
ing that all were dead.

There were four more precinct stations in
Mobile, and Jake and his assault team took them

out one at a time. Prior to each attack Willie had managed to neutralize their communication so that never, at anytime, was a warning flashed ahead. By the end of the day, the city of Mobile was under the complete control of United Free America.

When the citizens of Mobile turned on their television that night, they were surprised by what they saw. The broadcast started, not with praises to Allah, but with the Stars and Stripes, behind which was playing "The Star Spangled Banner." When the music ended, and the flag was taken away, there was no bearded man wearing a *dishdasha* and *taqiyah*, nor was there some woman in a burqa. What they saw instead was a very pretty young woman in Western dress—and not just any Western dress. She was wearing a low-cut blouse which showed cleavage. Many recognized her as one of the regulars on the Fox News Channel, from before it was shut down, along with all the other national networks.

"Citizens of Mobile," the young woman began.

"Tonight, there is cause for rejoicing, for tonight we have taken our first steps toward freedom. There are no SPS men to monitor our every move. Today, Mobile has joined with the freedom fighters from Pleasure Island. As of today, Mobile is now a part of United Free America, a new state, free of the American Islamic Republic of Enlightenment. Our guest

*tonight is Robert Varney, president of Pleasure
Island. President Varney, welcome, it is good of
you to be our guest tonight."*

*Bob smiled. "I've done dozens of TV
interviews over the years, and it has always been
a standard reply to say, 'thank you for having
me.' Tonight, though, I can say that and mean
it as I have never meant it before. Because my
being here, on this show tonight, is symbolic of
the freedom you mentioned in your opening.
Mobile is free!"*

During the interview, Bob gave credit to the
men who had carried out the raid that freed
Mobile, and he explained that there was an unlimited supply of natural gas. Also, by now, there
were more than a dozen places in Mobile that
could easily convert the cars and trucks to run
on CNG.

In the "before time" it cost as much as five
thousand dollars to convert a car to CNG, but
that was because most of the money was used in
making the car "green compliant." Bob explained that there were no such requirements
now, so the conversion could be made quickly,
simply, and inexpensively.

The *Moqaddas Sirata* regime had been publishing a newspaper in Mobile, called the *Way of
Enlightenment.* The owners of the paper, who had
stolen it from its original publishers, were run

off, and a new newspaper, the *Journal of Freedom* was started.

After leaving the TV station, Bob Varney, who had owned a newspaper after his retirement from the army, was standing in the pressroom when the bell rang. After that, the giant press started its run, slowly at first, then moving very quickly as the finished newspapers, printed, collated, and folded, began to pile up at the end of the press. He remembered fondly that one of the most exciting things a person could do was to stand in the pressroom when that bell rang and watch the presses start to roll. It is even more exciting, he realized, when the rolling press was printing a story that he had written.

Bob reached down to pick one up, and smiled as he saw the headline of the story he had written—though he had written this one without a byline.

FREEDOM ON THE MARCH

First Steps to Take Back America

Mobile, now a city of freedom, has proudly joined ranks with the newly formed nation of United Free America. All ties with the AIRE have been severed, and representatives of that illegal government, whether they be civilian officials, military personnel, or members of the SPS, are warned that if they attempt to reenter the city, they do so at their own peril.

Those citizens of our city who do not wish to become a part of this battle for freedom, are at liberty to leave without fear of reprisal. There will, however, be serious consequences for anyone who stays in the city for the express purpose of disrupting our mission of securing liberty and justice for all.

CHAPTER TWENTY-THREE

On the very day the city was liberated, Eddie and Jane surprised their parents by coming back home. Jane's mother came over to the Manning house to celebrate the homecoming.

"Oh, what a wonderful day this is!" Edna said. "I was pleased that Mobile is free, but to see you children here, I can't tell you how happy I am!"

Edna insisted on preparing a dinner for all of them, and during the dinner Eddie and Jane talked to them about YCEC 251. By mutual agreement, they said nothing about the fact that Jane was nearly raped, nor did they give any of the details of their escape, other than saying that Eddie had stolen an official car that had a remote device that opened the gate for them.

Paul Manning laughed. "Well, I never thought I would say good job to you for stealing a car. But in this case, son, I say good job."

They visited for a while longer, then Eddie surprised everyone but Jane when he announced that he couldn't stay.

"What do you mean you can't stay?" Paul Manning asked.

"There are a lot of our friends who are still in 251. We're going to get everyone out of there."

"What do you mean 'we'?" Edna asked.

"I mean Mr. Lantz and Mr. Varney, and the others in the Firebase Freedom team, the ones who freed Mobile."

"Eddie, you and Jane are safe now, and Mobile is free. Let those men do that. They know what they are doing, and you are way too young."

"I've grown up a lot in the last several weeks, Mom. I can help get the other kids out of there. I've been there, nobody in the Firebase team has. They need me."

"No," Edna said. "You're still a minor, and I refuse to let you go."

"Edna," Paul said. "He's not a child any longer. Let him go."

"But, Paul . . ."

"Let him go," Paul repeated. He put his hand on Eddie's shoulder. "Our boy has become a man. And I'm very proud of him."

"Thanks, Pop."

Later that same day Eddie met with Bob, Jake, Deon, and Tom to discuss the rescue of the detainees of the Youth Confinement and Enlightenment Center 251.

"Good intelligence is worth an additional ten men," Jake said. "You've been there, none of us have. We need you to tell us everything you know about the camp."

"I can draw a map of it, if that would help," Eddie said.

"Now you get the picture," Jake said. "Yes, that would help a lot. Draw a map for us, and put in every detail you can think of."

"All right," Eddie said.

Presented with a piece of paper and a pencil, Eddie began drawing the camp as he remembered it, first drawing the perimeter fence.

"What sort of fence is it?"

"It's a high, chain-link fence, with razor wire on the top. But it only goes around the north, west, and south side of the camp. There's no fence on the east side, because that's where the bay is."

"Any concertina wire?" Tom asked.

"Concertina wire?"

"Rolls of barbed wire," Tom explained.

"Oh, yes. It's all stretched out in front of the fence, and also on the other side."

He continued with his drawing, putting the number and approximate location of every guard tower around the compound.

"There are eight towers," he said. "Three on the north, three on the south, and two on the west side, but there are also gate guards on the west side, so that's the same as having three towers. The gate is on the west end of the camp, away from Weeks Bay." He pointed to the gate on his map. "There are two cabins just opposite each other, just outside the fence, and that's where the gate guards are."

"What will we find inside the compound?" Tom asked.

"Just as soon as you go in, there will be big building to your left. That's the administration building. There's never anybody there until about eight o'clock in the morning. Just behind the administration building are three more buildings. This bigger building is for the guards, the one right beside it is for the men instructors, and the one right across the road from that one is for the women staff members. The two buildings here in the middle are the classrooms, this one for the girls and this one for the boys. This big building right in the middle of the camp is the dining hall, and this big building back here, the one that used to be the chapel, is where the camp commandant lives."

"Are the staff members armed?" Jake asked.

"No, they aren't, but the guards are."

"How many guards are there?"

"I'm not exactly sure," Eddie said. "But we can figure it out. There are three on duty in each of the towers, and they change guards every eight hours. Plus, there are two guards who walk in opposite directions around the compound, and they change every eight hours as well. And there are two guards on duty at all times at these cabins just outside the gate."

"I imagine they change every three hours as well," Jake said. "So, let's see, three per tower would be twenty-four, three per gate cabin, would be six, and the two walking guards, if they are changed every eight hours, would be another six."

"That's thirty-six guards," Tom said.

"Yes, but, if we hit them at oh-three-hundred, there will only be ten on duty. The rest will be asleep."

"Asleep when we start," Deon said. "But they're bound to wake up pretty damn quick."

Jake chuckled. "I expect they will."

"Where are the kids, Eddie?" Jake asked.

Eddie pointed to two clusters of buildings. "These cabins are all connected. The ones on the south side of this road are for the boys, the ones on the left side of the road, also connected, are for the girls."

"How old are the kids?" Jake asked. "What I'm asking is, how much can we count on them helping themselves when we get in there?"

"We have two boys who are six years old, but the older boys will look out for the younger ones. I'm sure the same is true of the girls, but I have no idea what their ages are. They're all in burqas, so I've really never seen any of them, though I know there are some pretty young ones."

"The older boys you were talking about, you know them, so what do you think? Are any of them likely to panic, and cause us trouble?"

"No. I know everyone there between fourteen and seventeen. Tim O'Leary, Carl Edwards, Burt Rowe, I know for sure we can count on them.

"How many are there in the camp?"

"There are forty-six boys. And Jane told me there are fifty-one girls. Well, only fifty now that she's gone."

"Ninety-six," Bob said.

"The girls? What about them? Can they handle this when we start?"

Eddie thought of the girl who had come to tell him about Jane. "I'd be willing to bet that the older girls will be as dependable as the older boys," Eddie said. "I know one of them helped me rescue Jane."

"Who was it? It might be good to know?" Deon asked.

Eddie shook his head. "She was wearing the burqa and I didn't ask who she was. I didn't want to know, in case I got caught."

Jake put his hand on Eddie's shoulder and squeezed. "You're a good man, Eddie."

"Yes, you are," Bob said. "And this," he pointed to the map Eddie had drawn, "was a good clear report."

"Tom and Bob are right, this will help us a lot. But we'll take it from here," Deon said.

"What do you mean, you'll take it from here?" Eddie asked.

"I mean you've done your part. We'll take it from here."

"No. I'm going too."

"There's going to be shooting," Deon said. "There's no need for you to be risking your life."

"What if there is shooting? It won't be any more dangerous for me, than it is for the kids who are still there, will it? Besides, in two more months, I'll be seventeen," Eddie said. "My grandpa was in Vietnam when he was seventeen."

"He's got a point," Bob said. "I served with some seventeen-year-olds in Vietnam. They were dependable, honorable, and when called upon, courageous. I say if Eddie wants to go along, more power to him."

"All right, Eddie," Jake acquiesced. "You can come."

"Thank you," Eddie said, beaming with pride.

It was three o'clock the following morning when Jake, Deon, Tom, Mike, Eddie, and seven others approached YCEC 251. They arrived in five school buses so they would have transportation for the young internees. They stopped the buses on Sarah Ann Beach Road, about two hundred yards south of the main gate. There was a heavy growth of woods just west of the compound.

"All right, Mike," Jake said, pointing to the

trees. "Use the woods as your cover, and go around to the north side of the compound and lay in some C-4. When you get planted, give me a call. I'll give you the word as to when to blow it. That should provide a diversion to bring several guards there. Deon, use the trees to get as close to the main gate as you can. Wait one minute after Mike's charge goes off, then blow yours at the main gate. As soon as your charge goes off, we'll come barreling through in the buses."

"Right," Mike said.

Equipped with small two-way radios, Mike and Deon set out to complete their mission. Jake, Tom, and the others waited by the buses. It was quiet except for the incessant call of the whip-poorwills, and the singing of the frogs.

Tom slapped at a mosquito.

One of the men took a leak against the wheel of the bus.

"Good idea," Jake said. "First time I went into combat, I learned from a very good man, Sergeant Clay Matthews, that best thing you can do to get ready is take a piss."

Jake and all the others joined him.

"Freedom Six, Freedom One on station, package delivered," Mike's voice said over the two-way radio.

Jake spoke into the radio. "Freedom One, go."

The order was followed by the loud thump of

an explosion . . . which was followed by shouts of confusion from inside the camp.

"Freedom two, are you counting?"

"Roger, at twenty," Deon replied.

"Get the buses started!" Jake ordered.

Now a new sound was introduced to that of the whippoorwills and frogs as the five buses started their engines. They waited until they heard a second explosion, then Jake, in the first bus, ordered the driver to go ahead. The five buses, accelerating as quickly as they could in the distance they had, roared the two hundred yards down the road, then through the gate, which had been blown from its hinges by Deon's blast.

The buses drove up to the dining hall, then stopped. There, the assault teams poured out of the buses. The target buildings were taken under by M72 rocket launchers. There were explosions inside the buildings, quickly followed by flames.

Many of the guards had responded to the first explosion, and now, as they came running back into the middle of the compound, they were taken under fire by the assault team, all of whom were firing automatic weapons.

As the firefight was under way, Eddie, as previously directed, ran into the boys' barracks.

"Everyone, get down on the floor, but get dressed as quickly as you can! Older boys, look after the younger ones!"

"Eddie, is that you? We thought you were dead! What's going on?" Carl called.

"We're getting you out of here. Stay here until you get the word. Carl, you, Tim, and Burt, keep everyone in here, and keep your heads down until you get the word. Then, when you do, run like hell, go outside and get onto the buses."

"I'm scared!" one boy of about ten said.

"Tim," Carl shouted. "Take care of Billy. The rest of you, you heard the man. Just keep your heads down and stay where you are."

Eddie nodded at Carl, then ran across the road, even as the gunfire continued. He heard the pop of a bullet as it zipped close by, and though he had never before been exposed to such a thing, he knew exactly what it was.

When he stepped into the girls' barracks, he gave them the same instructions he had given the boys, to get dressed, get down on the floor, and wait for further instructions. Some of the younger girls were crying.

"Barbara Carter!" Eddie shouted. Jane had told him she was the natural leader of all the girls.

"Eddie! What's going on?" Barbara asked.

"We're here to get everyone out," Eddie said. "Keep all the girls inside, and down on the floor until you get the word. Then when you leave, get onto the buses outside—but not until you get the word!"

All the time Eddie was giving his instructions, the sound of gunfire could be heard outside.

With the boys and girls in both barracks notified, Eddie ran back outside. Like the others of the assault team, he was armed, but he was carrying a pistol only. As it turned out, he needed it, because just as he left the girls' barracks, he saw one of the guards coming toward the barracks.

The guard swung his automatic weapon around toward Eddie, but when he pulled the trigger nothing happened. Frustrated, he pulled the bolt back and let it forward to clear the chamber, but before he could pull the trigger again, Eddie had already brought his pistol up.

Eddie had never fired a real pistol before, though when he was younger, he had a pellet pistol. He had also fired pistols in video games, so his action was almost reflexive. He pulled the trigger, then saw a dark hole appear in the guard's chest. The guard got a surprised look on his face, slapped his hand over the wound, then, with blood streaming between his fingers, he fell.

Inside the compound the battle continued, though the guards, who had been caught by surprise, were unable to mount a very spirited defense. More than half of the defenders fled into the woods. Those who stayed to fight were killed, and within five minutes, it was all over.

The camp commandant had fled with the others. The three men and two women of the faculty were brought out of their quarters, but weren't harmed.

"Who are you?" one of the male instructors asked.

"We are the ones who have taken over," Jake

replied. "The SPS and the *Moqaddas Sirata* are no more."

By now all the boys and girls were brought out of the barracks, where they were loaded onto the buses.

"What are you going to do with us?" one of the two women asked.

"Nothing," Jake said. "You're free to go or stay, I don't care which."

The members of the faculty looked at each other in confusion, but said nothing.

"Jake, we're all loaded!" Deon called.

"You folks have a nice day," Jake said to the five who remained behind. He climbed onto the bus, and the vehicles left the compound. The children in the buses were just now coming to grips with what had happened.

"We're free!" Burt shouted, and everyone in the bus cheered loudly.

CHAPTER TWENTY-FOUR

Lancaster, Pennsylvania

"It's started," Gregoire said with a broad grin. He hit his fist into his hand. "I knew they couldn't hold us down. Two hundred and thirty-eight years of freedom can't be so easily erased."

"It's just one city, George," Riley said.

"Yes, it's starting with one city," Gregoire replied. "But I'm telling you, Mark. Today it's Mobile, but when people around the country hear that, there will be more cities taken back, New Orleans, Dallas, Atlanta, Louisville. No matter what these *Moqaddas Sirata* bastards do, or say, they can't hold down the wave of freedom, once the movement starts."

"I hope you're right."

"How much longer until broadcast?"

"Thirty seconds," Riley said. "Are you ready?"

"Yes, open with me here, I'll walk across to

there," he said, pointing out his blocking in the makeshift studio.

"Ten seconds," Riley said.

Gregoire stood in position until Riley brought his hand down. He smiled at the camera.

"Hello, America.

"The city of Mobile, Alabama, has been liberated. Freedom fighters from United Free America freed the city from the oppressive occupation of Ohmshidi's personal military force, the State Protective Service. Not only was the city freed, but so too were the almost one hundred young people who were being held prisoner in the nearby youth concentration camp.

"All across America there are groups, and even individuals, who are fighting for the freedom and liberty we had so long enjoyed, before the disastrous presidency of Mehdi Ohmshidi. I will continue to keep you informed so that you can take hope in our eventual salvation.

"Long ago our founding fathers pledged their lives, their fortunes, and their sacred honor to secure liberty for the people. We have such people among us today. And to those of you who are engaged in this fight, you have the thanks of all America, and I know that God's blessings are upon you. To those of you who have not joined the fight, ask not what they can do for you, ask rather, what you can do for them.

"Good night, and God bless.
"This is George Gregoire, telling you to take
back America!"

Muslimabad

Ohmshidi wasn't watching the broadcast, but Hassan was, and watching with him was a man named Caleb Brenneman.

"You are sure that if I tell you, you will free my brother?" Brenneman said.

"Yes, yes, he will be set free."

"You will find George Gregoire at the house of Solomon Lantz in Lancaster, Pennsylvania," Caleb said. "He is passing himself off as Lantz's uncle, as Amish, but he is English. When you find him, he won't look like he does on the television. He is being made up to look very old."

The Harry S. Truman Building

Once more, the Great Leader, President for Life Ohmshidi, was summoned to the office of Mohammad Akbar Rahimi.

"Do you know what this is?" Rahimi asked, holding out a bill.

"It looks like currency of some sort."

"It is. It is the currency of the breakaway state, United Free America. They are calling the currency Freedom Dollars."

Ohmshidi chuckled. "What does it matter if they print their currency? It can't be of any value."

"Their currency has gained international

recognition, and is exchanged at an established rate throughout the rest of the world."

Ohmshidi's eyes widened in disbelief. "That can't be true. How can money they print be worth anything, unless it is backed?"

"It is backed by at least fifty million Moqaddas in gold," Rahimi said.

"They have to be lying about that. They don't have any gold."

"They have convinced the World Bank that they have gold. I don't think they could do that if they didn't actually have it."

"How would the World Bank know, anyway? I mean, suppose they did have that much gold—they are isolated, there is no way for them to reach the World Bank."

"Not as isolated as they once were. They have now taken Mobile and the Mobile airport. It is also my understanding that there were four airliners on the ground at Mobile when the city fell to the rebels. The crews of those aircraft have gone over to the rebels, and the rebels have now established their own airline."

"To fly where? I'm certainly not going to recognize them, so they won't have clearance into any airport in the AIRE."

"No, but they can establish international flights to Mexico, the Bahamas, Jamaica, South America. From there, they will have access to the rest of the world."

"Imam, some people made a demonstration. It is nothing, we will soon have it put down."

"See that you do. I will not have our plans for this country to be the center of a world caliphate, put into jeopardy by a group of revolutionary infidels."

"I will make certain that these apostates cause us no more trouble," Ohmshidi promised.

"What about the Ultimate Resolution?"

"The Ultimate Resolution is well under way, Imam. I have put the Janissaries in charge of the operation. They are well aware of what must be done to solve the Jewish problem."

"Ohmshidi, as these things develop, you must keep me informed. Don't make me send for you as a schoolmaster must do for a wayward student."

"I will keep you informed, Imam," Ohmshidi promised.

Plano, Texas

American Islamic Republic of Enlightenment
Department of Relocation for Jews—
Muslimabad, AIRE

Obey Ohmshidi

Mr. and Mrs. Sam and Sarah Gelbman
2117 Davenport Court
Dallas, TX
Subject: Acceptance Letter—Relocation

Dear Mr. and Mrs. Sam and Sarah Gelbman:

In the name of Allah, Most Gracious, Most Merciful, congratulations! Your names have been selected to participate in the Jewish Relocation Program.

The JRP is designed to provide an area where Jews who have been unable to assimilate into the way of truth and enlightenment, may, by agreeing to abandon all personal holdings, relocate to an area to be chosen which will concentrate all apostates into a controlled area whereby you may practice your own religion.

In order to be processed, you must have this letter of appointment in hand when reporting to the Jewish Relocation Center in Plano, Texas.

In the name of Allah, the Most Beneficent, peace to you.

> Kareem Ali
> Commandant
> Jewish Relocation Program

Obey Ohmshidi

Once one of the biggest churches in America, Preston Acres Fellowship Church in Plano had been taken over by the *Moqaddas Sirata* Muslims. Although the church had been converted to a mosque, it was now being used as a processing center, and a sign spread across the front of the main building proclaimed its purpose.

JEWISH RELOCATION CENTER

This had once been the church of over 30,000 Christians, but over the last two weeks at least two thousand Jews had been processed there. A loudspeaker greeted the crowd of more than five hundred who had gathered this morning.

"Obey Ohmshidi! Please have your appointment letter in your hand, and your identity cards pinned to your shirt or jacket. Without your appointment letter and identity cards, you cannot be processed."

Sam and Sarah Gelbman were among those who were to be processed today, and they stood together, clutching the appointment letter they had received.

"We'd better get our ID cards pinned to our shirts," Sam said.

"Obey Ohmshidi! Please have your appointment letter in your hand, and your identity cards pinned to your shirt or jacket. Without your appointment letter and identity cards, you cannot be processed."

"Sam, I don't know," Sarah said as she pinned Sam's ID card on for him.

"You don't know what?"

"I don't know how I feel about this. There's something about it that just isn't quite right."

"Sarah, you were the one who was pushing to get this letter. You said you wanted to go somewhere, where we would be free to live our own lives."

"I know I did. But I'm having second thoughts now."

"Sarah, I know you don't want to leave our home here," Sam said. "I don't blame you. It took us years to get it just the way we wanted it. Besides which, we are about to lose it anyway—you know that as well as I do. It's about to be taken away from us. But there are some things more important than just having a nice home; and being able to live in a place where people aren't breathing down our necks every minute is one of those things."

"Obey Ohmshidi! Please have your appointment letter in your hand, and your identity cards pinned to your shirt or jacket. Without your appointment letter and identity cards, you cannot be processed."

"How do you know that's where we're going?"

"Where else would we be going? You read the same article I did. There is a huge tract of land out in West Texas where they are relocating everyone who doesn't want to convert. And it makes sense when you think about it. I expect they don't want us any more than we want them. And this letter says that we will be free to practice our own religion."

"Obey Ohmshidi! Please have your appointment letter in your hand, and your identity cards pinned to your shirt or jacket. Without your appointment letter and identity cards, you cannot be processed."

"I wish they would change that announcement," Sam said. "It's driving me nuts."

"Sam, let's don't do this. Let's go back home," Sarah said.

"Now why in heaven's name do you want to go back home? We talked about it when the offer came out in the paper, and you agreed that we would do this. It's not like we're being forced to move, we are the ones who applied for the letter."

"Obey Ohmshidi! Please have your appointment letter in your hand, and your identity cards pinned to your shirt or jacket. Without your appointment letter and identity cards, you cannot be processed."

"Jesus, will you shut the hell up with that announcement? We've heard it already," Sam said, his irritation growing.

"I'm scared. There's something about this that I don't like."

Sam put his arm around his wife. "It'll be all right," he said. "I know you're a little nervous. Who wouldn't be? But I'm sure it will be all right."

"We've been married for ten years, Sam. You know that when I get these kind of feelings that I'm usually right."

"What has you so frightened?"

"These aren't policemen. They aren't even the regular SPS. They are Janissaries. You and I both know that the Janissaries are the worst."

Sam sighed. "All right, if you are that worried about it, we won't go. Come on, we'll go back home. Though, I don't know how much longer we'll be able to stay there."

"Thank you," Sarah said.

The two started back toward the door, but they were stopped by a couple of the men in black uniforms.

"Where do you think you are going?" one of them asked.

"We've changed our mind," Sam said. "We're going back home. Here's our letter."

"It's too late. You've already received the letter, you will be relocated."

"That's silly," Sam said. "I'd think you would be glad that we've changed our mind. That leaves room for someone else."

"You will be relocated. Now, get back in line."

"I will not get back in line. I told you . . ."

That was as far as Sam got before the Janissary hit him on the side of his head with his pistol. Sam went down to his knees.

"Sam!" Sarah shouted.

"I said, get back in line," the Janissary repeated.

Sarah pulled a tissue from her purse and put it to the side of Sam's head.

"What are you doing? Why did you hit him like that? Are you crazy?" she asked.

"I didn't hit him hard enough to hurt him. Now the two of you get back in line like I said."

Sarah helped Sam to his feet. "Come on, Sam. We'll go. Maybe it won't be so bad."

"Obey Ohmshidi! Please have your appointment letter in your hand, and your identity cards pinned to

*your shirt or jacket. Without your appointment letter
and identity cards, you cannot be processed."*

Holding a tissue to the wound on the side of
his head, Sam walked with Sarah to the table by
the side door where someone was checking the
appointment letters and ID cards. Unlike the
Janissaries and their black uniforms, this man was
in civilian clothes. As soon as he identified the
person, he would find their name on a printout,
then make a mark beside it.

"What happened to you?" the man at the table
asked as Sam and Sarah approached.

"I . . ."

"He fell down," Sarah said, quickly, before Sam
could say what actually happened.

"Yes, well, be careful getting onto the bus."

"I'll look out for him," Sarah said.

"What did you tell him that for?" Sam asked
once they were outside the building, and walking toward the ten buses that were parked along
the street.

"I think it's best we aren't perceived as trouble-
makers," Sarah said. "At least, not until we get to
where we are going."

As they approached the buses they saw several
more black-uniformed Janissaries standing on
the sidewalk.

"Which bus do we get on?" Sam asked.

"Do not address me, Jew, without the proper
salute."

"I beg your pardon?"

"The proper salute, Jew!"

Sam made a fist of his right hand, crossed it across his chest, and said, "Obey Ohmshidi."

"You will get on this bus, she will go on one of the others," the man answered. Sam noticed that he did not return the salute.

"What?" Sam replied, protesting loudly. "Wait a minute, what do you mean we go on separate buses? This is my wife!"

"Men and women are not allowed to travel together. It's the law of *Moqaddas Sirata.*"

"What the hell do I care about the law of *Moqaddas Sirata?* We're Jews, remember? The Jewish relocation program? Does that ring a bell with you?" Sam held up the letter of acceptance.

"Get on the bus, Jew, or we will put you on the bus," the Janissary ordered.

"Do it, Sam," Sarah said. "I'll be all right."

"You go over here," the officer said to Sarah, pointing to another bus.

Sam felt a lump in his throat, and a pressure behind his eyes as he watched his wife being led away. He climbed onto the bus, then settled in the third seat back from the door, on the right side of the vehicle. He sat there, staring through the window as the others were brought out of the building to load onto the buses, and he watched as the men and women were separated.

Sam began to think about the recurring dream that had been plaguing him for the last three years. In that dream some event would separate him from Sarah, and he would be unable to locate her. Often the dreams would be so disconcerting that he would wake up in the middle of the night, breathing hard, his heart beating rapidly, able to calm himself only when he reached over and felt his wife lying beside him.

Now that nightmare was coming true. Or, was this just another dream? Yes, that was it! That had to be it! This was no more than a bad dream. He had certainly had them enough to be able to recognize them. Sometimes when he realized he was having a bad dream, he could will himself to wake up, and he decided to do that now.

Wake up! Wake up! He told himself.

The bus engine started with a loud roar, and Sam didn't awaken, because he was already awake.

"My God," Sam said quietly. "It isn't a dream. It's a nightmare, and it has come true!"

Sam saw the other buses pulling away, and he realized to his horror that he didn't even know which bus Sarah was on.

Sarah knew about Sam's recurring dream, and as the buses drove off, she thought about her husband and the terror he must be going through, now that his worst nightmare was coming true. She held onto the hope and the prayer that they would be reunited once they reached their destination, but when she realized that the buses weren't traveling together, she began to lose hope.

Sam was a strong man, a veteran of the war in Afghanistan who, as lieutenant and platoon leader, had been awarded the Silver Star for bravery in battle. Sarah knew that he could face death calmly, but, like many strong men, he had his Achilles' heel, and in his case it was separation anxiety.

"Hang on, Sam," she said quietly. "Hang on to the thought that I love you, no matter where you are, no matter where I am, and know that our love will keep us together."

The bus rolled on, far into the night.

CHAPTER TWENTY-FIVE

It was twenty-four hours later when Sam's bus passed through a gate into some sort of compound. There was a "Welcome" sign just inside the gate.

Welcome to Jewish Ultimate Resolution Camp 26
Earn Your Freedom by Working
Obey Ohmshidi

Looking through the window, Sam could see nothing but men, but maybe it was because the women were all inside somewhere. When the bus stopped, an official stepped in through the door. "Everyone off the bus!" he called. "Follow me for your in-processing."

"Where are the women?" one of the other passengers asked. "We were separated back in Dallas."

"All of your questions will be dealt with during the in-processing," the Janissary officer said.

"What about our luggage?" another asked. "I didn't see it loaded onto this bus."

"You won't be needing your luggage."

"How is it that we don't need our luggage?"

"You'll be issued clothes."

"What do you mean, issued clothes? I have my own clothes. I didn't come here to have you take care of me—I came here to take care of myself. Now, where are my clothes?"

"Let's go, everyone off the bus," the guard said, without answering the man's question.

As Sam stepped down from the bus he was able to look around, and what he saw caused his knees to grow weak. This wasn't merely a place where they would be in-processed. This was a prison camp. There was no other way to describe it. And, of the ten buses that left Dallas, this was the only one that came to this particular camp. The only people he saw were the Janissary guards, dressed in their black uniforms, and other men, dressed in nondescript gray shirts and trousers. He saw no women anywhere and he had no idea where Sarah was.

The in-processing took place in a building that was set apart from the other buildings, which were long, low, barracks-type buildings. The in-processing building was set up like a classroom, with several rows of chairs facing the front. On the front wall was the red, beige, and blue portrait of Ohmshidi over the words "Obey Ohmshidi."

Below the portrait was a banner.

EARN YOUR FREEDOM BY WORKING
OBEY OHMSHIDI

"Freedom?" one of the men asked when he read the sign. "What do you mean, earn our freedom? I'm already a free man. I came here of my own free will, remember."

"Sit down, Jew!" one of the guards said to the man who asked the question. "Sit down, and keep your mouth shut."

A moment later, one of the Janissaries stepped to the front of the room to address them.

"I am *Sarhag* Kareem Ali. *Sarhag* means colonel, so when you speak to me, you will address me in this fashion: 'Sir, Jew,' then give your name, '*Sarhag* Ali, I beg permission to speak.' If I, or any other official whom you may address sees fit to grant you permission to speak, we will tell you so. You will then proceed by saying, 'Sir, Jew,' then give your name, and then say whatever unimportant thing it is you have to say. Do you understand?"

Nobody responded, so he pointed to someone in the back row. "You, back there, do you understand?"

"Don't we say 'Obey Ohmshidi' before we talk to you?"

Suddenly one of the uniformed guards at

the back of the room hit the man on the side of his head.

"Evidently, you did not understand how to address me," Ali said.

"I do, I do!"

The man was hit again.

"Do you understand, now?" Ali repeated.

Now the hapless man understood. "Sir, Jew Friedman, *Sarhag* Ali, I do understand, sir."

Ali smiled.

"Well, Jew Friedman, I congratulate you. You learned quickly. And now, to answer your question, you do not salute and say, 'Obey Ohmshidi' when you speak to us. The salute and greeting is an honorable exchange between citizens of the American Islamic Republic of Enlightenment. You are Jews, you are not citizens, therefore you are not accorded the privilege of an honorable exchange."

"What does that . . ." one of the men started, then remembering, he started over. "Sir, Jew Bernstein. *Sarhag* Ali, I beg permission to speak."

"You may speak," Ali said.

"What does that sign mean?" Bernstein asked, pointing to the "Earn your freedom by working" sign.

"It means exactly what it says," Ali said. "What about the sign do you not understand?"

"I don't understand . . ." Bernstein started, but his response was interrupted by a blow to the side of the head from one of the guards.

"Sir, Jew Bernstein. I don't understand any of it. We came here of our own volition. We applied to come here. But this is nothing like I expected. Where are our wives?"

"Your wives are in another camp, undergoing orientation," Ali said.

"Sir, Jew Bernstein. We were never told we were going to be separated. I came here by choice, therefore I expect to be able to leave anytime I want, regardless of what that sign says."

"The situation has changed," Ali said. "You are Jews."

"Sir, Jew Bernstein. Yes, we are Jews. We were Jews when we applied for the letter of acceptance, we were Jews when we got on the bus, and we were Jews when we were born. So how can you say that the situation has changed?"

"There has been a public outcry all across the land about the Jewish situation," Ali said. "The people have demanded that we do something about it."

"My God!" one of the others said. "So you have set up concentration camps?"

One of the guards started toward the last man to speak, but Ali held up his hand in a benevolent gesture, preventing the guard from hitting him.

"These camps are for your own safety," Ali said. "I think you do not understand how much hatred the people have for you. If we were to allow you to continue to live among decent Muslims, they may rise in righteous indignation, and we can't be responsible for what would happen."

"What do you mean you can't be responsible?" Sam asked. "It is your policies, the policies of this new order, that have created this atmosphere of hatred. I never felt hated before."

"Believe me, you were. All Jews were hated, but because Jews controlled the press and the entertainment industry, the nation was inundated with Zionist propaganda. Lies were told about the so-called holocaust when everyone knows there was no such thing."

"My God, you are insane," Friedman said.

Ali lifted his hand toward two SPS officers who were standing in the back of the room. They moved quickly to Friedman, grabbed him, then started toward the door with him.

"What is this? What are you doing?" Friedman shouted in fear.

"Jew Friedman, you are about to provide an object lesson for the others. We will not tolerate insolence or insubordination in this facility."

"Sir, Jew Bernstein, what are you going to do to him?"

"What we do to him is none of your concern," Ali said. "But take a lesson from this." Ali pointed to the portrait of Ohmshidi. "Obey Ohmshidi," he said.

* * *

After the orientation, the newcomers were taken to a building where they were told they would take a shower.

"No! My God, no!" one of the men shouted.

One of the Janissaries in charge laughed. "This is not a gas chamber," he said. "This is a shower. We will remain in the same building with you as you shower. We wouldn't be here if we were to use gas, now, would we?"

The guards did remain in the same building with them as they showered, and all during the shower the guards laughed and pointed to the naked men, singling out ones who were less endowed than the others, and making fun of him.

"Hey, Jew, what happened to your pecker? Did the *mohel* cut too much off when you were circumcised?"

The other guards laughed, and the rest of the naked men looked away in shame, not wanting to add to the humiliation of the one who was being singled out.

"Jew, you have a new name," the guard said. "From now on when you speak, you will say, 'Sir, Jew Tiny Pecker,' then say whatever it is you have to say. Have you got that?"

The man said nothing, and suddenly a whip lashed out to strike him across his bare back and buttocks.

"I asked if you've got that."

"Yes," the man replied quietly.

Again the whip lashed out. "Have you got that?"

"Sir, Jew Tiny Pecker. Yes, sir."

"Ha!" the guard with the whip said. He looked at the others. "I do believe Jew Tiny Pecker has learned his new name."

Again, the other guards laughed.

The guards handed out new names to some of the others, Jew Fat Ass, Jew Fag, and Jew Dick Face.

After the shower the men returned to recover their clothes, only to discover that they were gone. In their place were gray trousers and shirts, all the same size. For the smaller men the uniforms hung from them, while the larger men could barely get them on. Fortunately, Sam was of average size, and his clothes fit.

That night, after a full day of orientation, if the constant barrage of insults could actually be called that, the men went to bed. This would be the first night since their marriage that Sam had not gone to bed with Sarah.

Not long after they were in bed, the door to the barracks opened, and the guards shouted at them.

"Let this be a lesson to you, Jew bastards!" One of them called, then they heard a loud bump on the floor.

"Oh my God, it's Friedman," one of the men said.

"Is he hurt?" another asked.

"He's dead."

Jewish Ultimate Resolution Camp 49

The women had also been given new clothes, but in their case the clothes were black burqas. At first Sarah resented it, but then she decided there was some advantage in being able to hide herself from the camp guards, nearly all of whom were women, dressed, not in Burqas, but the black uniforms of the Janissary Auxiliary.

As she lay in bed that first night, she wondered about Sam. Where was he? What were they doing to the men?

"Sam," she said quietly. "Sam, know that I am thinking of you. Know that I love you."

Jewish Ultimate Resolution Camp 26

When Sam and the others awakened the next morning, they were shocked to see, hanging from the rafters, the man the guards had called Jew Tiny Pecker. It was obvious he had hung himself, because he had tied his shirt and trousers together to use as a rope.

The others cut him down, put his clothes back on him, then laid him, gently, alongside the body of Rob Friedman.

Sam learned that day what the sign "Earn your freedom by working," meant, because he, and all the other prisoners with him, were taken out, under guard, to work a farm. For the first time in his life, he learned what it meant to chop cotton.

He and the others had been working for two weeks, and Sam had blisters on his blisters. His back hurt so much that he could barely walk, but he knew better than to let any of the guards know this, because he knew what that would mean. If a person was nonproductive, he was eliminated.

"Hey, Sam," Ben Bernstein said one day, as they were in the field, chopping. He spoke so quietly that only Sam could hear him.

"I know where our wives are."

"What? Where?" Sam said, speaking louder than he intended.

"Shh!" Ben warned, and both looked around to see if any of the guards heard him.

It appeared that the guards had not heard.

"Where are our wives?" Sam asked again, this time speaking as quietly as Ben had.

"They are in Sanderson."

"Sanderson? I know Sanderson, it's twenty miles west of here."

"How do you know Sanderson?"

"I was in the trucking business, remember? On 90, we came through Dryden and Sanderson between Del Rio and Alpine. Sanderson and Dryden are the only two towns in Terrell county. What are the women doing there? Are they working in the fields?"

"No, they're making uniforms for the SPS."

"Where is the camp?"

"It's at the end of Carlisle Road. Do you know where that is?"

"I know exactly where it is. And it makes sense to put the camp there, because it would be out of the way from the rest of the town. But there are good people who live in Sanderson. I can't see them going along with having a concentration camp there."

"There's nobody left in Sanderson now but the Janissaries and plant managers, and the women they have working there. They've moved all the natives out of town, just like they have here, in Dryden."

"Thanks, Ben," Sam said.

That night, for the first time since Sam and Sarah had been separated, Sam felt a sense of calmness. He wasn't lost anymore. He knew where he was, and he knew where Sarah was.

And he began working on a plan.

CHAPTER TWENTY-SIX

Mobile

There was a limited amount of jet fuel at the Mobile airport, but none left at what had been, at one time, the Mobile Coast Guard base. Jake and Bob flew the Huey from Fort Morgan to the Mobile airport, where they took on enough fuel to bring the fuel on board to 240 gallons. That was the first time the helicopter had been topped off in well over a year.

With the helicopter at full fuel load, Jake and Bob decided to make a scouting flight around their newly acquired territory. Jake was in the right seat, the command seat on the Huey, and Bob was in the left. As they flew, Bob was doing a search of all the radio frequencies. Most of the frequencies were quiet, then he picked up a broadcast that came in quite clear.

"When we get to Mobile, what's our target?"

"The National Leader has declared Mobile a free fire zone."

"So, we just set up the pieces and start firing?"

"Yes. Remember, our only mission at this point is to spread around a little terror."

"Ha! I'm gonna enjoy this."

"Put that on the ADF," Jake said, and Bob tuned in the automatic direction finder. The needle swung to the azimuth from which the radio signals were coming, and Jake turned to fly in that direction. They flew for another half hour, then, near the town of Greenville, Bob saw them.

"Down there," Bob said. "I see ten trucks headed south. Four of them are pulling artillery pieces . . . looks like 105s."

"Yeah, I see 'em, M777A1 Howitzers," Jake said. "What do you say we go back and set up a little surprise for them?"

They started back to Fort Morgan at VNE speed, and Jake called Willie on the way.

"Willie, put Deon on."

"Roger," Willie said.

A moment later, Deon's voice came up. "Six, this is Three, over."

"Three, get an assault team ready. And we'll need some heavy armament. This is for an immediate operation."

"Will do, Six."

When Jake landed at Fort Morgan twenty minutes later, Tom Jack, Deon Pratt, Marcus Warner,

Willie Stark, Mike Moran, and Jerry Cornett were waiting for them. All were armed with M-240 machine guns, and in addition the attack team was equipped with two FGM-148 Javelin anti-vehicle missile launchers.

Jake landed, then shut the engine down just long enough to brief them.

"There are ten trucks," Jake said. "Now, let's say that each truck is eighteen feet long. Four are pulling M triple seven Howitzers that are thirty-five feet long. Allow a hundred feet between each vehicle, that means the column will be right at four hundred yards long, depending on the distance between. So the first thing we'll do when we get there, is set up two roadblocks, four hundred yards apart. That will give us a contained kill zone. Do we have any C-4 left?"

"Yeah, we got a lot of it from the SPS armory in Mobile," Tom said.

"Good, we'll use it."

"Damn," Deon said.

"What?"

"This is the American army we are about to attack. These are guys I served with, and fought with. I never imagined myself setting up an ambush. Hell, that's what we had to deal with in Iraq and Afghanistan."

"First of all, Deon, I would be willing to bet that you never served with a single one of these men," Tom said. "The army, like the navy, was totally destroyed by Ohmshidi. There is no army anymore. These are SPS goons."

"Yeah, you're probably right."

"Let's get mounted," he said.

"Damn!" Bob said with a broad grin.

"What is it?"

"This will be the first combat insertion I've done since Vietnam."

"Yeah?" Jake pulled the starter trigger and the blades started to turn. "Well, if you've done one insertion, you've done them all." Using the beeper switch, he beeped the RPM up into the green, then lifted off.

Bob knew the area better than Jake, and he recommended that they set down at an abandoned service station at exit 34. Jake landed just east of the abandoned building so the helicopter could not be seen from the road. Then, he deployed the team.

"Not you, Bob," he said.

"What do you mean, not me? Are you an age bigot?"

Jake chuckled. "You're our reserve. If I get hit, you'll have to fly us back."

"Yeah, all right, I can see that. But don't get hit."

They found a Chrysler that, though it could no longer be driven, could be pushed, and they filled it with C-4 plastic explosive. They pushed it out onto the road, then moved back four hundred yards behind where they found a Chevrolet, and filled it with C-4.

"I love it," Tom said. "These cars are from the auto companies that Ohmshidi stole from the stockholders."

The C-4 in both cars were set to be exploded by two-way radio, broadcasting on a certain frequency. He left Willie and Marcus on the Chevy.

"There are ten trucks," Jake said. "Count them, when the tenth one goes by, push this car on the road, then back out of the way."

"Right," Marcus said.

Jake spread the rest of them out along the side of the road, then waited. There was very little traffic on what had once been a very heavily traveled artery that stretched from Mobile all the up to Chicago.

A 2010 Ford came by.

It was ten minutes before another vehicle passed them, this one a 2003 Dodge. Both cars merely steered around the Chrysler, which looked no different from all the other abandoned cars along the interstate. It wasn't even the only car in the middle of the highway

"Major!" Deon called from the top of a berm that ran parallel to the highway. Deon was looking north with a pair of field glasses. "They're comin'!"

"How far?"

"No more'n a mile, I'd say."

Tom keyed the mic on his two-way radio. "Willie?"

"I'm here."

"Did you read that?"

"Roger."

"All right, stand by."

Deon came back down from the berm then, and Jake took his radio. He changed it to the detonation frequency, then put it down so that he wouldn't inadvertently key the switch and activate the trigger signal that would set off the explosives.

"Here they are," Deon said.

"Stay down."

The men stayed out of sight behind the berm.

Jake watched as the first truck came by, the back of the truck filled with uniformed SPS men. Then he keyed the mic on the radio, and was rewarded with a stomach-shaking explosion as the Chrysler went up in a huge, rolling ball of flame.

"Go!" Willie said, over the radio, indicating that the Chevy was in position and that he and Marcus were clear.

As the vehicles came to a stop, Tom triggered the explosion in the Chevy, trapping the convoy between the two burning cars.

"All right, take out the heavy guns!" Tom ordered, and almost immediately two missiles were launched, and two of the guns were destroyed. At the same time the other members of the attack team opened fire on the SPS personnel using M-240 machine guns.

There was very little resistance from the SPS troops, and those who weren't killed in the initial attack ran, most of them abandoning their weapons. It was all over within five minutes. Tom, Deon, and the others of the attack team came out from behind the berm and completed their work by tossing thermite grenades into each of the trucks. They also took care of the remaining Howitzers by damaging the breeches so that they couldn't be fired.

"Gather up the weapons," Tom said. "We can use every piece of armament we can find."

Fifteen minutes later, with at least two dozen undamaged M-4 rifles, along with several containers of ammunition, the attack detail regathered at the helicopter.

"Whoa! We can kick some major ass now!" Deon said as, laughing, he and the others climbed back into the helicopter for the flight back.

They landed at the Mobile airport to take on more fuel, and were met there by several of the town's citizens who had heard the news that there had been troops coming down to reclaim Mobile.

"President Varney, we want you to come on TV tonight and give a report to the city," Barney Caldwell said. Caldwell had been the mayor of Mobile, before the SPS took over and appointed their own mayor. That appointed mayor left town shortly after Mobile was retaken, and Caldwell moved back into the job.

"All right," Bob said. "I'll be glad to."

Caldwell looked at the other men who had taken part in the interdiction operation.

"And, I think it would be great if you would all just drive down Government Street and let our citizens see you, and cheer you," Caldwell said.

Caldwell had made several convertibles available to Bob and the others, and as they drove on into town, both sides of Government Street were lined by cheering citizens. That night Bob Varney went on the one remaining television station to address the citizens of Mobile. Sitting behind the news desk, he couldn't help but think of the last time he was in this studio. Then, it had been to promote his novel about the 8th Air Force during World War II.

The book had sold very well, and as he recalled that interview, he remembered thinking how good life was then, how he and his wife had realized their dream of buying a beach house, and how his publisher wanted as many books as he could write.

Now, all that was gone, and he was navigating his way through a world that was still very alien to him.

"President Varney, you'll be on in ten seconds," the floor director said. "You'll hear the voice-over introduce you."

Bob nodded, then watched the floor director hold up a clenched fist. He counted off the last five seconds by lifting one finger at a time.

"Ladies and gentlemen, President Bob Varney," the voice-over said.

A red light on the camera came on.

"Good evening," Bob said. "Over the last three and a half years, beginning with the election of Mehdi Ohmshidi, our lives have undergone some major, and, most I am sure will agree, unpleasant changes. It began innocently enough with a presidential election. We have had many presidents in our history, some better than others, but always there was the power of the ballot box so that we could, every four years, vote to sustain or to replace the person we had chosen to lead us. And, we even had the power of impeachment, so that if the sins of our elected officials were too severe, we could remove them from office, short of re-election.

"It was not until this last election that we, by our own hand, cast the ballot that destroyed our republic. For with that ballot we elected Mehdi Ohmshidi. Now, Ohmshidi has declared himself president for life, and our precious heritage has been taken from us."

Bob let that comment sink in for a moment, then he smiled at the camera.

"But we Americans are a resilient people, and, town by town, county by county, state by state, we will *take back America*!"

Although Bob was not speaking before an audience, several who were in the TV studio cheered, and their reaction could be heard over the air.

"Today the illegitimate government of an illegitimate entity, the so-called American Islamic Republic of Enlightenment, sent a reconnaissance team in force to our city, intending to bombard us with artillery fire. At this point it isn't clear whether they thought that, by intimidation, they could take the city back, or whether they had no idea of recovery at all—but only the intent to kill as many of us as they could.

"I am happy to say that we successfully intercepted their attack and totally destroyed their force. But, you may rest assured that any future force that Ohmshidi may direct toward us will be much larger, and much more lethal, so we must be ready for it.

"Therefore I am asking, tonight, that anyone within the reach of this broadcast who has any military experience, report to the Hank Aaron baseball field tomorrow at thirteen hundred hours." Bob smiled at the camera. "If you have military experience, I won't have to tell you what time thirteen hundred is.

"Now, I address this to those of you who converted to *Moqaddas Sirata*. If your conversion was genuine, and you wish to continue to practice that perversion of Islam, you are free to do so . . . but . . . you are not free to condemn, or to interfere with, any other citizen in the practice of their religion.

"And finally, I tell you this. We are in a state of war with the American Islamic Republic of Enlightenment. Anyone who gives aid and comfort to the enemy shall be treated as a traitor, and will be dealt with. If you think you cannot live under these principles, leave now! We will make no effort to stop anyone from leaving. But if you leave, we will not let you return.

"God bless all who join our struggle for freedom. And I bid you all a good night."

CHAPTER TWENTY-SEVEN

Bob and Jake were both surprised by the number of military volunteers who showed up at the ball park the next day. Many were wearing bits and pieces of military uniforms, several were wearing the complete uniform, some were old enough that the uniform they wore had, on the right sleeve, the patches of MACV and USARV, units that were specific to Vietnam. Jake took a count and determined that there were at least seven hundred who had showed up. That was more people than they had weapons for, but they decided that they could acquire the weapons later, if need be.

After some organization, they broke the assembly down into army and navy, explaining to the air force and marine veterans that, for the time being they could only support an army and navy. The first job would be to organize them into functioning units, and to do that, he asked those who had been officers and noncommissioned officers to report to him.

"For now, I'm putting you men on your honor," he said. "Don't be giving yourselves spot promotions. I need leaders, but more than that, I need honesty. If you represent yourself as something you aren't, we will find out about it, and once we find out, you'll no longer be of any use to us."

"I was an NCO" one of the men said. "But I was only a buck sergeant, I don't know if that's high enough for you.

"For now, I would say that we could use the experiences of anyone who served as an NCO, E-5 and above," Jake said.

The man smiled. "Then you've got me."

His call for officers and noncommissioned officers produced a cadre of some thirty men, ranging in rank from full colonel down to buck sergeant.

"Damn," Jake said quietly. "I'm just a major, two or three of these guys have me outranked."

"No they don't," Bob said. "I was a chief warrant officer, now I am the commander-in-chief, and that gives me the authority to appoint you, general."

Jake laughed. "General Lantz. Yeah," he said. "I like the sound of that."

"Gentlemen," Bob said, speaking to the assembled officers. "I am President Bob Varney. This is General Jake Lantz. I'm going to turn this over to him."

"Hell, Major, you've come up in rank quite a bit since I saw you last," Ed Tadlock said. "Look at you, you're a general now."

"Ed!" Jake said, starting toward him with his hand extended. The two men shook hands. "Bob, I want you to meet another chief warrant officer. This is Ed Tadlock. We were together at Mother Rucker when everything collapsed."

"I've been wanting to meet you," Tadlock said. "You wrote *Barracks Ballads*, didn't you? About warrant officer pilots in Vietnam?"

"Yes."

Tadlock laughed. "That's the funniest damn book I've ever read in my life. I was in Walter Reed where they were trying to get shrapnel out of my ass when someone gave me that book. I knew it had to be a warrant who wrote it."

"I don't know that book," Jake said.

"Trust me, Jake, you wouldn't like it. It tells the truth about how every commissioned officer needed a warrant to wipe his nose."

"Well, that's better than having a warrant wipe my ass," Bob said, and the others laughed.

"But, you've just been given a spot promotion, Ed. As of now, you are a lieutenant colonel."

"What the hell makes you think that's a promotion?"

"You're just going to have to live with it," Jake said, laughing. "I need all the help I can get."

After the initial organization, Jake asked Tadlock to have dinner with him at a restaurant that was near the TV station. He remembered the last time he had seen Tadlock, it was just after General Von Cairns had committed suicide.

Chief Warrant Officer-3 Edward Tadlock was waiting just outside the door to the Post Headquarters building when Jake and Clay arrived in Jake's Jeep SUV.

"I waited out here," Tadlock said. "I don't mind telling you, it's creepy as hell in there."

"How do you know it was a suicide?" Jake asked. "Did he leave a note?"

"No, there was no note. But the pistol is still in his hand."

"Let's have a look."

The three men went back inside the building which, as Tadlock had said, was completely deserted.

"I'm taking off," Tadlock said. "I'm going to Missouri. I own a small farm there, I'm going back to work it. My wife and kids are already there, waiting for me."

"Do you have enough fuel to make it all the way to Missouri?"

"I'm driving a diesel, and running it on jet fuel. I bought thirty gallons extra from someone that I didn't ask any questions as to where he got it."

"Well, good luck to you, Chief," Jake said.

When they stepped into the general's office, he was

still sitting in his swivel chair, facing the window that looked out over the parade ground.

"I left him just the way I found him," Tadlock said.

Jake walked around to get a closer look at him. He shook his head. "Damn," he said. "He was a good man. I hate to see this."

"Ohmshidi killed him," Tadlock said. "Yeah, von Cairns may have pulled the trigger, but Ohmshidi killed him."

"I can't argue with that," Jake said.

"So now the question is, what do we do with him?"

"Does he have any next of kin?" Clay asked.

"He's divorced, I know that," Tadlock said.

"He has a daughter somewhere," Jake said. "If we looked through all his things, we could probably find out where she is. But then what? The way things are now, what could she do with him?"

"We can't leave him here," Tadlock said.

"Let's bury him out there on the parade ground, under the flagpole," Clay suggested.

"Damn good idea, Sergeant Major, damn good idea," Tadlock said.[2]

"What happened to you?" Jake asked as the two men sat down to a meal of barbecue pork steak. "I thought you were farming in Missouri."

---

2. *Phoenix Rising*

"Yeah, I was. But there were too damn many of Ohmshidi's officials around then, telling me that I could do this, and I couldn't do that. So I just decided to leave. When I heard that Mobile had been freed, my wife, kid and I came down here. We've only been here a few days."

"Well, I'm damn glad to have you here. I want you and your wife to come on out to Fort Morgan. After all, you're on my payroll now."

"Payroll? Wait a minute, you mean I'm going to get paid for being in your army?"

"Yes, with Freedom Dollars. And don't worry about them, they are real currency."

"Sounds good enough to me," Tadlock said. "Oh, what about my eighteen years? Does that count? Can I retire in two more years?"

"Ha. You can if you want to, and you'll get the same retirement pay Bob gets."

"Why do I have the feeling that's nothing?"

"I don't know. Maybe because it is nothing," Jake answered with a laugh.

"Do you ever think about the army? I mean the way it was in the before time."

"I think about it all the time," Jake said.

"I do too. I think about the general, and how Ohmshidi same as killed him. And I think about the way we buried him."

"Yeah, I remember that as well."

* * *

Clay went to the general's quarters to get his dress blue uniform and he and Jake dressed the general, to include all his medals. While they were doing that, Tadlock rounded up as many officers and men as he could, including seven men who would form a firing squadron to render last honors, and one bandsman who agreed to play taps.

Now the general lay in a main-rotor shipping case alongside a grave that three of the EM had dug. There were over fifty men and women present, in uniform, and in formation. The general was lowered into the grave, and Jake nodded at the firing team. The seven soldiers raised their rifles to their shoulders.

"Ready? Fire!"

The sound of the first volley echoed back from the buildings adjacent the parade ground.

"Ready? Fire!"

Rifle fire, which, during his life, the general had heard in anger, now sounded in his honor.

"Ready? Fire!"

The last volley was fired, and those who were rendering hand salutes, brought them down sharply.

The bandsman, a bespectacled specialist, raised a trumpet to his lips and with the first and third valves depressed, played Taps.

Jake thought of the many times he had heard this haunting bugle call, at night in the barracks while in basic training, and in OCS. He had also heard it played for too many of his friends, killed in combat or in aircraft accidents.

The young soldier played the call slowly and stately, holding the higher notes, gradually getting louder, then slowing the tempo as he reached the end; and holding the final, middle C longer than any other note before, he allowed it simply and sadly to . . . fade away.[3]

---

3. *Phoenix Rising*

CHAPTER TWENTY-EIGHT

Lancaster

"*Ja?* What do you want?" Solomon Lantz asked, when he answered the door. There were two men standing there, both wearing black uniforms. Behind the two men were two vehicles, a truck and a van.

"You are Solomon Lantz?"

"I am."

"We are told that you have a relative living with you. An uncle by the name of Jacob Yoder."

"*Onkel Jakob ist nicht hier,*" Solomon said.

"Where is he?"

"He has gone back to Illinois."

"You are lying, Lantz. Now, aren't you ashamed of yourself? I thought Amish never lied."

"What do you want with him?"

"Oh, so now you are changing your story. You

are telling us that he is here, you just want to know what we want with him. Is that it?"

"I have not said that he is here."

"Then, you won't mind if we have a look around your place. Actually, it doesn't matter whether you mind or not. We are going to have a look around."

The speaker turned toward the truck, and ten men jumped down, all of them carrying submachine guns.

"Gregoire?" the officer who had been doing all the talking said. "Gregoire, if you are here, you had better come out. Otherwise we are going to kill this man and everyone in the house. Then we'll find you."

There was no answer.

"I hope you are here, Gregoire," the Janissary officer shouted. "Because I'm going to count to ten, and when I get to ten, I'm going to start killing. The only way you can stop it is by coming out. If you aren't here, and this is all just a terrible mistake, I'm still going to start killing when I reach ten."

Again, there was nothing but silence.

"One . . . two . . ."

The counting continued until the officer reached seven.

"No, wait!" a voice called from within the barn. "We're coming out!"

Gregoire, now without the makeup that made

him appear to be an old man, came out of the barn with his hands raised. Two others were with him, a man and a woman.

"Who are these two people?" the commandant of the Janissary team asked.

"Mark Riley and Jennie Lea," Gregoire replied. "My producer and my makeup woman."

The commandant nodded his head, and the other Janissaries began shooting. Both Mark Riley and Jennie Lea went down.

"No!" Gregoire shouted. "No, God in Heaven, why did you shoot them?"

"We had no orders to bring them in alive," the commandant said. "To do so would just be an added burden."

"You are mad!" Gregoire said. "You are stark, raving, mad!"

"Come with us now," the commandant said. "Or we will kill more."

"No, no, I'll go with you," Gregoire said. "Please, I beg of you, don't shoot anyone else!"

Solomon Lantz watched as the men in uniform put Gregoire in the van. The others climbed back into the van and the truck, then the two vehicles sped off, raising a billowing cloud of dust as they left.

The man and woman who had been killed, Mark Riley and Jennie Lea, lay dead in the dirt between the barn and the house. Solomon would see to it that they were given a decent burial.

Cartersville, Georgia

Chris Carmack and Kathy York drove into town in a dark green 2011 Camry. Four miles south of town, at the junction of routes 61 and 113, they had hidden a silver 2007 Chrysler Town and Country minivan.

Now, on Main Street, they drove by the Bank of Submission, which, in the "before time" had been known as Regions Bank. They drove around the block, stopped, and switched drivers, so that now Kathy was driving.

"Park in the lot, and keep the right door open," Chris said. He kissed Kathy, but the kiss stretched out a little longer than a quick buss.

"On the other hand," he said. "We could move over there in the far corner and, uh, fool around a bit."

"I'm supposed to be a man, remember? What if someone sees us?"

"Yeah, I guess you're right.

"On the other hand, if you want to take this up later," she said with a little chuckle.

"That's a promise?"

"That's a promise."

As Chris got out of the car to walk into the bank, Kathy slid down in the car so that anyone who just happened to glance in wouldn't have a close enough look to see through her disguise.

There were two customers in the bank, and Chris went over to the table and began filling out a check. He waited until both customers were gone, then he stepped up to the teller's window.

"I have a check here for several dollars, and I wonder if you could cash it," he asked.

"Sir, we no longer deal in dollars."

"Oh, yeah, what is it called now? Moqaddas? What a dumb-assed name for money. But money is money. I'll take it in Moqaddas."

"How many Moqaddas?"

"I don't know. How many Moqaddas do you have?"

"What? Why would you ask such a thing?"

Chris pulled his pistol and pointed it at the teller. "Because I intend to take everything you have. I'm not greedy, just whatever you have in that drawer will be enough for me."

The teller opened his drawer and started emptying it.

"Do you have a little bag, or a pouch of some sort?" Chris asked.

"I have a leather deposit pouch."

"Yes, that would be very nice," Chris said. "Thank you."

The teller put the money in the pouch, then handed it across to Chris.

"Thank you very much. It's been quite a pleasure doing business with you today," Chris said. He turned to leave, but halfway to the door, a bell rang.

"Robbery! The bank is being robbed!" the teller said.

Chris ran to the door, but when he tried to open it, he discovered that it had been locked by remote.

"Drop the money!" someone shouted, and looking toward the sound of the voice, he saw the bank security guard. The security guard was pointing a gun at Chris.

Chris knew that, even though the security guard was pointing the gun at him, he still had the advantage. From his years as a contract shooter for the FBI and CIA, he know the concept of reaction. If the guard did not shoot until he saw Chris making his move, it would be too late, because three-fourths of the time required to make a fast shot is in thinking about it.

Chris shot and the security guard reacted in shock when he was hit in the chest by the bullet from Chris's revolver. The security guard dropped his pistol and slapped his hand over the wound in his chest. Chris picked up a chair from behind an empty desk and used it to smash out the window in the front door. Then, he stepped through the opening the broken window provided, and sprinted quickly to the car. Kathy sped off as soon as Chris was in the car, even before he got the door closed.

Fifteen minutes later, they drove back into town, this time in the silver minivan, and stopped in front of a restaurant. Now, Kathy was wearing a burqa. They could hear sirens, and they saw several people standing out in front of the restaurant.

"What happened?" Chris asked, as he and Kathy stepped out of the car. "What's all the excitement about?"

"I'm not sure," someone wearing a waiter's garb said. "Somebody said the bank was just robbed."

"You don't say. You haven't closed the restaurant, have you? I mean, we can still get dinner?"

"Yes, come in. I'll seat you."

"Very nice of you," Chris said.

Chris and Kathy sat at a table in a restaurant that was less than three blocks from the bank they had robbed. Through the window they could see the police cars going to and fro, always importantly, always with the lights flashing and the siren going.

"As my grandmother would say, the police are running around like chickens with their heads cut off."

"Oh," Kathy said. "Given the way things are now, saying something has its head cut off isn't a good analogy."

Chris chuckled. "You've got a point."

After dinner, Chris and Kathy checked into a motel.

"Do you have proof of marriage?" the motel clerk said.

"Yes. Why, do you think we would live in sin?"

Chris asked. He showed the motel clerk a marriage license he had bought, identifying them as Mr. and Mrs. Dan Morton.

"Very good, Mr. Morton, your room is 128, at the far end."

Chris took the key, and fifteen minutes later, he and Kathy were in bed, watching the nightly news.

"All praise be to Allah, the merciful. Whomsoever Allah guides there is none to misguide, and whomsoever Allah misguides there is none to guide. You must live your life in accordance with the Moqaddas Sirata, the Holy Path. Those who do will be blessed. Those who do not will be damned.

"There was a bank robbery in Carterville this afternoon. Witnesses say that the bank robber got into a green Camry. It is believed that these are the same two men who have robbed five other banks in the last six weeks. One of the men is described as medium height, with dark hair and a dark beard. There is no description of the driver, who has never been seen outside the car.

"The amount of money taken was forty thousand Moqaddas."

"What?" Chris shouted to the TV. Why, those lying bastards! There was less than ten thousand in that drawer."

"Ha," Kathy said. "It would appear that we weren't the only ones to rob the bank today."

"Apparently we weren't," Chris said. "And the hell of it is, the teller, and whoever else was involved, got away with more than we did."

Muslimabad

Gregoire was brought in to the Oval Office, where he stood, his hands cuffed behind his back, in front of the Resolute Desk. Janissaries, in their black and silver uniforms, stood to either side of him. Ohmshidi was sitting with his feet propped up on the desk.

"Gregoire, as far as I know, you may be the only person ever brought into this office wearing handcuffs."

"That may be so," Gregoire replied. "But you are the first traitor ever to occupy this office."

The Janissary to Gregoire's right gave him a sharp jab in the side, and Gregoire's knees buckled from the pain.

"I've invited you here so we could talk," Ohmshidi said.

"I wouldn't exactly call this an invitation."

The guard started to hit him again, but Ohmshidi stopped him with a lift of a hand. Ohmshidi chuckled.

"You're right. It wasn't exactly an invitation," Ohmshidi said. "But you are here, nevertheless, so we may as well have a conversation."

"All right."

"Why have you been so opposed to me?" Ohmshidi said. "From the very beginning, from the first day I was elected, you have been a thorn in my side. Why?"

"Because from the time you started your campaign, with your promise to be a transformative president who would fundamentally change America, I considered you to be the greatest threat to our republic since the civil war," Gregoire said. "But I was wrong."

Ohmshidi smiled. "Ahh, so now that you are my prisoner, you are willing to admit that you were wrong?"

"Yes," Gregoire said. "It turns out you were an even greater threat. We survived the Civil War. We didn't survive you."

"You say you didn't survive, I say you evolved. The government I have put in place is the most efficient government ever on this continent. In less than one year we have come from a nation that was on its knees, to a vibrant, new nation, no longer the enemy of the world. My government has brought peace to this nation . . . peace through *Moqaddas Sirata* . . . the Holy Path."

"If this nation was on its knees, it is because you took it to its knees," Gregoire said. He shook his head. "The mystery to me is how the hell you ever got anyone to vote for you in the first place. You had absolutely no experience of any kind. You had never earned so much as one penny in the private sector. You held two elective positions, one as a state senator who cast no vote in two years, except present. Then you had another very unremarkable two years as a U.S. senator. Just how did you get elected?"

"I was elected, because the people of America were ready for a change," Ohmshidi said. "They had stood by helplessly to watch as America waged war on Islam. They had watched the American Jews take over the financial industry, the media, the entertainment industry."

"The media? The mainstream media, and their shameless fawning over you, is what got you elected, and now you are attacking them?"

Ohmshidi smiled. "Well, there, you see, you wondered how I got elected. It just came from your own mouth. The media elected me. That is, all the media except that extreme right wing cable news service that billed itself as, what was it? Fair and Objective? Well, you see what happened to them. The people overwhelmingly supported my Fairness Doctrine, which got them, and you, knocked off the air."

"How do you know the people supported it? Neither they, nor their elected representatives, ever got the opportunity to vote on it. It was one of your executive orders."

"Yes, but in your case, it didn't work, did it? Somehow, you managed to get back onto TV, to do your damage. Well, you will do no more damage. I am going to make an example of you, Mr. Gregoire. I am going to hold your trial on national television, then, after you are found guilty, you will be publicly executed."

"Have you ever heard of Nathan Hale?" Gregoire asked.

"No, who is he? Is he another right wing bigot?"

Gregoire smiled. "I didn't think you would have heard of him."

CHAPTER TWENTY-NINE

Jewish Ultimate Resolution Camp 26

While chopping cotton, Sam managed to break off a piece of the hoe handle, about as long as a policeman's nightstick. He was able to get it back into the barracks without its being discovered. At a little after one a.m. the next morning, he got up and sneaked out of the barracks.

Sam had killed when he was in Afghanistan, so the concept of killing, if it was an enemy soldier, was not foreign to him. His plan called for him to kill one of the roving guards, and that's what he intended to do, unless the guard killed him.

Sam stayed in the shadow of the barracks, waiting for the guard to come by. The first time he came by, he was too far away. If Sam committed himself, he would be seen before he could get close enough to the guard. The guard's second pass was the same as the first—he was still too far away.

Sam knew that he was going to have to do something to attract the guard over to him, so on the third pass, he began raking the billy club against the side of the barracks building. The guard heard it, stopped, and looked over toward the building.

Sam had already checked out the visual, and he knew that under the current conditions, he couldn't be seen by the guard. He raked the club across the side of the building again, and this time, as Sam hoped he would, the guard came over to investigate. Sam waited until the guard was practically on top of him, then he brought the club down, hard, over the guard's head.

The guard went down and Sam knelt beside him, hitting him again and again until he was sure he was dead. After that, he stripped the guard and donned the black uniform, dressing the guard's body in his own clothes.

Now, dressed in the black uniform of the Janissary, Sam picked up the guard's rifle and began walking guard. He knew, from observation, that this relief would be over at two o'clock, which was less than an hour from now. He knew, also, that the gate would be open about five minutes before two, to allow the new relief in. It was Sam's plan to measure his circuit so that he would be even with the gate when it opened.

Steadily, and with a measured gait, Sam continued "walking guard" to complete the duty of the man he had just killed. He was at one corner on the side of the compound where the main gate was, when it was opened and the new relief came inside. As he knew they would, they gathered in formation for a moment before they were released to relieve the guard.

Sam slowed his gait until the new relief began to scatter through the compound. He walked through the open gate holding a handkerchief over his nose and mouth, sneezing as he did so.

"If you're catching the flu, don't be coming around me," the man in the gate house said.

Without lowering the handkerchief from his face, Sam lifted the other hand and waved. He walked straight to the parking lot, then hit the remote key he had found in the guard's pocket, until he found the car. He wasn't challenged as he drove away.

The first part of his plan, escape from Camp 26, was relatively easy. But he had had several days to come up with the plan, and, more importantly, to scope out the compound.

Now, though, he was going after Sarah. He had not seen the compound where she was being kept, and didn't know which barracks she would be in. Then, as he thought about it more, an idea came to him, and he smiled. It would either work perfectly, or it would get him killed. And if it didn't work, then he would just as soon be killed.

He drove at nearly ninety miles per hour,

reaching Sanderson no more than fifteen minutes after he left Camp 26. It helped that he knew Sanderson, and Carlisle Road, so he knew where Sarah would be.

Women's Jewish Ultimate Resolution Camp 49

Sam drove right up to the gate house, got out of the car, then sprinted to the door. Jerking it open he saw someone sleeping at the desk.

"Wake up!" he demanded.

The man awoke.

"What is your name?" Sam asked.

"Lewis."

"Lewis, I have urgent orders from *Sarhag* Kareem Ali."

"What are the orders?" the sleepy guard asked.

The first part of Sam's plan had succeeded. He had not been recognized and challenged immediately.

"The Jew Gelbman has escaped. We believe he will be coming here to try and get his wife. *Sarhag* Ali wants me to take her back to Camp 26. Bring her to me at once."

"What is his wife's name?"

"Jewess Gelbman."

Lewis tapped the name into a computer. "We have two Gelbmans here. Samantha and Sarah."

"Sarah," Sam said. "Bring her to me, and be quick. Even now, the Jew Gelbman might be here."

"She's in barracks number three, fourth bed

on the left," Lewis said. "All the guards have cell phones, I'll call." He picked up the phone and punched in a number. "Simmons, are you near barracks number two? Good, get the Jewess Gelbman, fourth bunk on the left, and bring her to the gate. Don't ask questions, just do it."

Sam stepped over to a window and looked out. The next big challenge would be what would happen when they brought Sarah in. If she gave a sense of recognition, it could spoil everything.

He decided he would stay at the window with his back to her, when they brought her in, hoping she wouldn't recognize him right away.

Although he only waited, according to the clock on the wall, seven minutes, each minute seemed an hour long. He was afraid that at any moment, the phone would ring, and it would be the authorities from Camp 26.

"What is this? Why have you brought me here?" Sarah asked as she was brought into the gate house. The sound of Sarah's voice was so wonderful that Sam had to fight to keep from calling out to her.

"Shut up, you Jew bitch!" Sam said, making his voice as hostile as possible. "I'll ask the questions."

He turned then to look at Sarah, praying that she did nothing to give him away.

"Lewis, do you have something for me to sign before I take the Jewess with me?"

"No!" Sarah said. "No, I want to go back to the barracks. Please, don't make me go with him."

She had caught on right away! Sam knew that she would.

"Shut up," Lewis said. "You have no say in this." Lewis typed a receipt into the computer, printed it out, and slid it across the desk to Sam.

Received into my Custody, by order of Sarhag Kareem Ali, the Jewess Sarah Gelbman.

Sam signed the name Otto Spear on the blank line, because he knew it to be the name of one of the Janissary guards back at Camp 26.

"Come on, Jew bitch," he said gruffly, grabbing Sarah by the arm.

"Ow! You're hurting me!" Sarah said. She turned back to Lewis. "Please, let me go back to the barracks."

Lewis laughed. "That's what I like, for our women to look at this as their home."

"Come on, you're wasting my time," Sam said, leading her out to the car. Opening the door he shoved her into the seat roughly, then he hurried around to the driver's side, and drove away. Not until they were at least a quarter of a mile down Carlisle Road from the camp did Sarah speak.

"Sam, God in Heaven, how did you do this?"

"It was easy. I just decided to wake myself up from the nightmare I was having."

"Oh, Sam, I love you so! I, I . . ." tears began streaming down Sarah's cheeks. "I didn't know if I would ever even see you again."

"We're not out of the woods yet. I'm sure that by now they've discovered the body of the guard I killed. And this is his car."

"Oh, you had to . . ."

"Kill someone? Yes, Sarah, I had to kill someone. But I look at it as no different from what I had to do when I was in Afghanistan."

"I'm not condemning you, my darling," Sarah said, putting both hands around his arm.

"Sarah!" Sam said. "Look!" They were passing a warehouse, and Sam pointed to an eighteen-wheeler that was sitting in the dark parking lot. "I recognize that truck! It's one of the ones we used to own in the before time!"

Driving into the warehouse yard, he parked the car, got out, and made a close examination of the big, Peterbuilt diesel truck. Even though the door had been painted over, he could see under the paint the shadow of the old markings:

MID-AMERICA TRUCKING
Dallas, TX
BL 80,000LBS

"I wonder if . . ." he said, then he reached under the left vertical stack, felt around a bit, and smiled. He pulled a little case out, opened the lid, and produced the key. "Yes!" he said, excitedly.

"Sam, what if there's someone sleeping in the back?"

"Yeah, maybe I'd better check."

Sam pulled the pistol that had come with the black uniform he was wearing.

"Sam, whoever it is, don't kill him."

"I won't," Sam promised. "If there's anyone there I'll just order him out. When he sees this uniform I don't think he'll give me any trouble."

Sam opened the door, pulling it open as quietly as he could. A light came on, on the floor, but not overhead. He stepped up onto the step, put his knee on the seat, and looked into the sleeper cab. It was too dark in the back for him to be able to tell if anyone was there or not.

Sam knew this truck well, and he knew where the toggle switch was that would turn on the light in the sleeper cab. He flipped it on, and the cab was flooded with light.

It was empty.

"Sarah, it's empty," Sam called down. "Get in, quick!"

Sam thought about dropping the trailer, but decided that once the word got out, a tractor without the trailer would stand out among the highway traffic more than a tractor-trailer combination. So, leaving it attached, he drove off.

* * *

They reached Del Rio, Texas, just before six in the morning. Turning right on Gibbs, he headed straight for the Mexican border, crossing into Mexico at Ciudad Acuña. The "open border" problem had been eliminated when the United States collapsed. The U.S. was no longer a destination for "illegal immigrants." Instead, the opposite phenomenon developed, with Americans fleeing to Mexico.

Sam's trucks had often crossed into Mexico to deliver or pick up cargo, and all that was required was a twenty-four hour commercial pass at the point of entry.

"You'd better take off that shirt before you get to the border check," Sarah cautioned.

"Yeah, good idea."

When he reached the checkpoint, a border guard, with a cigarette hanging from his lips, came out to the truck.

"*Necesito una visa commercial, por favor*," Sam said.

"*Diez Moqaddas*," the border guard said.

Fortunately, the guard whose uniform Sam had taken had been carrying a billfold with almost two hundred Moqaddas, so Sam had no problem paying ten for the commercial visa.

Two hours later Sam and Sarah were in a 2008 Toyota, having traded the truck for it to someone who didn't need the title to close the deal. When Sam crossed into the U.S. at Laredo, he was, again, wearing the black uniform of the Janissary.

The border guard approached the car, but seeing the uniform, stopped, and gave the closed fist over his heart salute.

"Obey Ohmshidi!" he said.

Sam returned the salute.

"You may go ahead, sir," the border guard said. Sam nodded, then drove on through.

"Sam, where are we going?" Sarah asked.

"Shortly after Ohmshidi was elected, I got a letter from Jake Lantz, an officer I met in Afghanistan. He was a helicopter pilot who carried me from place to place a few times. He said that if everything went south under Ohmshidi, he was going to hole up in a place called Fort Morgan, down on the Alabama coast. He invited me down, I should have taken him up on it."

"Do you really think he is there?"

"I don't know," Sam admitted. "But right now we don't have a lot of options left, do we?"

"I guess not."

CHAPTER THIRTY

Alexandria

The motel room was redolent with the hint of pheromones, and Chris and Kathy lay naked together in bed, just coasting down from having had sex. Chris's left arm was under Kathy, who was on her back beside him, and his hand cupped her breast, gently kneading the nipple.

"Now, if you don't watch out, you'll get me ready to go again, and you won't be ready," Kathy warned.

"Ha! Who says I won't be ready? Just not at this precise moment."

Kathy laughed, then, after a moment of silence she asked, "Chris, do you ever think of us as Bonnie and Clyde?"

"Bonnie and Clyde? What gave you that idea?"

"Oh, I just remember watching that movie a long time ago. And we're sort of like them, a man and woman, living together but not married, robbing banks."

"Did Bonnie dress like a man when they robbed the banks?"

"No, I don't think so."

"I saw that same movie, and seems to me like Clyde was impotent. Do you think I'm impotent?"

Again Kathy laughed. "Lord no," she said.

"Well, then, we aren't like Bonnie and Clyde. And we damn sure aren't going to wind up like them, shot down like dogs."

"That's reassuring," Kathy said, snuggling closer to him.

Clyde picked up the remote. "It's time for the news," he said. "Or at least, it's time for what passes for news." He pointed the remote toward the TV then clicked it.

The opening spiel had already started.

"*. . . guides there is none to misguide, and whomsoever Allah misguides there is none to guide. You must live your life in accordance with the* Moqaddas Sirata, *the Holy Path. Those who do will be blessed. Those who do not will be damned.*"

The newscaster appeared then, sitting in front of the Ohmshidi portrait. "*Obey Ohmshidi,*" he began.

The picture on the screen changed to that of the very recognizable George Gregoire.

"This is the traitor, George Gregoire. Great Leader, President for Life Ohmshidi, Allah's blessings be upon him, has tried Gregoire and found him guilty of treason. Tomorrow at one o'clock, there will be a public beheading of this traitor at the National Mall. The event will be televised for all to see."

"Damn!" Chris said, sitting up in bed.

"Do they really think anyone would want to watch someone get his head chopped off? Nobody is going to watch that," Kathy said.

Chris reached for the phone. "That's right, nobody is going to watch it, because it isn't going to happen." He punched in some numbers. "Gates? This is Carmack. Yeah, yeah, I know, I've sort of dropped out for a while. Look, could you meet me for dinner tonight, my treat? There's a kabob place over on Pennsylvania Street . . . yes, that's the one. Meet me there."

"Are we going out for dinner tonight?" Kathy asked after Chris hung up the phone.

"No, I don't want you seen. If this goes bad, I don't want you involved."

"What are you going to do, Chris?"

"Whatever has to be done," Chris replied.

Chris met Bryan Gates at Mehran Kabob Restaurant on Pennsylvania Avenue, within sight of the White House. The two shook hands, then found a table in the back of the room that was separated some distance from any other customer in the restaurant. Gates had been someone that Chris worked with in the CIA, and though Gates never knew about Chris's "contract killing" job, he did know that Chris had been involved in several very classified operations.

"What are you doing these days, Bryan?" Chris asked.

"Whatever I have to do to turn a buck. Or, I guess I should say, a Moqadda."

"Do you still have inside sources of information?"

Bryan broke eye contact, and shrugged, but didn't answer.

"And if you had that information, would you sell it?"

"Chris, are you wired? Are you still working for the government?"

"I swear to you that I am not," Chris said.

Bryan smiled, though the smile was strained. "You were trained to lie," he said. "I never did know exactly what you did for the company, but I did know that it was top secret. How do I know you haven't just taken your talent over to the SPS, or worse, to the Janissaries?"

"I was a contract killer," Chris said.

Bryan nodded. "Yeah, I thought it might be something like that."

"I'll give you another piece of news about me,

that if it got out, would have my head on the chopping block, literally. You will be the only one who knows this, and the only reason I'll tell you, is to show you that I represent no danger to you."

"What would that be?" Bryan asked.

"I've already given you some information, I told you I was a contract killer. Now, I'm going to ask you for some information. If you can supply it, I will give you five thousand Moqaddas, then I'll give you the incriminating information I spoke of."

"Five thousand Moqaddas?"

"I have the money with me."

"Where did you come up with money like that?"

"First, you answer a few of my questions, if you can."

"All right, ask. I'll see what I can do."

"Where are they keeping George Gregoire? In which jail?"

Bryan shook his head. "They aren't keeping him in any jail. He is being kept on the top floor in Grant Hall at Fort McNair."

"Grant Hall? Wait a minute, isn't that the old Federal Arsenal Penitentiary where the Lincoln Conspirators were tried?"

"You've got it. And it's not by mere coincidence that he is being kept there. According to Rahimi, Gregoire is the biggest traitor since the Lincoln conspirators, so he ordered that Gregoire be kept there."

"According to whom?"

"You mean you haven't heard of Mohammad Akbar Rahimi?"

"No."

Bryan chuckled. "You probably know him as Warren Church."

"Warren Church? Wait a minute! Do you mean that blowhard asshole college professor who was spouting off about how righteous those bastards were who murdered all those people on 9/11? And how they should be given medals?"

"That's the one I'm talking about."

"What the hell does he have to do with deciding where Gregoire is kept?"

"Ha! You really are out of it, aren't you? You probably think, like the rest of the country, that Mehdi Ohmshidi is in charge."

"Are you telling me that he isn't?"

"That's exactly what I'm telling you, my friend. The real person in charge is Warren Church, otherwise known as Mohammad Akbar Rahimi."

"How is it that he's in charge? I mean, what is his position?"

"Technically, he's the minister of culture. But that's much more powerful than it sounds, because he is the one who has the ear in all the Islamic capitals. He is their representative for the great caliphate they are trying to put together."

"An American is doing all that? He wasn't born Muslim, was he?"

"I don't know what he was born, but it certainly wasn't Muslim."

"Just out of curiosity, where does that son of a bitch stay?"

"He has an office in what used to be the Harry S. Truman Federal Building. But he is living at Fort McNair in the old house once occupied by the vice chief of staff of the U.S. Army."

"Whoa, so Gregoire is being kept in Grant Hall, and Church lives there?"

"Yes. Tell me, Chris, what do you want with this information?"

Chris shook his head. "Believe me, you don't want to know," he said. He smiled. "But the information is worth five thousand Moqaddas."

Chris took five packets from the small leather pouch he was carrying, each packet containing fifty bills in the denomination of twenty Moqaddas. He slid them across the table to Bryan, and Bryan glanced around the dining room quickly, then he picked the packets up and started putting them in his pockets.

"Enjoy your dinner," Chris said, getting up before they had even ordered. He had not shared with Bryan the self-incriminating information that he was the bank robber everyone was looking for, and Bryan was so involved with the money that he didn't ask.

* * *

It was just after midnight when Chris drove up to the Fort McNair gate. He stopped just before he went through the gate, then unfolded a map, and was sitting behind the steering wheel when the black-uniformed Janissary who was manning the gate walked back to him.

"What are you doing here? You can't come in here," the gate guard said, gruffly.

"I think I'm lost," Chris said. "I'm looking for this place."

"I don't care what you're looking for. Turn that car around now and leave."

The guard leaned over so that his head was even with the car window. When he did, Chris shot him between the eyes, using the same pistol, a Glock 19, with a suppressor, that he had used when he shot Shurayh Amaar. Again, the shot sounded no louder than a trigger being pulled on an empty chamber.

Very quickly, Chris dragged the body into the gatehouse, wiped away the blood, then put the body in the chair, positioning him so that to the casual glance, he appeared to be asleep.

Returning to the car, Chris drove next to the old, sprawling, brick house that was, at one time, the home of the vice chief of staff for the U.S. Army. Chris knew the house, because in the "before time," he once attended a cocktail party here.

Parking under the shadow of some trees, he left the car and walked across the grass, up to the house. He looked back and was pleased to see that, with the shadows, the car wasn't immediately noticeable. Moving up to a window on the side porch, he checked for an alarm system, finding one that depended upon a continuous flow of electricity, that would be broken when the window was raised.

"Damn, Church, you being such an important man and all, I was sure you'd have a more sophisticated system than this," Chris said, quietly.

Taking a copper wire from his pocket, he bypassed the alarm so that, even when the window was raised, the current flow would remain unbroken. Then, putting on night vision goggles, he slipped through the window, entering the house through the dining room. Because of the NVG he was able to see well enough to move through the house easily.

Two minutes after he entered the house, he was in a bedroom, standing over Church's bed. As he had done with Husni Mawsil, he gave Church/Rahimi an injection of Batrachotoxin. Then he put his hand over Church's mouth, so that when he opened his eyes, he couldn't call out.

"I'll only have to hold my hand here for a

couple of seconds," Chris said quietly, "because the first thing you'll lose is your ability to speak."

Chris took his hand away. "Go ahead, try to speak now."

All Rahimi could do was make a few grunting sounds.

"I thought so," Chris said. "Next, you'll lose the ability to breathe."

Even as Chris was speaking, Rahimi put his hands to his neck, his eyes open wide in terror.

"Yeah, dyin' is fun when you're doing it to helpless people, but not so much when it happens to you, is it?"

Rahimi gasped a few more times, then was quiet, his face contorted in death.

Chris left by the same window he had entered, then went directly to Grant Hall, which stood right in the middle of the parade ground. The front doors were locked, but Chris picked the lock easily.

The Janissary at the desk was looking at a men's magazine from the "before time" and was fondling himself as he was studying the picture of a beautiful, nude woman. Because it was so late at night, and the front doors were locked, he didn't expect anyone to come in. And because he was so lost in the nude pictures, he wasn't paying any attention. As a result, Chris was standing in front of his desk before the man even noticed him.

"What are you . . ."

That was as far as the Janissary got before

Chris shot him. He fell forward onto the desk, and Chris continued through the building.

Chris went up two flights of stairs to the third floor. This floor had been turned into a prison, like the one that once held the Lincoln conspirators. There was one Janissary sitting at a desk, reading, and there were two occupied bunks.

Chris walked right up to the man reading, shot him, then shot the two sleeping guards.

Gregoire, who had been awakened, stepped up to the bars and looked out with curiosity.

"Who are you?" Gregoire asked.

"Let's just say I'm a fan of yours, Mr. Gregoire, and I don't want to see you get your head chopped off tomorrow." Chris took the keys from the desk. "Oh, and don't let the fact that I'm dressed like a Muslim fool you. I just wear this shit to get by."

"I don't know if there are any more guards in the building or not," Gregoire said.

"I think I've killed them all," Chris said dispassionately as he unlocked the cell door.

"How . . . how many have you killed?" Gregoire asked.

"You mean today?"

Gregoire shook his head. "Never mind," he said. "I have a feeling this is something I don't need to know."

"Come on."

Chris led Gregoire downstairs, then out to the car.

"What about the man at the gate?" Gregoire asked.

Chris glanced at his watch. "If I'm guessing right, it'll be another half hour before the relief is scheduled, so if we're lucky, they haven't discovered him yet."

As they drove through the gate, Chris looked into the gate box. "Yeah, see, he's still asleep."

"You mean he's been asleep all this time."

"He'll be sleeping for a very long time."

"Oh." Gregoire didn't have to say anything else, he had a pretty good idea of what Chris meant. "Where are we going?"

"To tell the truth, I don't have an idea in hell. My only thought was to get you out of here."

"I have a suggestion if you're up to it."

"Sure, let me go pick up a friend first."

Half an hour later, Chris parked in front of the motel room he and Kathy had rented in Alexandria.

"Wait here for a second while my friend gets dressed," he said.

Gregoire stood in the shadows against the front of the building while Chris opened the door, then stuck his head in.

"Kathy, I need you to get decent," he said. "We have company."

"Company?" Kathy's sleepy voice replied from the darkness.

"Yeah, get dressed, we're going to take a trip."

"I'll dress in the bathroom," Kathy said. "Am I a man or a woman?"

Chris laughed. "You're a woman, darlin', all woman. And no burqa."

Kathy grabbed a suitcase and disappeared into the bathroom. Chris stuck his head back outside. "Okay, come on in."

Chris turned the light on, and invited Greg to have a seat. "Want a drink?" he asked.

"A drink?"

Chris pulled a bottle of whiskey from a bag. "Just because the Muzzies say we can't drink doesn't mean you can't still get it," he said.

"You know what, I think I would love a drink," Gregoire said, and Chris poured a little into one of the glasses that sat on the desk. Kathy came out of the bathroom then, wearing a western-style dress.

"Oh, my God!" she gasped when she saw Gregoire. She put her hand over her mouth. "You're . . ."

"Yeah, that's who he is, all right," Chris said, smiling. "George Gregoire, this is Kathy."

"I'm pleased to meet you, Kathy."

"I'm such a fan of yours!" Kathy said. "I can't believe you are here. What are you doing here?"

Gregoire smiled. "Well, I was just sitting around minding my own business when Chris stopped by and invited me to go with him. I didn't have anything else to do, so I said, 'Sure, why not?'"

Kathy laughed. "That's what you meant when you said he wasn't going to get his head cut off, isn't it. Oh, Chris, I love you!" Kathy kissed him.

"Well, now, I'm glad you did that, Kathy. I wanted to, but I didn't think it would be appropriate, I mean, us both being men and all."

"We have to get out of here," Chris said.

"All right," Kathy said.

They stepped back outside and Gregoire started toward the Ford.

"Wrong car," Chris said.

"Oh, I thought this is the one we came in."

"It is, but that doesn't mean it's the one we have to leave in. Pick us one out, Kathy."

"How about that gray Honda?"

"Yes, that's pretty nondescript," Chris said. He pulled a flat piece of metal from his pocket, stuck it down in the window, and popped the lock. He opened the door and the horn began to honk and the lights flash, but he reached under the dash and stopped it almost instantly. He signaled to the others and they climbed into the car. Again, Chris reached under the dash, connected a piece of wire, and started the car.

"I shouldn't be impressed by such a thing," Gregoire said. "But I have to admit, I am."

"Chris can pick any lock," Kathy said proudly.

"I believe it."

"Now, George," Chris said as he pulled out of the parking lot. "You said you had a suggestion as to where we might go."

"Yes," Gregoire said. "There are some people down in Alabama who have broken away and formed their own country. They call it United Free America."

"What part of Alabama?"

"Everything south of Mobile."

Kathy laughed. "I didn't think there was anything south of Mobile."

"Oh, yes, there's Gulf Shores," Chris said.

"Have you ever been there?" Gregoire asked.

"Yes, but it's been quite a few years. If they've broken away, what makes you think they'll let us in?"

"Because I have some information that I think they would like to know," Gregoire said, mysteriously.

CHAPTER THIRTY-ONE

Fort Morgan

"Son of a bitch!" Jake said angrily. "Are you telling me that this country actually has concentration camps for Jews, like they had in Germany during the war?"

"Well, not exactly like that," Sam said. "As far as I know, they have no gas chambers. And we were adequately fed." He smiled. "But they did work the devil out of us. Have you ever chopped cotton?"

Jake chuckled. "I never did, but my dad did, and he told me about it."

Sam and Sarah had arrived the day before, and were given an apartment right next to Tom and Sheri in the row of connected rooms that had been built when Jake and his team first arrived.

"I'll have to find some way to earn my keep," Sam said.

"Ha, I have just the job. We have money now. I'll have Bob appoint you as Secretary of the Treasury. That will be a paying position."

"Secretary of the Treasury?"

"Well, yeah, I mean, you're Jewish aren't you? And everyone knows that Jews are good with money."

"Jake!" Karin scolded.

Sam laughed. "If anyone else said that, I'd be offended. But I am good with money. And I do need a job."

Two days later, Chris, Kathy, and George Gregoire arrived at Gulf Shores. Gregoire created quite a stir when he arrived, so much so that a pot-luck dinner was held at the Holy Spirit Episcopal Church, which had also been the site of their declaration of independence. Gregoire was invited to speak, and though he only spoke for a few minutes, the audience was uplifted by his words, which concluded with:

"I can tell you now that there are at least twenty other groups like yours, including one group of American Muslims who call themselves American Scimitars. And while none of these other groups have the geographical advantage you have in establishing your own country, they have been conducting guerrilla operations all over the country, with some success. You haven't heard of it, of course, because none of the AIRE media has covered it. And I haven't spoken of it over any of my broadcasts, because I didn't want to take a chance on saying anything that might put these brave freedom fighters in jeopardy. But there have been some highly visible operations, such as attacks on military convoys and bases, and against SPS squads acting as Sharia-compliance enforcement, as well as the neutralization of all the missile sites and nuclear weapons that were once in the U.S. arsenal."

"All of them?" Jake asked.

Gregoire nodded. "Yes, all of them. I can tell you, with some authority, that AIRE does not have access to any nuclear weapons. Let me repeat that. AIRE has no nukes. We can thank God, and the wisdom of the American military who were in direct charge of those weapons. As soon as they saw the direction the country was going, they neutralized the weapons, doing so in such a way that none of them can be reactivated.

"The most important figure in the so-called American Islamic Republic of Enlightenment is not Mehdi Ohmshidi. Ohmshidi is only the front man for a cabal of Islamic plotters who plan to establish a world caliphate where everyone will either conform to their religion, or be killed. And the principle spokesman for that group was a man named Mohammad Akbar Rahimi. He was the one who pulled the strings for Ohmshidi."

"Who?" someone asked.

Gregoire smiled. "It's no surprise that you have never heard that name, for his success depended upon being unknown, behind the scenes. But though you may never have heard of him as Mohammad Akbar Rahimi, you may have heard of him as Warren Church."

"Warren Church? You're damn right I've heard of that son of a—" Remembering they were in a church, Tom stopped and covered his mouth in embarrassment. "I mean, yes, I've heard of him."

The others laughed.

"You are speaking of him in the past tense," Bob said.

"Yes, I am. Rahimi is the one who ordered my arrest," Gregoire said, "and he was the one who was going to have me beheaded. And he would have, had not a man in shining armor come along to slay, and I mean literally slay, the dragon. I'm talking about Chris Carmack."

Gregoire held his hand out toward Chris, and the others applauded him.

"All these groups I've spoken about, these freedom fighters, to the man and woman, are dedicated to the principle of taking our country back from the despots who have usurped control.

"And I promise you, it will be done!"

The applause that greeted his final words was thunderous, and for a while afterward, he stayed and met just about everyone who had come, one on one, signing hundreds of autographs.

The next day Chris and Gregoire met with the group who now lived at Fort Morgan. They were here to discuss the information Gregoire had brought.

"Before I was captured, I was acting as a clearinghouse for several other groups that are just like your group," Gregoire said. "Well, not exactly like your group; you are the only ones who have actually declared your independence. You are probably also the group that is best situated to take advantage of a situation that is developing, a situation that can net you several million gallons of refined gasoline."

"Several *million* gallons?" Bob asked.

"Twenty-one million gallons, to be exact," Gregoire said.

"How? I mean, where is this gasoline?"

"It's on board the *Khoramashur*, a tanker ship that will be coming into the port of New Orleans on the twenty-second of this month. There was some talk of capturing the tanker."

"The twenty-second is only twelve days from now," Jake said. "That doesn't give us much time to come up with a plan."

"Maybe not," Bob said. "But twenty-one million

gallons of gasoline would really be something. That would keep us going for a year."

"And we don't have to come up with a plan," Gregoire said. "We already have a plan. All we have to do is implement it."

"What is the plan?"

"The tanker is being escorted by two destroyers," Gregoire said. "They were formerly of the U.S. Navy, but now they belong to Iran. The officers of the tanker, and one of the destroyers, are Iranian. The crews of both the tanker and one destroyer are all Iranian as well. But the other destroyer, formerly named the *John Paul Jones*, now called the *Shapur 1*, has Iranian officers, but American crewmen, eighty percent of whom served on the old *John Paul Jones*. And that includes its former captain and executive officer."

"Would that be Stan Virdin?" Tom asked.

"Yes, that's the one," Gregoire said. "You know him?"

"Yes, I do. He was a damn fine officer."

"And a good American," Gregoire said. "He is the one who came up with Operation Tight End."

Tom chuckled. "Still reliving his glory days, I see."

"Glory days?"

"He was a tight end at the academy."

"All right," Jake said. "Let's hear about Tight End."

"Every American on board the *Shapur 1* has pledged their allegiance to the revolution. They are going to take over the ship, then sink the other three destroyers. With the escort gone we can put an assault team on board the *Khora-mashur*, then bring it to Mobile."

"Something like this is going to have to be well coordinated," Jake said. "And I don't see how we are going to be able to do that."

"Virdin has a satellite phone that nobody knows about."

"Then all we need to do is find a satellite phone."

"We have one," Willie Stark said.

"What? Since when? Where did we get a satellite phone? How did we get it?"

Bob laughed out loud. "Jake, I could have used you when I owned the newspaper. You would have been a good reporter, you just demonstrated the formula for all news articles: what, when, where, and how."

Jake laughed as well. "They're good questions, I can see why reporters ask them. What about it, Willie, can you answer them?"

"Yes, sir. Well, you know what a communications geek I am. When we took Mobile, I found the phone in one of the police stations, so I took it."

"Good for you, Willie. That was pretty farsighted of you. I should have thought of that."

Willie laughed. "I have to confess there was nothing farsighted about it. I just wanted it, so I took it."

"Does it work?"

"I've never tried to use it, but I have checked it over. Yes, it does work."

"Suppose we do get hold of Virdin, how will he know we are legitimate?"

"Yes, well, we might have a problem there," Gregoire said. "I was going to get an authenticator code, but I got captured before I did. And if he's heard I was captured, he probably thinks the whole thing is off now."

"There's no way he hasn't heard you were captured," Chris said. "When he got you, Ohmshidi figured he had such a coup that it was broadcast to the whole world."

"Maybe we can still pull it off," Jake suggested. "Tom, how well do you know this guy?"

"We were classmates," Tom said.

"Is there anything you can say to him, something that maybe only the two of you will know?"

"Uh, yeah, there was that time in Norfolk that, uh, well, this was before Sheri and I were married, and it's pretty embarrassing."

"Good," Bob said.

"What do you mean, good?"

"If it's embarrassing, that minimizes the chances of others knowing about it."

"Yeah, I guess you're right."

"What is it?" Jake asked.

"I don't have to tell everyone, do I? At least, not until I actually have to use it."

The others laughed. "I guess not. All right," Jake said. "We're going to have to come up with our own plan as to how we take over the tanker. We'll need to put enough men on board to do the job, and that will definitely take at least two helicopters. Bob, are you up to flying one of them?"

"Damn straight I am," Bob answered enthusiastically. "There is a Hughes 500 at the Mobile airport. We can get six in there. And twelve in the Huey."

"That'll give us eighteen," Tom said. "I doubt there are that many crewmen on board the tanker, and they for sure won't be armed."

"Once we establish contact with Virdin, we'll need to keep track of the location of the ships. We'll hit them when they are about fifty miles off shore," Jake said.

"All right. All we have to do now is make contact with Virdin, and let him know our plans," Bob said.

Ten days later—at sea with the Shapur 1

The convoy of the tanker and two destroyers were off the southern tip of Florida when Stan Virdin's satellite phone vibrated in his pocket. Walking to a part of the ship where he could be relatively alone, he answered.

"Virdin."

"1994. It was all your fault, Stan, if you had hung on to that short sprint-out pass, we would have been within field goal range, and we would've beaten Army twenty-three to twenty-two. But you dropped the ball and we lost twenty-two to twenty."

"I didn't drop the ball. It was over my head."

"You could've caught it. You just didn't try hard enough."

"Who the hell is this?"

"Let's see if this tells you anything. Norfolk, Virginia, August of '96, we got drunk at the Red Dog and took a cab home."

Virdin was quiet for a moment, then he said, "Yeah? What's wrong with taking a cab when you're drunk?"

There was laughter at the other end of the phone. "Because the next morning, neither one of us could remember where we left it."

Virdin laughed as well. "Hello, Tom. It's been a while."

"It's been too long," Tom said. "But now that we've made contact, I hope it won't be long before we get together. Say about fifty miles from port."

"What are you saying?"

"What was the position you played? Tight end."

"I thought with principle gone, the deal was off."

"He's not gone. He decided not to stick around."

"I'll get in touch with you tomorrow," Virdin said. "After."

After hanging up the phone, Virdin got in

contact with the others on the crew who had been briefed on Operation Tight End.

"It's on," Virdin said.

"All right, what's our first move?" Rick Adams, Virdin's one-time XO asked.

"We'll wait until they start their afternoon prayers, then we'll lock them in the wardroom. After that, we make certain that everyone is with us . . ."

"What if we find some who aren't?" Adams asked.

"As you know, Rick, most of these men served with us in the before time. I have absolute confidence in them. If we have to be wary of any of the others, I think they'll let us know. And even if they do resist us, we'll have them significantly outnumbered."

"You're right, I don't think we'll really have a problem."

"Now, here's the drill. We'll take control of the ship, and I'll contact the people who are going to take the tanker. As soon as we get word they're coming, we'll put ourselves between the tanker and the *Jamaran*. We will then inform the *Jamaran* that we have taken the ship, and have guns and missiles trained on them. More than likely, they'll stand down."

"If they don't?"

"If they engage us, we'll sink them," Virdin said.

"I'll make certain we have the target acquired," Adams promised.

"Okay, men, let's take this ship."

"Aarrgh!" one of the sailors said, laughing. "It's just like the *Mutiny on the Bounty*."

"Hah. I saw all three films of *Mutiny on the Bounty*, and I didn't see either Clark Gable, Marlon Brando, or Mel Gibson say 'aarrgh'!" one of the others said.

"I'm saying it. Aarrgh."

The men laughed, and Virdin was glad to see that they seemed to be loose, and in good spirits.

"All right, those of you I've chosen to come with me, come now. The rest of you, go to your assigned stations. Man the guns and the missiles."

With all tasks assigned, Virdin and ten men proceeded to the wardroom. There were two entrances to the wardroom, and Virdin made certain that both were covered before he opened the door and stepped inside.

"I have taken command of this vessel!" he shouted.

"How dare you interrupt prayers!" the Captain said angrily.

"Oh, go ahead with your prayers," Virdin said. "I'm just here to tell you that I have taken the ship, and you six men will be confined here in the wardroom until further notice. So as far as

I'm concerned, you rag-headed bastards can pray all you want."

Virdin stepped back outside, and the doors were secured. He called Tom Jack.

"The *John Paul Jones* is standing by," he said.

CHAPTER THIRTY-TWO

"Sir, we're getting a blinker signal from the *Jamaran*," a signalman reported.

Rick Adams picked up a phone. "Captain, blinker signal from the *Jamaran*."

"I'll be right there," Virdin replied.

Virdin was on the bridge in less than half a minute. "Still getting the signal?"

"Yes, sir," the signalman replied. "They want us to come up on channel thirteen—156.650 megahertz."

"Go to the frequency and bring it up," Virdin said.

The radioman responded, and all on the bridge could hear the hail in Iranian-accented English.

"*Shapur 1, I wish to speak with Captain Najib. Please respond.*"

Virdin picked up a microphone and looked at his signalman.

"Your mic is hot, sir," the signalman said.

"This is Captain Stan Virdin, commanding the *John Paul Jones.* Go ahead, *Jamaran.*"

"Where is Captain Najib?"

"He is in our custody. I have taken the ship," Virdin said. "Out," he concluded.

"Now let's see what he does next. Lieutenant Adams, what kind of activity do you see?" Virdin asked.

Adams was looking at the other destroyer through his binoculars. "Cap'n, they're clearing away their missile tubes."

"All right, gentlemen, it looks like we've come to the 'show,' and the *Jamaran* is about to throw the first pitch," Virdin said.

The tension increased as the others on the bridge looked at each other.

"I have the con. Sound general quarters," Virdin ordered.

Hitting a button that sounded a Klaxon throughout the ship, the boatswain's mate of the watch brought the silver call, cupped in his right hand, to his lips and let fly a long shrill whistle. His voice then barked over the 1MC.

"Now general quarters! Now general quarters! All hands, man your battle stations, surface action!"

Again, the Klaxon sounded, and again the boatswain's mate's whistle rose in pitch, then fell.

"Now general quarters! Now general quarters! All hands, man your battle stations, surface action!"

From bow to stern, the clatter of ladders resounded under their footfalls as sailors grabbed vests and helmets and rushed to their stations.

"Rick, I'll be in CIC," Virdin said as he headed for the Combat Information Center.

"Aye, aye, sir!" Adams responded.

The CIC, located belowdecks just under the bridge, bristled with radar screens, infrared imaging screens, computer monitors, and an array of switches and dials. Virdin picked up the phone as soon as he reached his battle station. *"Weapons!"* he barked.

"This is Langley, sir. Weapons manned and ready!"

"The Phalanx guns?"

"Aye, aye, sir."

"Missiles incoming, sir!" one of the CIC operators called out.

Up on the bridge, Adams stepped up to the window and watched as two anti-ship missiles were launched from the *Jamaran*. They were wicked looking, leaving a long trail of fire behind them as they streaked through the gray sky toward the *John Paul Jones*.

Everyone on the bridge braced themselves for the impact, then the ship echoed with the sound of the four Phalanx weapons firing. Long streams of fire, representing several thousand rounds per minute of forty-millimeter shells, lashed out toward the two incoming missiles. Both missiles were destroyed, and cheers could be heard throughout the ship.

"Look like any more activity?" Virdin asked, down in CIC.

"I'm not reading anything, sir. If you ask me, they've shot their wad."

"I'm going back to the bridge."

"Aye, aye, sir."

Virdin hurried through a short companionway, then up a ladder.

"Cap'n's on the bridge," the boatswain's mate reported.

Virdin picked up the phone.

"Weapons?"

"Weapons, aye. This is Langley, sir."

"Well done, Mr. Langley, well done," Virdin said. "Now, run out the five inch guns and bracket the son of a bitch."

"Fire for effect, sir?"

"No. Just bracket the bastard. Let's see what he does."

"Aye, aye, sir."

"Let me have the glasses, Rick."

Adams handed the binoculars to Virdin and he lifted them to his eyes and watched as the massive guns of the *John Paul Jones* fired toward the *Jamaran*. The Iranian destroyer lay helpless in the water as it was bracketed by a barrage of five-inch shells, falling on either side. This was the recognized signal to the captain that the ship was bracketed, and the next barrage would be on target.

"Okay, let's see what he does now," Virdin said. "He knows we have his range, and he knows that we know he can't stop us."

Virdin could see into the bridge of the *Jamaran*, and he saw someone standing at the window, looking back toward him. He knew that it was the captain, and he knew that the captain of the *Jamaran* knew that he had been beaten.

The Iranian destroyer made a wide turn, then left at flank speed.

"Stand down, Mr. Langley," Virdin said into the bridge phone. "Our friend is leaving now."

Fort Morgan

"Major Lantz," Willie called.

"Don't you mean General Lantz?" Marcus asked.

"Yeah, General Lantz. I've got Captain Virdin on the horn."

"Thanks," Jake said reaching for the phone. "This is Jake Lantz."

"I'd feel better if I could talk to Tom Jack."

"No sweat, I don't blame you," Jake said. "Just a moment." Jake lowered the phone, then called out. "Tom! He wants to talk to you."

Tom trotted over to take the phone. "What's the matter, Stan? Does talking to a general intimidate you?"

"I just wanted to be sure I wasn't stepping into something," Virdin said. "Tell your general I have the ship."

"What about the other destroyer?"

"It ran off with its tail tucked between its legs."

"Any sign of any activity on board the tanker?"

"I've called them, but they haven't responded. They have to know that something is up, though. How long before you can get here?"

"How far off coast are you?"

"According to our GPS we're exactly 42.7 miles off coast."

"We'll be there within half an hour," Tom said.

Tom shut down the phone and handed it to Jake.

"All right, Bob, let's spool up. Gentlemen, climb aboard!"

Just under twenty minutes later the UH-1D and the Hughes 500 approached the *Khoramashur*. The tanker ship was 1,300 feet long, with the superstructure on the after deck taking up 200 feet. That left 1,100 feet of deck, as flat as the deck of an aircraft carrier, which would make an easy landing platform.

There was a gun mounted in the door of the Hughes 500, and the plan was for Jake, who was flying the Hughes, to come to a hover just in front of the bridge, providing cover for Bob to land the Huey.

Deon was manning the door gun, and when he

pointed it at the bridge, the helmsman and the officers all ducked below the windows.

Two men appeared on top of the superstructure, armed with AK-47s. Deon opened fire and both of them went down.

"Deon, throw a few rounds into the bridge, just to get their attention," Jake said.

Deon fired a short burst, and bits of shattered glass flew from the windows. Then a stick came up with a white flag attached to it.

"Ha! They just surrendered!" Deon said.

"All right, Bob, make your insertion," Jake said.

Fort Morgan

Willie punched a few keys on the computer, then adjusted the video camera.

"All right, Mr. Gregoire," he said. "We'll be up on the bird in five, four, three, two, one."

Jake and the others were watching the TV monitor and they saw the intro come up, the Stars and Stripes waving on the screen, with the national anthem behind.

"Ladies and Gentlemen," Bob said, providing the voiceover. "From the Capital of United Free America, we bring you George Gregoire."

Gregoire's familiar figure filled the screen then.

"Hello, America.
"Yes, I'm still here, thanks to the bravery of a real hero. And now, I am among real heroes,

*men and women who have not given up, men
and women who have started a new nation,
conceived in liberty, and dedicated to the
principles of personal freedom, self-
determination, and sacred honor.*

*"This week, the brave soldiers of United Free
America captured a fully armed destroyer which
will keep the gulf open so we can enter into
commercial trade with other nations of the
world. We have also acquired a tanker full of
refined fuels, gasoline, diesel, and jet fuel.*

*"In addition to an army and navy, we also
have an air force, consisting of the very latest
in jet fighter aircraft, as well as a functioning
industry to build more ships, aircraft, and
wheeled vehicles.*

*"In short, ladies and gentleman, United
Free America is a fully armed and totally self-
contained nation of free men and women. We
welcome anyone who wants to come join us, to
help us attain our ultimate goal.*

"What is our ultimate goal?

*"First, I want you to see some of my friends
here, the brave men and women who, by their
courage, determination, and dedication to the
principles of honor and duty, guarantee that
we will reach that goal."*

The camera showed Jake Lantz, Karin Dawes,
Deon Pratt, Julie Norton, Marcus and Becky

Warner, Bob and Ellen Varney, Willie Stark, Tom and Sheri Jack, Chris Carmack, Kathy York, James and Cille Laney, Jerry and Gaye Cornett, Mike Moran, and Sam and Sarah Gelbman.

All twenty smiled, and raised their fists as they shouted the motto of the UFA.

"Take Back America!"

THE BEGINNING